12/30/2020

Matt

Enjoy the read!

The Silver Cord

THE LILY LOCKWOOD SERIES: BOOK TWO

D1520089

Alison Caiola

The Wonderland Press
New York

Printed in the United States of America

THE WONDERLAND PRESS, NEW YORK

First Edition: January, 2015

10 9 8 7 6 5 4 3 2 1

ISBN-13:9781508475040

ISBN-10:1508475040

Library of Congress Control Number: TXu001903243

Caiola Alison. The Silver Cord

Cover artwork by Eric Hutchison

Cover design by Inbeon Studios

Author photo by Jen Rozenbaum

For my son, J. D., with love.

Acknowledgements

This acknowledgment page is a great opportunity
To thank the people who mean the world to me.
So I beg a moment of your time,
To do so now, in this rhyme.
To John Campbell—my agent, a voice on the end of a phone,
You have become my dear friend and mentor, as our relationship has grown.
Steven Schnurman—you are so loving and true blue—like no other,
Even when you pretend to act like my bratty kid brother.
Donna Harris-Richards—my Pali, my bestie, my cherished sister-friend,
We shall be the keeper of each other's secrets 'til the very bitter end.
To my nephew, Jesse—you did a fine job checking military strategies and names.
Now who said that nothing good can come from playing video games?
To my dear cousins Alissa, Melinda and Pammy,
Thanks for being supportive friends as well as loving family.
To Joyce, Anita, Elyn, Jimmy, Lita, Patt, Tania, Ken, Art, Jill, Jeanne H. &
Jeanne N.
Cheerleaders all—I am blessed and honored to call you my family of friends.

When a silver cord ties two hearts together, neither time nor distance can sever the bond.

—Alison Caiola

Prologue

The prisoner drifted in and out of consciousness. Moments of oblivion were a welcome reprieve from the pain, which stemmed from the harsh body blows he had received from the fat, sweaty guard. Two other guards held the prisoner's arms while the third, larger one pummeled his body. The prisoner's head throbbed and his eyes were swollen shut. As the hours passed, the metallic taste of blood became more pervasive. The prisoner's hands were tied and his eyes newly blindfolded, so he could not see when the next blows would be delivered, nor could he protect himself when they landed.

A group of ten uniformed sentinels burst into the room, shouted loudly in a language the prisoner did not understand, and tied him to a chair. The prisoner told them he knew nothing and that he was unable to understand what they were saying. He pleaded with them to bring someone into the room who spoke English, but the more he pleaded, the louder the guards laughed.

A few minutes later, the fat sweaty one emerged from the group, wielding a large sledgehammer. He smiled, stepped closer to the prisoner, lifted the heavy hammer slowly, swung it back, and pounded the prisoner's left kneecap. Hot, searing pain resulted from the crippling crunch. The guards untied the prisoner and left him screaming on the floor, writhing in pain.

From that moment on, their dark faces and uniformed bodies became indistinguishable. The prisoner strained to listen for the steel boots that would again kick open the door and, soon thereafter, his head. It was sweltering in the room and the heat had reactivated the stench of urine, blood, feces, and sweat embedded in the cracks and crevices of the tiny space.

He remembered his mother's garden at home and tried to conjure the scent of the heavily fragrant Texas Mockorange and Gardenias that lined the driveway.

He would ride his bicycle out of the garage and speed past the aromatic hedges, holding his nose to ward off the aromas that competed desperately for attention.

The prisoner thought of his parents, certain that the physical agony he was experiencing was nothing in comparison to the emotional pain his situation was causing them. He could not bear bringing even the smallest discomfort to them. He was one of the lucky ones: a golden son in a family where everyone not only loved each other, but also liked one another, too. Their home was located on five acres out in the country. It had been in his mother's family for generations—all proud Texans to the very core.

He and his brother spent summers in a Tom Sawyer-like bliss, making forts, climbing trees, and riding horses. On the hottest days, they'd swing for hours on the ropes their father had tied atop the two tallest elm trees, next to the crystal-blue lake. They'd let out Tarzan-worthy yodels before plunging into the ice-cold water.

No matter what memory he conjured up, his mind always wandered to the recent past and he thought of her. He could almost smell the fragrance of her hair when she stepped out of the shower; the mischievous twinkle of her eyes, a tip off that she was about to say something sarcastic. Her laughter rang like a bell, starting low and slow, then escalated in pitch and speed. How she would always tilt her head to the right and stare into his eyes a few seconds before kissing him. Her kisses tasted of peppermint. He memorized every inch of her body. She was generous with it—never holding back. He marveled at the change in her face when they made love and how it took on a primal look of fierce pleasure.

He tensed as he heard the stomping of their boots on the floor down the hall. He could feel the vibration through the thin walls even before hearing their voices and loud laughter. Too soon the door would open and he prayed that this time it would be swift. He heard her laughter, felt her body underneath his, gazed into her hazel eyes, kissed her lips—the taste of peppermint…

Crack. Crack. Crack. Lightning. Darkness.

Chapter 1

Tap, tap, tap. Her fingers flew across the keyboard with lightning speed. There was a knock on the door but Lily ignored it and continued typing. Another three knocks, this time more insistent.

Lily didn't look up from the keyboard. "Not now. Please go away."

"Miss Lily, the baby—she's very sick."

Lily pushed back her chair, jumped up, and ran to unlock the door. Her housekeeper, Gladys, was standing on the other side, chubby arms folded across her abundant breasts, with a cat-that-ate—the-canary grin on her round face.

"My God, what's wrong?"

"Nothing. Little Miss Daisy Rose is fine, sleeping soundly. She's perfect—like a little angel. Don't you remember you said, 'Gladys, no matter what you have to do, just make sure I stop my writing when Mr. Fernando gets here?'"

Lily breathed a sigh of relief. She was annoyed, but in all fairness to her housekeeper, she had indeed instructed Gladys to do this.

"So Mario called from the lobby. Mr. Fernando is on his way up now."

Gladys started walking toward the front door, then turned dramatically to say, "Now you know for sure that you're not the only actress in this house, right? Watch out, 'cause I may be the one up for the award next year." Gladys laughed. Lily smiled and went back into her office, closing and locking the door behind her.

She walked over to her desk, read the last paragraph she had written, and pressed "Control S" on her laptop. Today Lily was on a writer's roll, one that didn't come often to her. But today the words were flowing fast from an invisible faucet and she was hesitant to slow the momentum, lest it dry up forever.

1

Her first book had been extremely well received and lauded by critics and readers alike. But while writing her second book, she found the process more slow-going—to the point where she actually fell into an agonizing spell of writer's block. In fact, she seriously wondered if she would be able to successfully complete a second novel—one that people would be drawn to read. What if she were only capable of authoring that one book? What if the first one was a fluke? She often wondered how long it would take and how many books she would have to write before she felt like a *real* author. Sometimes, especially after a fruitless writing session, she would come down so hard on herself that she felt perhaps she should give up writing altogether and stick to what she knew best and was good at—acting. Acting was the reason that particular day promised to be an exciting one.

The door knob turned but did not open. "How many times do I have to tell you to leave the door unlocked?"

Lily opened the door and once again, Gladys was standing on the other side.

"And how many times do I have to tell you that you are not my mother, you are only my housekeeper." Lily said.

Gladys's face turned beet red. "Only your housekeeper? Really, is that what I am—only your *housekeeper*? Someone should've told me that twenty years ago when I sat with your mother, by your sick bed, all night long, taking turns with Daisy wiping the sweat that was dripping from your forehead. Or the time, when you were 16 years old and I picked you up from that party because you were drunk and afraid to call your mother. Then I had to clean the puke off of you, before I put you into bed."

Gladys spun around and stomped down the hall toward the front foyer.

Lily called after her, "Gladys, come on, don't be mad. I didn't mean it like that."

When her housekeeper refused to reply, Lily went back into her office, closed the door, and made sure not to lock it. Gladys had been her mother's housekeeper since Lily was a child and even though she was often overbearing, Lily knew Gladys loved her—and now loved her daughter, too. Lily had to remind herself that Gladys had been her rock since Daisy passed away.

Moments later, the door flung open and Fernando burst into the room. His assistant Stefan, carrying a small table and two large canvas bags, trailed behind shyly. They made quite the pair—Fernando with his movie-star good lucks, tall, with a full head of lustrous hair, standing next to the homely Stefan, bald and a mere 5'2", who, as usual, was doing all the heavy lifting. Fernando practically ran across the room and grabbed Lily's cheeks with both hands.

"It's a beautiful day to get dolled up and stand in front of millions of people to accept your very first Tony Award for Leading Actress in a Play, isn't it my love?"

A flutter of butterflies engulfed Lily's tiny stomach. "Don't say that, Ferny. You'll make me barf, truly.

"Nonsense, you're a Lockwood, and, as everyone knows, Lockwood women never get shaken." He winked at Stefan, "Stirred, but never shaken." He threw his head back, gave his long brown hair a dramatic flip and laughed.

After catching his breath, Fernando stepped back, folded his arms, and took a good look at Lily. "Now, darling, tell me that you've showered already."

"Sorry, I got caught up in my manuscript and lost track of the time," she said sheepishly.

"Of course you did, Miss New York Times Bestselling Author." He clapped his hands twice and proclaimed, "Chop, chop: Get into the shower right now."

"Boy, you would make a fantastic drill sergeant."

"Oh I think not—that 'don't ask, don't tell thing' would seriously cramp my style. Now, go!"

Lily saluted, "Yes, sir, on my way, sir." On that note, she hurried out of the room.

With the precision of a seasoned scrub nurse, Stefan began to lay out what Fernando fondly called his "weapons of mass creation": liquid and powder foundation, eye shadows, false eye lashes, lipsticks, bottles and jars of hair gels, conditioners, hairspray, various-sized flat and round brushes, barrel curlers, flat irons, and a high-speed blow dryer.

As was their routine, Fernando watched him like a hawk. When Stefan put out and straightened the last item, Ferny nodded his approval and said, "While she's in the shower, I'm going to visit the little princess."

He walked down the hallway and opened the third door to the right. No matter how many times he entered this room, he was always struck by the mural of hundreds of hand-painted roses, in every shade of pink imaginable that adorned the wall behind the white crib. He walked in and nodded to the nanny, Margaret, who was seated in the rocking chair, knitting, over in the corner of the room. His eyes glanced at a photo of Lily's beloved mother Daisy that had a place of honor on top of the dresser next to the changing table. Daisy had been one of his dearest friends and the photo had been taken only a few months before she died tragically in a car crash. Her wide smile looked as if the camera had caught her in mid-laughter, her green eyes twinkling mischievously. His gaze lingered on the picture for a few seconds. There would never be another Daisy; she was one in a million. The familiar feeling of loss washed over him as he sighed and tiptoed over to the crib.

Baby Daisy Rose, in purple and pink pajamas, was sound asleep, her face almost completely covered by tousled blond ringlets. Fernando smiled, knowing that in years to come he would be the one tasked to tame those curls, just as he had done for her grandmother. He gently pushed her hair away from her face and marveled at how much she had changed in the past three weeks since he and his partner, Tommy, had babysat her.

They were playing horsey and he was down on all fours while Daisy Rose was seated on his back. Her chubby fingers grabbed and pulled at his long mane as he pranced around the room. Daisy Rose squealed with delight. Tommy, of course, was right behind them every step of the way, hands outstretched to catch the toddler if she tumbled. In retrospect, Ferny realized that this scenario summed up their relationship perfectly: Fernando was the wild card, changing directions on a whim, while Tommy was always nearby—Fernando's safety net—arms outstretched always ready to catch him. Their roles fit them like the Italian suits that line their walk-in closets. The last ten years were proof positive that opposites not only attract but that they can successfully endure the ups and downs of life.

Fernando marveled at how much the toddler resembled her beautiful mother. He adamantly told anyone who would listen that she looked nothing like Jamie, whom he called "the social-climbing actor who happened to be the sperm donor." Fernando would rather die than say it aloud, but he was surprised at how Jamie had stepped up and taken responsibility for the baby. Well, time would tell with that one. He had never liked Jamie, but he liked Jamie even less after the way the actor had blatantly cheated on Lily. Jamie would be forever dead to Fernando.

Lily, her hair wrapped in a towel, entered the room in a long white bathrobe and stood next to her dear friend for a good moment, watching her child breathe in and out. Thankfully after Daisy Rose was born, Lily had found renewed joy in life. They all did. After Daisy's fatal accident, they had become a small army of the walking wounded. Lily, of course, had suffered the most. Losing a mother—and one as extraordinary as Daisy—was unfathomably painful. Lily and Daisy had been closer than any mother and daughter whom Fernando had ever met. How on earth would Lily recover? Time does not heal all wounds; Fernando knew that was bullshit. And then, when Robbie left her, it added weight to Lily's downhill free-fall. The birth of Daisy Rose had brought not only into their world this precious child who lay sleeping in front of them, but also a deep sense of renewal and hope for them all.

Fernando nodded that it was time to go. They left the room and quietly closed the door, allowing the princess to sleep undisturbed.

"Voilà. I present to you Audrey Hepburn 2.0." Fernando held the mirror up behind her so that Lily could see the back of the masterpiece that had taken nearly two hours to create. The chignon was stunning, very *Breakfast at Tiffany's,* with a modern 21st-century twist. Fernando had added one of Daisy's antique crystal hair ornaments above Lily's bangs. She stood up and turned around to get a glimpse of every gorgeous angle. The golden highlights in her chestnut hair sparkled and brought out the flecks of yellow in her large, hazel eyes. She spun around and hugged Fernando.

"Thank you, thank you, Ferny, I love it!"

"Of course you do, darling. Was there ever any doubt?" Fernando nodded his head, giving Stefan the go-ahead to start packing up.

"Have to leave, lovey. Donna's waiting, I'm going to do her hair and makeup and then I'll get dressed. The limo will pick us up at 5:00 p.m. and then we'll swing by and pick you up about fifteen minutes later. This will give us plenty of time to walk the red carpet together, wave to your myriad adoring fans, and even give an interview or two."

Lily shook her well-coiffed head and smiled. "You, sir, are a media whore."

"*Moi?* How could you say that? Is it my fault that the cameras love me?"

Lily caught Stefan's eye and they both began to laugh.

Fernando walked toward the door and scowled at the other two, "Whatever are you two cackling about?"

Lily put her arm around her cherished friend, went up on her tip-toes and kissed his cheek, "Do you know how much I love you?"

Fernando smiled, "Of course. I'm extremely lovable, *everyone* knows that."

Lily shook her head and smiled as Fernando swept out of the room.

"The Tony Award for the best performance by a leading actress in a play goes to…" As if flawlessly choreographed, Donna grabbed Lily's right hand and Fernando her left. Lily smiled because even through her death grip, she could feel the trembling in Donna's hand. She glanced affectionately at her late mother's best friend and partner in crime. She had been the keeper of her mother's secrets since grade school, more than forty years ago. As soon as she heard that Lily was up for a Tony Award for her role in *The Smallest Life,* Donna didn't hesitate for a nanosecond. Without a word from Lily, she canceled the last leg of her European concert tour and winged her way back to NYC to be at her god-daughter's side. They both knew why she was there; no discussion was needed.

Lily turned to Fernando, who would be mortified to know that his hand was clammy. In fact, he would unquestionably deny this to the death. The renowned hairstylist never left the house if, from the top of his head to the bottom of his feet, didn't absolutely scream FABULOUS! Lily thought Fernando looked awesome, like a young Antonio Banderas in his chic Tom Ford tuxedo. Lily turned her attention back up to the stage and waited for the presenter to make the announcement that would put the four nominated actresses out of their misery. She held her breath while the presenter, one of Broadway's hottest male actors, clumsily opened the envelope and retrieved the results card from its snug hiding place. He looked at the audience and triumphantly called out, "Lily Lockwood, *The Smallest Life*."

Did they actually call *her* name? For a second she didn't trust her ears, so she quickly glanced around to see if anyone else had stood. But when Fernando all but yanked her arm out of its socket to get her out of her seat, she knew this was the moment she had been waiting for since she'd been a little girl.

Walking up the long aisle to the stage, Lily remembered the day, more than twenty-one years earlier, in the kitchen of their postage-stamp-sized two-room apartment in Greenwich Village. It was before her mother, bestselling author Daisy Lockwood, had sold her first book. Money was tight and her mother's dear friend Donna, then a singer on a dinner cruise ship that circled Manhattan every night, lived with them. Lily must have been about eight or nine years old. Her mother and Donna were washing dishes when Lily walked into the kitchen and proudly announced, "Mama, Auntie D, I'm going to be a movie star." Her mother knelt down and said, "You can be whatever you want when you grow up, Lily Girl."

"That's the thing, Mama—I wanna be a movie star *now*.'

"Honey, you're too young to be an actress. As you get older, you'll have plenty of time to decide what you want to be. You can be an actress or a doctor or an architect—you can be anything you want, after you graduate college."

Lily folded her arms and stomped her foot. "I need to be an actress *now*—I just have to be. And if you can't help me do it, why then, you are the meanest people in the whole wide world!"

After two weeks of whining, begging, and strategic intervention from Donna, Daisy finally acquiesced and allowed Donna to introduce Lily to her agent. The talent agency had a children's department and within weeks Lily was cast in her first commercial. Small parts in television and movies followed, and the rest, as they say, is history.

And now that her name had been announced a few moments earlier, Lily found herself at the steps leading up to the stage.

Dear God, please don't let me trip and embarrass myself in front of millions of people. She imagined herself taking a vaudeville-style flying leap, head first, landing spread eagle on the stage. But even though the pencil-thin, stiletto heels on her crimson-colored Manolo Blahniks were well over six inches high, she managed to make her way gracefully up the steps to the center of the stage without incident.

She looked magnificent in her short, black, satin Oscar de la Renta strapless cocktail dress. Earlier in the day, when Fernando piled her long, dark hair into the messy chignon and braided in some hair extensions to give it extra volume and texture, Lily wasn't at all pleased.

"I don't need extensions, Ferny, my hair is thick enough." Lily complained as she sat in front of the bedroom mirror while Fernando worked his magic, his arms flailing grandly like a frantic orchestra conductor.

He stopped abruptly, glared into the mirror and asked, "Who was named Top Stylist in the Country by *Allure Magazine,* little lady?"

"You."

"Correct. And who was named Hairdresser to the Stars in *Glamour Magazine, In Style* AND *Vogue.*"

"You."

"Right, again!" Fernando spun Lily's chair around dramatically and looked into her eyes.

"So, who then, knows best, may I ask?"

"But it's *my* hair."

"Now, that's where you are wrong, my darling." Fernando flipped his own long locks out of his face for added emphasis. "When you are walking the red carpet tonight, in front of millions of people, your hair belongs to *me!*"

Lily laughed and had to admit the result was spectacular: Not one lovely lock was out of place, in front of the theater filled with her peers and millions of viewers watching at home. She held her Tony in one hand and her thank-you cheat sheet in the other. When the audience stopped clapping, Lily opened the crumpled piece of paper that, for the past hour, she had clenched tightly, in her hand for dear life. She looked at it, took a deep breath, and feigned a smile. She couldn't remember who anyone was or why she was supposed to thank them. Not one person; zilch, zero, nada, no one! Her mind was a complete blank.

"*Fuck me!*" She quickly looked up at the audience because, for a split second, she thought she had said it out loud.

"Thank you. You have no idea how much this means to me. I would like to thank the members of The Broadway League, the board of directors, and members of the advisory committee of the American Theatre Wing for this award. I would like to ask the producers, director, and my fellow actors to please stand, because without them, I would never be here, in front of you, today." She prayed that her nerves wouldn't get the best of her, and that when they stood, she would finally remember their names. They stood and luckily she remembered.

"I would like to extend my deepest thanks to our producers Stan Marsh and Leonard Patel, our director Richard Klein, and to the playwright, Favia De Larusso, for the rich, beautiful words that I have the honor to speak every night . . . and four times on the weekend!" The audience laughed. "I would also like to thank my cast mates Jodee Carter and Manny Rodriguez for being talented, generous, and supportive.

Lily took another deep breath and willed the tears that were rapidly filling her eyes not to fall. "Many of you know about the death of my dear mother, Daisy. I would like to dedicate this award to her." Lily's tears escaped and flowed down her cheeks. "She would have been incredibly thrilled and proud to share this evening and this honor with me. From the time I was a child, I knew that I wanted to be an actress. My mother supported me always and helped me realize my dream. This award is as much hers as it is mine." Lily held the statue up triumphantly and pointed upward. "For you, Mom." The sniffles from the audience were drowned out by the burst of applause and onset of music.

Two handsome model-types escorted Lily backstage to speak to the press. As she made her way, she thought of Robbie —something she did perhaps a half a dozen or more times per day. She wondered if he might be watching television that night. She imagined him, relaxing on his couch, randomly channel surfing and stopping on CBS just as the camera closed in on her face, accepting the Tony. Would memories of their time together flood back to him? Did he even *miss* her? She shook her head as if to erase the picture of him that she held in her mind's eye at all times. As far as she knew, Robbie was not even back in the States.

She reached backstage and it was sensational bedlam—every actor's dream. There were on-camera reporters and press everywhere, interviewing the winners and the presenters. There were film and stage actors laughing and drinking champagne. She surveyed the large area and in one corner alone she counted four Academy Award-winning directors. The cameras were flashing, nonstop, so the area took on a strobe-like effect. Before she could walk over to the press, Fernando, comb in hand, rushed over to her. "Congratulations, baby. That was incredible. And *my* hair looked fabulous on stage, too!" They both laughed. "We were pretty impressed with your speech. I didn't realize you had memorized it."

"I hadn't." Lily smiled and handed him the crumpled piece of paper she was still holding tightly. He started to read and she laughed when she saw Fernando's eyes widen.

Baby wipes

Diapers

Balmex

Orange Juice

Eggs

Whole-wheat bread

"The correct list is unfortunately sitting somewhere on my kitchen counter, unnecessarily awaiting its big TV debut!"

Before Ferny could say a word, her cell phone rang and her home number appeared. Fernando rolled his eyes.

"I have to get it, it's the nanny. Hello?"

"Congratulations, Mommy." It was Jamie.

"Thanks. Wait—what are you doing in my apartment?"

"Margaret called and asked me to come by. Her daughter was rushed to the hospital with appendicitis or something like that. So Daisy Rose and I are spending the evening together. We were just watching her glamorous mother win a Tony Award. Looking smokin' hot, by the way."

"Thanks. Are you okay? I mean, if you have plans I can always call Tommy to go over and watch the baby."

"Lily, she's my daughter too, you know. There's nowhere I'd rather be than right here."

"I've got a slew of parties to attend tonight, so I don't know what time I'm going to be home." The noise backstage increased after another win was announced. Lily had to cover one ear to hear.

Jamie said, "Don't worry, I'll crash on the couch. I'll be fine."

"Sorry, I can't hear. If you don't mind staying, you can sleep on the couch or in the guest room, whatever you want."

Even though Lily was grateful that Jamie was taking care of Daisy Rose, she felt strangely uneasy about it. They had not slept under the same roof since their break-up more than two years earlier when she discovered that, while shooting a movie on location, he had cheated on her with his curvy co-star. What's more, he had used her mother's car crash and hospital stay to orchestrate a paparazzi photo opportunity.

Popular talk-show host, Maryanne Watson, walked over to Lily, stuck a microphone in her face, and began asking her a machine gun-full of questions. Within seconds, Lily was back in the moment as Best Actress, clutching her Tony as the pain of the last few years was, temporarily at least, forgotten.

Chapter 2

The limousine stopped short and the Tony Award that was propped up on the leather seat next to Lily, fell over.

"This was the best night, ever." Lily straightened the award, lifted her fluted glass in a mock toast, and downed the last of the Cristal champagne.

"It certainly was," Donna said. "I don't remember the last time I danced that much. My feet are killing me." Donna took off her shoes, draped her long legs across Tommy's lap, and pointed her toes in Fernando's direction, indicating that she wanted a foot massage.

"You're kidding, right? Do I have to be the one to do *everything* for *everyone?* Fernando warmed up for his limousine dramatic debut. The rest sat back and watched the show. "Not only did I wake up at the crack of dawn before the roosters…."

"There are no roosters on Manhattan's Upper East Side, my love," Tommy replied.

"Metaphorically speaking, of course. Now allow me to finish. I *struggled* to make each of you beautiful for this soirée…"

"He *struggled* to make us beautiful?" Lily laughed, as they all joined in. "I will have you know, my good sir, that I was on the list of the ten most beautiful actresses last year."

"Hmmm, that was *last* year." Fernando sniffed.

Another burst of laughter.

"If not for me, where would you all be?" He continued, "I'll tell you where: the Worst Dressed List, that's where." The other three roared.

"And to think, after fully dressing the ungrateful lot of you, I only had mere moments to prepare myself."

Tommy patted his hand. "Darling, you were getting ready for a full three hours."

"Well it wasn't enough time. I could have used at least another hour."

"You were the handsomest man at The Tonys," Donna assured him. Tommy shot her a look. "Of course, Tommy was a very close second."

"Guys, I appreciate everything. Thank you Ferny for all your hard work. And thank you all for all your support—tonight and always."

"We'll be there for you every step of the way, Pali." Donna hugged Lily. Lily smiled because "Pali" had always been Donna's nickname for her mother, Daisy. "I know you will, Auntie D. I know you all will. I'm blessed to have you. Mom sure knew how to pick good friends." They sat in silence, thinking of Daisy.

"For God's sake, Donna, give me your big ole' size ten feet and let me rub them," Fernando said, breaking the now-somber mood.

The limo pulled up in front of Lily's East Side apartment building. The doorman, Mario, who was dozing on a chair by the entrance, woke up on cue, jumped to his feet, and rushed over to open the limo door before the driver had a chance to walk around the car.

The doorman extended his hand for Lily and said, "Congratulations Miss Lockwood, on winning the Tony. I knew you would win. I said to my wife, 'That girl has gone through enough tragedy the past couple of years, with—well, you know, she's overdue for something good.'"

"Thanks, Mario." Lily turned around, leaned her head back into the limo, and blew kisses to her friends. Tommy jumped out and gave Lily a hug.

"I couldn't be more proud of you, even if you were my daughter." Tommy had tears in his eyes.

Lily kissed him on the cheek. "Thanks Tommy, I appreciate it."

"Now you get upstairs and kiss that gorgeous child of yours. And tomorrow you get right back to writing your manuscript. When can I expect to see it?"

"Stop being a slave-driving editor and give me a hug."

She walked into the lobby and Mario ran ahead to press the UP button on the elevator. When it arrived, Lily got in and he followed. Mario turned the key and pressed "P" for penthouse.

The doors closed, shook twice, and began its slow ascent. Mario looked at Lily's reflection in the mirror and said, "I knew this day would come. I knew that one day you would be a star and win lots of awards. Even when you were a little girl you were special— different from the other kids in the building— more talented, much more refined."

Lily turned to Mario and chuckled to herself because the doorman had obviously forgotten the hundreds of times he had chided her for making noise while running through the lobby with her little friends. Mario would shake his head and mumble something about 'little spoiled brats' under his breath.

Lily smiled as they rode the rest of the way in silence. The elevator door opened into her apartment's spacious circular foyer. She kicked off her stilettos, walked across the imported marble tile, and proceeded to stroll down the hall into the den, where Jamie was asleep on the couch. Daisy Rose lay peacefully on his chest, her face snuggled between his neck and shoulder. They breathed in unison.

Lily looked at them— father and daughter—and felt a stab of regret. While growing up, hadn't she wished, practically every day, that her father and mother would stay married? Back then, she prayed that one day the phone would ring and that when she answered, it would be her father on the other end of the line. He would say that he was calling to tell her that she and her mother were wonderful and beautiful and that he realized he'd made a big mistake and wanted to move back home. The phone call never came and neither did her father.

She and her mother spent summers on her grandparent's farm in Southold, a bucolic town on the east end of Long Island's North Fork, surrounded by vineyards and the beautiful Long Island Sound. During the many town parades, she would watch little girls sitting happily atop their father's shoulders to get a better view of the floats. Lily had to look away so as not to cry.

Now here she was doing the same thing to her precious daughter. Granted, Jamie was in Daisy Rose's life, for now at least. But who knew how long that would last? Jamie was certainly not the most reliable person she knew. But he was wonderful with Daisy Rose and had been helpful and attentive whenever Lily needed help. He had also been aggressively pursuing Lily to get back together with her, even before the baby was born. He'd been telling her how much he had changed and how genuinely sorry he was. He had even stated, more than a few times, that losing Lily was his biggest regret. If she would have him back, he would spend the rest of his life making it up to her.

She blocked every advance that he made, physically and emotionally, arguing that she couldn't move past what had happened. Was she still upset that he had acted like a jerk and cheated on her? Well, people certainly can change as they mature. Hadn't *she* changed over the past couple of years? She was no longer the spoiled, helpless girl she had been when they were together. Or was it something else? Was she holding out for Robbie's return? In a few months it would be two years since he had left; certainly by now he must be back in New York City. There was no contact, no email, not even a text to indicate that she had even crossed his mind. He might very well be, at this moment, living with someone else, or, worse, he might even be engaged or married.

She sighed and gently picked up Daisy Rose, whose little body repositioned itself so that her head was now snuggled upon Lily's neck. Lily kissed her pink cheek, breathed in the sweet scent of baby lotion and powder and then walked Daisy Rose into the nursery.

A half hour later, Lily lit the fragrant row of candles that lined the sunken tub in the master bathroom. She dimmed the lights, walked to the oversized glass shower, and turned on the water. She tested the many showerheads mounted on the tiled ceiling and walls to make certain they were adjusted to the gentlest rain setting. Then she stepped into the shower and caught her breath as the water hit her body. As she closed her eyes, she thought of Robbie.

The memory of their first night together suddenly flashed through her mind. It was the night before her mother had died. She'd spent that day—as she had done since the days after the accident—sitting vigil at her mother's hospital bedside. By that time, they had moved Daisy into the hospice ward and everyone knew that it would be only a matter of days before she would pass.

Robbie was at the hospital, visiting his brother David, who had been the other passenger in Daisy's car the night of the crash. That evening in the hospital, Robbie saw how weary Lily was and volunteered to drive her home. Once they arrived at the farmhouse, he ordered her to relax in a hot tub while he cooked dinner for her.

Lily obeyed and soaked for a stress-releasing, prune-inducing hour and emerged feeling almost normal. When she walked downstairs and entered the kitchen, Lily couldn't believe her eyes. Robbie was in the middle of the room, wearing her Gram's old apron, surrounded by mixing bowls, spices, and utensils that must have been leftover from the glory days when Grams had cooked large meals at the farm. Lily looked at him and thought Robbie must be the best-looking guy she'd ever seen. Not only was he 6'1" with wavy-brown hair, but he also had a gorgeous smile with dimples for miles and had a way of holding himself confidently. He was comfortable in his own skin.

Lily opened the oven and saw two perfectly overstuffed pot pies happily baking their little hearts out in her mother's rarely used oven.

"Are you kidding me? Pot pies? You made them from *scratch*? Pot pies are my very favorites. But I thought they only came frozen."

Robbie removed his apron and asked, "While the pies are in the oven, would you mind if I get cleaned up?"

"Oh, of course you can. Just go up the stairs, take a left, and the bathroom's right there." While Robbie headed upstairs, Lily walked back into the living room, stretched out cat-style on the couch, and listened to the rain on the roof. She was transfixed by the fire dancing in front of her. Earlier in the evening, while leaving the hospital, she had felt dejected, grumpy, and tired. But now, thanks to a long soak in the tub, the presence of Robbie, and the promise of a hearty meal, she finally felt relaxed.

Robbie seemed like one of the good ones. Now *he* was someone her Mom would have chosen for her. She could hear Daisy now: "Lily of the Valley, he's handsome, he has manners, he loves his mother, he's a doctor, *and* he is not an actor!" Lily laughed to herself because, in the past, she would have totally avoided this type of man. If it was someone her mother wanted her to be with, unfortunately that was the big, fat kiss of death for that guy. She wouldn't give him a second glance. Jamie fit right into her then-picture of terrific. Cute, hot body, out-of-work actor and her mother absolutely did not like him from the minute they met.

Robbie emerged fresh from cleaning up and they sat down to eat. The meal was extraordinary and after the final crusty crumb had been devoured, Robbie suggested they move to the living room and sit near the fire. Once they were comfortably seated on the couch, Lily asked Robbie to tell her all about the organization he was involved with, Doctors Without Borders.

"It's actually called *Médecins Sans Frontières*, an international medical humanitarian group that was started in the early 1970s by doctors and journalists." He leaned toward Lily. His eyes lit up and she could see how passionate he was about the subject.

"It provides independent, impartial assistance in more than sixty countries to people whose survival is threatened. They have to be impartial while they provide first-rate medical care. But, Lily, while the care they give is important, they must also remain politically impartial to atrocities taking place in these third-world countries. You can't imagine what's going on there. You wouldn't believe the things I've seen." He shook his head and closed his eyes briefly, as if to block out terrible memories.

He drank his wine and continued. "They're not supposed to get emotionally involved, ever, but while giving medical care to the people of Rwanda, the group was able to call for an international military response to the genocide they were witnessing. And in 2004 and 2005, they called on the United Nations Security Council to pay greater attention to the crises in Darfur."

"It sounds amazing, Robbie. It must feel rewarding to know that you're making a difference in so many lives."

"Well, I know it made a difference in my life; that's why I volunteered for another mission."

"So when do you leave and where will you go?" She had asked, trying to ignore the lump that was growing in her throat.

"That depends. I'm supposed to leave in a couple of weeks. I know I'll be going to Africa. Not exactly sure what part they'll send me to. Wherever I'm needed most, I imagine. I'll be gone for almost nine months this time."

The lump was now the size of a boulder, and Lily swallowed hard.

He smiled at her. "Anyway, enough about me. Tell me about your acting. My mother is a huge fan of your show. I've never seen it, but she says you're a big star."

"Oh no you don't," Lily protested. "You really expect me to talk about my unimportant role on a silly television series after hearing about your life-saving work in third-world countries? I think not, Dr. Rosen." She stood up and kissed him on the cheek. "Thanks for dinner and for staying with me, but it's getting late and I'm exhausted."

"You go on to bed, Lil, and I'll clean up the dishes. By that time, the fire will be out. I'll lock up when I leave. Have a good sleep, I really enjoyed our evening together."

Before she had a chance to say anything, the phone rang. Lily recognized the number as the hospital switchboard and stared at the phone for a second, afraid to answer it for fear of what she might hear at the other end.

"Hello?"

"Miss Lockwood, it's Lydia, your mother's nurse." Without realizing it, Lily had grabbed Robbie's hand for support and squeezed tight.

"I'm just calling to tell you that there are some substantial changes. Your mother's breathing is considerably more shallow and faster than it was this afternoon."

"Shallow and faster—what does that mean, exactly? What should I do? Should I come back to the hospital? I want to be with her when…"

"Stay home. Get your rest. We still have time. Tomorrow, I am sure, is going to be a trying day for you. I will certainly call you if anything changes."

Lily thanked her as she released her death grip on Robbie's hand and hung up. She relayed the message to Robbie, who looked genuinely pained. "I'm here for you, Lil, whatever you need."

Her feet felt leaden as she struggled up the stairs and into her mother's bedroom. Her heart was racing, and even though she was dead-tired, she knew that sleep would not come easily. Everything felt like it was moving in warp speed and it was beyond her power to slow it down. What was she going to do without her mother? How could she live in a world without Daisy? A surge of grief and loss overtook her and she was swept away in waves of sadness. Already there was an emptiness, a physical void that she'd never experienced before. For the first time in her life, she felt truly alone. All she could do was lie on her stomach, bury her face deep in her mother's pillow, and sob.

Robbie knocked at her bedroom door. "Lily, are you all right?" He sounded concerned. "May I come in?"

Lily was in a full-blown ugly cry and couldn't stop the tears from flowing. In between sobs and gasps, she hiccupped uncontrollably.

The door slowly creaked open and Robbie walked over to the bed. She turned over and sat up. He hugged her and the floodgates opened even wider. She wept while he rocked her. She couldn't control herself. She didn't even try. Yet before long her tears slowed down and finally dried up. She took a breath and wiped her face.

"I'm scared to be alone tonight; will you stay here and sleep next to me?"

"Of course I will. Just lie down and relax." He plumped the pillow and pulled the blankets over her, took off his shoes, and was careful to lie on top of the covers, next to her. He stroked Lily's hair and told her that he was there for her and wasn't going to leave, not as long as she needed him. Lily finally fell into a much-needed sleep.

Sometime in the middle of the night, she awoke, turned to him, and laid her head on his chest. While she'd been asleep, he had taken off his shirt and had slid under the covers.

His breathing was calm, so she knew Robbie was in a deep sleep. Lily felt him stir and with his eyes still closed, he tenderly began to stroke her hair. Without a word, he kissed the top of her head. Her heart beat so hard and fast that she thought it very well might catapult out of her body. She took a deep breath to quiet her nerves and stroked and kissed his chest.

They were both fully awake by that time, but neither one of them uttered a word. They didn't have to. It was clear what was happening and words would shatter the almost mystical feeling that was building in that moment.

Robbie kissed her and pulled her on top of him. He took his time; his lips were soft, and his kisses that started out tentatively became deep and passionate. His capable hands found their way under her nightgown, which he lifted gently over her head and tossed aside. His mouth never left Lily's as he caressed her neck and back. His hands skillfully traveled down her body and rested on her bottom. He squeezed and pulled her in to him. Her body immediately responded. With ease, he gently turned her so that he was on top. He tantalized her breasts with his mouth, flicking his tongue over and around her nipples. She felt on fire and arched her back, wrapping her legs tightly around him and drawing him into her. He pulled back, looked into Lily's eyes; smiled at her and slowed way down. He lifted his hips away from her and when he moved back, his body just barely touched hers. He teased her, played with her, almost entering, and then he pulled away. He did this over and over again, until Lily was in a red-hot frenzy and couldn't take it. All the anger, sorrow, and frustration she had been feeling the last week fueled her; she finally pulled him into her, hard. The moan that escaped her was a sound she had never heard herself make before, almost as if it came from the very depths of her soul.

Now, standing under the shower, trancelike, Lily poured the lavender soap gel into her hands and washed her neck, shoulders, and breasts. She closed her eyes and imagined Robbie was there with her—that *his* hands, not hers, were slowly caressing her body—and that *his* hands were between her legs. She slowly opened her eyes and saw him standing there, watching her. In her dream state, she did not stop touching herself. She closed her eyes again.

Her lack of protest was an unspoken invitation to Jamie that he could proceed. He undressed and stepped into the shower behind her, kissing her neck and shoulders. His hands covered hers as she continued to touch herself. As if perfectly choreographed, they moved in sync to their own rhythm and to that of the falling water. It was sensual dance, one they'd shared hundreds of times before. She lifted her arms over her head and placed them around his neck, pulling him to her. She leaned into him and let the water wash away all the memories that had lingered for far too long.

Chapter 3

"My ears must certainly be clogged, because it sounded almost as if you said you'd actually *slept* with Jamie." Jessica grabbed and shook her left earlobe in a mock gesture of clearing her ears. It was the day after The Tony Awards and Lily was having an early dinner at her favorite bistro, the Spring Street Natural Restaurant and Bar, in Soho, with her three gal pals—Jessica, Kristin, and Jodee—before she had to head uptown for her evening performance at The Broadway Theater.

She had known Jessica and Kristin since grammar school, but it was only recently, since she'd moved back to New York, that they had reconnected and renewed their friendships. They'd been extremely close growing up; in fact, in the late 1980s their teachers used to call them "the Madonna triplets" because they dressed like miniature versions of the pop star. Every day they would come to school wearing miniskirts and black leggings, with bows adorning their long hair, numerous black bracelets dangling from their wrists, and lace fingerless gloves covering their hands. Long chains with large crosses always swung from their tiny necks. Kristin and Lily, the two brunettes, were envious of Jessica's blonde hair, since it gave her look a more authentic Madonna edge.

The trio was inseparable. They were together every day after school, and most weekends had a sleepover at one of the girls' homes. The families spent holidays together, because the girls couldn't bear to be apart.

When Lily and Daisy moved three thousand miles away to California, it was hard for Lily to maintain her close relationship with Jessica and Kristin. Phone calls were difficult because of the three-hour time difference and expensive long-distance charges. So she lost touch with them through the years. When Kristin and Jessica read in the newspaper that Daisy had passed away, they reached out to Lily and the trio quickly renewed their friendship. Jodee recently joined the group to make an even four.

Jodee was Lily's outspoken co-star in *The Smallest Life,* and from the first day of rehearsal they became fast friends. Jodee's claim to fame, besides being a talented Broadway actress, was that she closely resembled the singer Beyoncé. So much so that she couldn't walk down the street without at least ten people stopping and asking "Beyoncé" for her autograph. After a while, it was easier for Jodee to simply sign the autographs and continue on her way. She signed her own name and explained to Lily it was a marketing strategy that helped build her "brand." Lily introduced Jodee to the other two and the trio became an even four. The women now shared their lives, their stories, and their clothes with one another.

"I said I had sex with Jamie," Lily smiled sheepishly. "There wasn't much *sleeping* going on."

The waitress walked over to the table. "Can I get you ladies anything else?"

"Yes a lobotomy for my good friend over here." Jessica pointed to Lily. The other three laughed.

"Just the check please," Kristin waited until the waitress was out of earshot. "Lily must have a very good reason for sleeping with the guy who almost single-handedly ruined her life. Let's hear what it is."

"Well, he is Daisy Rose's father…"

"Oh girl, do not even *think* of going there. The 'baby daddy' excuse won't fly at this table." Jodee picked up her fork and swung it around for added emphasis.

"Well, I'll admit I was a little tipsy last night." Lily smiled. "He was sleeping on the couch, holding the baby. They looked so adorable together that it melted my heart."

"So take a photo, don't fuck the douchebag!" Jessica picked up her wine glass and clinked it with Jodee's and Kristin's.

Lily ignored them and continued. "Well the truth of the matter is that sex with Jamie was always hot. And, might I remind you, I haven't been with anyone since…well, you all know. Anyway, later on, when the baby woke up, Jamie got her and brought her into our bed. For the first time, it felt like we were a real family. It was nice, it really was. Anyway, he told me that he loved me, always has, always will."

Jessica rolled her eyes "Should I be the one to say it?" the other two nodded their heads.

"First of all: bullshit. Second: can I remind you of a certain pre-production party you attended in Beverly Hills?"

"You don't have to remind me, trust me, I clearly remember." The waitress dropped off the check. Lily snatched it up before the other three could reach for it and took out her American Express Platinum card. "It's on me. Let's call it the Tony post-win celebratory dinner."

"Or we can call it *the trying to buy our silence so we don't give you a hard time, 'cause you screwed up* dinner." Jodee said.

Kristin gave Jodee a "behave-yourself" look. "I can totally understand. You didn't plan it—it was a one-time thing—let's call it an accident."

"Seriously, an accident? Like they *accidently* crashed their bodies into one another because it was so dark in the room?" Jodee asked.

Lily laughed along with her friends. "Listen, I know that even though you're all outspoken and certainly don't hold back one single itsy bitsy iota of a judgment that you may have about the decisions I make in life, you all love me." She stood up.

"I've got to run and pick up a dress I saw at *bebe*. Jodee, do you want to come with? We can share a cab to the theater."

"And miss all the shit they're gonna say about you after you're gone? No way." Jodee winked. "That's the best part."

"Okay. And Kristin, thanks for sticking up for me against these she-devils, but it wasn't a one-time thing. As a matter of fact I'm having dinner with Jamie tonight after the show." As her friends groaned, Lily blew them a kiss and left the restaurant.

Later on, in the cab ride to the theater district, Lily received a text from Margaret, Daisy Rose's nanny:

Miss Lockwood thank you ever so much for visiting Eaven, she loves her doll. I will be back to work in a few days.

Earlier in the day, before she met the girls for dinner, Lily visited Margaret's seven-year-old daughter who was recovering in New York Presbyterian Lower Manhattan Hospital from the emergency appendectomy she had had the night before. When the elevator doors opened onto the Pediatric Ward, Lily was greeted by two nurses, who had been contacted by the security guard on the main floor to advise them that the famous actress was on her way up. Both nurses were dressed in bright-pink scrubs and had miniature stuffed animals clipped to the sides of the stethoscopes around their necks.

The shorter of the two nurses stepped forward; her wide smile produced the deepest dimples Lily had ever seen.

"I'm Melinda and this is Trisha. You're here to visit Eavan Murphy, is that right? Lily nodded.

"Come, we'll take you to her room." Trisha said. As they walked up the wide hallway Lily was amazed to see that the walls were saturated with rainbow-colored murals of animals, children, and fairy-tale characters. Lily nodded and smiled at the parents who were walking up and down the hallways with their children, many of whom were connected to intravenous drips that hung from rolling stands. She couldn't even begin to imagine how heartbreaking it must be to see your little one go through a serious illness or injury. Lily's heart went out to all of them and she felt immeasurably grateful that her own little girl was healthy.

The nurses stopped in front of room 405. "Here's the room. If there's anything you need, please let us know. Oh, and do you mind taking a photo with us?" Before Lily could answer, Melinda and Trish moved closer to her. Trish pulled her cell phone out of her pocket, extended the arm that held the phone, and rapidly clicked the camera three times.

"That should do it, thanks so much." The two nurses giggled as they walked toward their station.

There were six beds in the room: three on each side of the dormitory style room. Lily had to fight back tears because the children looked so helpless in their large hospital beds. Two of them were bald—side effects from the rounds of chemotherapy they had received—and wore knitted caps to keep their heads warm. Parents, whose faces were etched with worry and eyes bleary from countless sleepless nights, surrounded their beds. One child was crying as the nurses stuck him with a needle for a blood test. One by one the adults looked up and were surprised to see Lily Lockwood smile at them as she walked to the far end of the room.

A little girl with two long blonde braids that framed her heart-shaped, freckled face was propped up in bed quietly listening intently to a story her mother was reading to her. Lily stood a few feet away, not wanting to interrupt. She listened to the familiar brogue and saw Margaret's animated face as she softly read to Eaven. Margaret stood up when she noticed her famous employer quietly standing nearby. "Miss Lockwood, what a lovely surprise." She leaned in to her daughter. "Eaven, this is Miss Lockwood. You remember, I take care of her little girl."

Eavan's blue eyes widened when she saw what Lily was holding. Her little arms were already outstretched in anticipation when Lily handed her a beautiful doll with long blonde hair.

"Oh how nice, but you shouldn't have!" Margaret looked back at her daughter. "What do you say to Miss Lockwood, darlin'?"

"Thank you so much! This is the prettiest doll I've ever seen in my whole entire life!" Eaven hugged the doll. "Do you think it would be all right to braid her hair so that it looks like mine?"

"Of course. Here, I'll do it for you." Lily took the doll and braided its hair so that it looked identical to its new owner.

Lily visited with them for another hour. She was intrigued by how smart and funny Eaven was. Lily was dutifully impressed by the bandages that covered the incision on the child's tummy when Eaven proudly revealed them to her.

When it was time to leave, she gave Lily a big kiss and thanked her again for visiting. Margaret walked Lily out of the room to the elevator.

"I am glad that Eaven is doing so well. It must have been scary. I can't even imagine."

"Oh you have no idea," said Margaret. "When my husband called me last night, I could hear Eaven screaming in pain. Thank goodness Mr. Jamie was able to come over to take care of Daisy Rose and I was able to leave. We got Eaven to the hospital just before her appendix burst. I can't even bear to think about what might otherwise have happened to her."

Lily squeezed her hand. "Well you don't even have to think about that, thank goodness."

"The doctor said if she continues to do as well as she's doing, we can bring her home tomorrow afternoon."

"Take as long as you need to be with her." Lily said, to Margaret's relief.

"You know, Miss Lockwood, I feel so lucky to have found steady employment working for a person as kind as you. When people find out you're my boss, they always ask me for "the inside dirt. I tell them that Lily Lockwood is a fine woman, a wonderful mother, and a good employer. Now I can happily add that you're also considerate and compassionate." Then Margaret did something she had never done before: She hugged her boss.

The driver slammed on the brakes and Lily's phone fell from her hands. Lily retrieved it and tightened the seat belt that she had neglected to secure when she first got into the cab.

Lily thought about the events that had taken place the night before. Had Jamie not been available to take care of Daisy Rose after Margaret's hasty departure, he would not have been there when she got home and they would not have made love.

She sighed when she thought about the conversation she'd had with her friends earlier in the day. They had not been wrong in their opinion of Jamie. She had told them on many occasions—probably too many—the events that had led to her break-up. Suddenly she found herself thinking about that fateful night that turned out to be the beginning of the end in her relationship with him. She and Jamie had been invited to a Hollywood party at producer Harvey Leder's house in Bel Air. Jamie had recently landed the coveted lead role in the movie, *Standoff in Sante Fe* and the party was a pre-production meet-and-greet for the actors, their significant others, and the director before principle shooting was to begin a few days later in New Mexico. The director and producer wanted everyone to get to know each other before they went on location.

During the party, when Jamie was off speaking to the director, Lily headed for the bar to order a Mojito. A pretty blonde girl walked over to her. She was about 5'8", with long, stick-straight hair, and a smokin'-hot body. She introduced herself as Natalie, Jamie's love interest in the upcoming movie.

"I'm so glad you're okay with me and Jamie." Natalie smiled and took a sip of her Martini

"Excuse me?" Lily said.

"Okay with the talk we had. I mean——he said you were."

"What talk?" Lily asked. Her radar was going off in all directions like fireworks on the Fourth of July.

"Well, it was after I found out that I got the role of Cassandra. I was actually at The Coffee Bean. You know, the one on Cross Creek Road in Malibu?"

Lily nodded.

"Jamie came in. We knew each other from the auditions and found out we'd both been cast! Amazing, huh? So, anyway, he sat down and we talked for a couple of hours. I told him it was important to me that my character and her relationships be authentic. So I was candid with him. I told him I have to be completely committed to my character; I'm the type of actor that has got to be in the moment for it to work."

"Meaning?" Lily asked.

"Well, if I have a love scene with an actor in a film—as I will in this one—I make sure to fuck him beforehand. A lot. This way we're really comfortable and take all our passion and chemistry and put it into the film."

Lily felt the blood rush to her head.

"So when he thought it was a great idea, I asked him if his girlfriend would mind. He told me that you were a real pro in the business and would be cool with it. I thought, wow, she must be rad!

When the party ended, as Jamie and Lily were driving home, Lily told Jamie everything Natalie had said. "You're joking, right?" Jamie laughed.

"No, I'm not joking. That's what she told me."

"Babe, she was just pulling your chain. It's not true, I swear,"

"Then why would she have said it?"

"Why do people say shit? I don't know. Ask her."

That evening when Jamie was in the bedroom packing, his clothes were all over the place, and his suitcase was open on the bed. The reality hit Lily: He was going away for six weeks and would be alone with a girl who'd already told Lily she planned to have sex with Jamie and that he was definitely into it.

"I don't believe you, Jamie, when you deny what you obviously said to that girl."

"I don't give a shit what you believe." He started throwing the clothes into the suitcase. "Lily, be smart and just leave me alone."

"Jamie, I'm not stupid. Why would she say that to me, knowing I would confront you about it? Why would *anyone* do that to another person? You're lying!"

"Lily, you're a spoiled bitch who doesn't know when to shut her fucking mouth," he yelled. His face was beet red, and one large vein was bulging from the left side of his neck.

"I want you to admit the truth!" Lily screamed just as loudly. Jamie slammed his fist against the wall, leaving a huge hole.

He stood in front of Lily, grabbed both her wrists, and through clenched teeth said, "You listen to me, Lily. If I wanna fuck someone, I'll fuck them. And you can't do shit about it!"

Early the next morning Jamie got into a town car that would take him to the airport and into Natalie's arms.

Weeks later, while Lily sat at her mother's bedside in the University hospital I.C.U, the news about Jamie and Natalie hit the wires and it became a feeding frenzy of gossip. Lily had to endure seeing footage of them together whenever she turned on the TV. Photos of them walking hand in hand and kissing appeared on the cover of every tabloid lining the checkout counters of every supermarket in the country. Of course Jamie denied that anything had happened between them and told Lily that the whole thing was a publicity stunt concocted by the executive producer and studio. True or not, Lily had had enough and finally ended their relationship.

She willed herself to shake off the memory of that time, which still made her sick to her stomach. She had decided that morning that if she and Jamie were going to give it another try, she would have to forgive, forget, and pray he changed as much as he claimed to have. This could be a second chance for them. They could start over with a clean slate. Hopefully, with time, she would forget the bad stuff they'd gone through and they could be a *real* family. Didn't everyone deserve that?

Lily looked out the cab window at the traffic on 8th Avenue. She checked the street sign and realized they were only near West 33rd Street and still had another 20 blocks to go. She glanced at her phone and saw that it was already 6:45 p.m. Shit, her call time at the theater was 7:00 p.m. and with this traffic, she would definitely be late. Leaning closer to the front seat, Lily said, "Excuse me, do you think it might be better to take 6th Avenue to 47th Street, then swing over to Broadway to avoid this traffic?"

"Sixth Avenue is a friggin' mess. Lady, I'm the professional here, so unless you want to switch seats, let me do the driving, huh?" he snarled.

Lily leaned back, shook her head, and smiled. She remembered another taxi ride she'd taken with her mother and Aunt Donna many years earlier. She must have been around eight years old, since it was before she started acting and before Daisy had sold her first book. They were riding in a taxi going uptown from Greenwich Village, which for them was a luxury. They hardly ever took cabs, since they couldn't afford them. Even though Daisy worked two jobs, money was always tight for the single mother. So the mother and daughter were frequent travelers on the subway. So much so that by the time Lily was five years old she could recite all the #1 Line subway stops, in the correct order heading uptown. She would recite them to the same tune as the ABC song. Lily proceeded to sing it to herself:

Christopher Street, 14th, 18th,23rd, 28th, 34th-Penn Station! 42nd –Times Square! 50th, 59th-Columbus Circle! 66th-Lincoln Center, 72nd, 79th and 86th Streeeeeet!

But this one night, she was dressed up in her finest, as were her Aunt Donna, and her mother, because they had gotten free tickets—orchestra seats—from a friend who was in the Broadway musical, *Les Misérables*. Daisy had helped the actress by getting her an audition for the show with a casting director at Johnson-Liff Casting who happened to be a regular customer at the restaurant where her mother was the hostess four nights a week. The woman landed a role in the chorus and the tickets were her way of thanking Daisy. The show was coincidentally playing at The Broadway Theatre, the same theater where Lily was currently headed.

Twenty-one years earlier, the three of them had ridden in one of the big old-fashion yellow cabs, the kind you don't see any more in Manhattan. It was the model that had had a small pull- up metal seat behind the driver, and faced the other passengers in the back. Lily was proudly seated on it, facing her mother and Aunt and watching the traffic out of the rear window.

They were stuck in a major traffic jam on 8th Avenue. The taxi sat without moving for a good ten minutes. When they finally did move, it was only a few feet and then traffic was stopped yet again. Impatient drivers honked their horns loudly which did nothing but add to everyone's tension. Daisy was visibly nervous and checked her watch every few minutes.

"Are we going to miss the curtain going up, Mommy?" Lily asked

"Oh honey, I certainly hope not. We left the house with plenty of time to get there."

Donna checked her watch for the hundredth time. "Pali, I don't think we're going to make it on time."

"One thing I know for sure— Lily is not going to miss any part of her first Broadway show!" Daisy handed the driver a five dollar bill, opened the passenger door, and got out. She waved to Donna and Lily, "Hurry up, ladies, we're on the move. Les Miz or bust!"

Holding hands and laughing gleefully, they ran up Eighth Avenue. People walking on the street smiled and moved aside, allowing the giggling trio to pass. They were out of breath, but right on time, when they finally arrived at the box office. Within minutes, Lily was seated between her mother and Donna, eagerly waiting for the curtain to rise. After the show, Lily knew, without a shadow of a doubt, what she wanted to be when she grew up. She was bitten by the acting bug and all these years later she still felt the same.

Lily glanced out the passenger window at the traffic, which fortunately had opened up. The driver was able to reach Broadway fairly quickly. "Can you turn on to 53rd and stop at the stage door on the left?"

The driver looked at her in the rear-view mirror and his whole demeanor changed. He actually smiled.

"Hey, I know you. You was that actress on that TV show. Damn, what's the name of it? My wife loves it. Me, I can't stomach all that drama crap. All the kissing—the crying—it gives me a headache. I told my wife, 'Selma that shit don't happen in real life.' She tells me 'Shut the fuck up, Harry.'

Lily bit her tongue so she wouldn't laugh. Oblivious, the driver continued, "What was the show called again? Wait don't tell me. It's on the tip of my tongue. Oh you know—shit— that hospital show.

"Uh huh, that's right." It had been a few years since she'd starred in *St. Joes* and Lily actually missed it, especially the cast and crew. Her manager, Franny, had called last week to tell her that because the ratings had gone south since her departure, they were asking for her to return. They promised her a great storyline and a big fat paycheck. Initially she dismissed the idea. She thought about Robbie. What if he wanted to get in touch with her and she was back in LA? Even Lily knew how ridiculous that was. Surely if he wanted to find her— anywhere on the planet— he certainly could. There was only two more weeks until her play closed and she needed to decide what she was going to do next. She promised Franny she'd give it serious thought and would let her know by next week. She got out of the cab and walked through the stage door, clocking in at 7:00 p.m. on the nose.

After the show, Jodee stopped by Lily's dressing room and knocked on the door.

"Hey, girl, you decent? Well maybe after last night I shouldn't use the word *decent...*"

The door quickly opened, Lily, still in her robe, shushed her friend, grabbed Jodee's arm, pulled her into the room, and closed the door.

"Now was that necessary?" Lily sat down in front of the mirror and continued to take off her stage makeup.

"Oh yeah, absolutely necessary until you come to your damn senses." Jodee sat on the corner of the dressing table, picked up one of the many perfume bottles from the antique silver tray, sprayed it on her wrists, and inhaled. "Okay, this one—I'm borrowing." Lily took it out of her friend's hands and placed it back where it belonged.

"Listen, I understand that it's a bit of a shock to everyone, but they'll just have to get over it. And be nice to Jamie when you see us together."

"Now I know you're out of your damned mind."

Lily picked up the perfume bottle that her friend coveted and held it up. "I'll tell you what. If you behave and are your charming self when you see Jamie, this is yours to keep. Deal?"

Jodee jumped to her feet and shook Lily's hand. "Deal."

She snatched the perfume bottle out of her co-star's hand before her she could renege.

"Done. But I'll tell you right now, you'd better come up with some pretty fancy bribes to shut the other two up."

As Lily applied her street makeup, she looked at her friend in the mirror. "How bad was the shit they said about me after I left?"

Jodee smiled. "Well, how bad is *bad*? You know, it's all relative."

Lily looked at Jodee and said, "On a scale of 1 to 10, with 1 being the kindest and 10 being the three of you at your bitchiest."

"An 11, definitely." Lily frowned and Jodee gave her friend a hug.

"Listen, after everything that's happened between you and Jamie, give us a little time to get used to the idea. We love you and we'll come around."

Lily walked over to the closet and retrieved a black shopping bag with *bebe* written in large pink letters on the front. "Great audience tonight, huh?"

After opening night, Lily had quickly learned that each audience has its own unique personality. Tuesday night audiences always tended to be their worst crowds. Laughter didn't come as easily to them as it did to audiences on other nights. The parts that usually make the audience gasp don't even seem to register on a Tuesday-evening crowd.

As a matter of fact, last Tuesday, as they took their bows, Jodee whispered to Lily, "If you stuck a broomstick up your butt and swept the stage floor, you wouldn't get one damn reaction from this crowd." Lily burst out laughing.

But this Tuesday was different. The crowd was on the edge of their seats and Lily felt that it almost had the electricity of an opening night.

She took the garment out of the bebe bag and smiled at the pink tissue paper that neatly wrapped the dress.

Jodee said, "Yeah, all you have to do is win the Tony every Monday night and we'll have a Tuesday night audience that isn't completely comatose." She watched Lily unwrap the paper, pull out a beautiful black-jersey, sleeveless, high-neck dress with a key hole that promised to reveal just the right amount of cleavage. Lily slipped into the dress and felt it hug her curves perfectly.

"Pretty sexy for a week night; what do we have planned?"

"*We* don't have anything planned. I told you, I have a date with Jamie." Lily put on her black platform, open-toed Christian Louboutins, and looked at herself in the mirror. "Do you think I need to run a flat iron through my hair?"

"No, you look great—too good for that little shit."

Lily took back the perfume bottle and held it up to remind Jodee of their deal.

"Okay, give it back. I'll be cool, no worries."

A few minutes later, Jodee and Lily emerged from the dressing room and walked down the stairs to the waiting area by the stage door. Jamie was standing there, hands in his pockets, talking and laughing with a couple of girls from the wardrobe department.

Lily smiled when she saw Jodee's eyes widen. Jamie was hot: He was 6'2", had blonde hair and high cheekbones—a young Kevin Bacon or River Phoenix with a smidgen of Brad Pitt thrown in. He was athletic without being too muscular, and had a killer six-pack.

When Lily saw the girls talking to Jamie, she felt a surge of jealousy. She wondered how long it would take for her not to remember Natalie every time she saw Jamie speaking to another girl. Could she ever fully trust him again?

As Jamie looked up, he saw Lily coming down the stairs and let out a long whistle. He walked over to her, extended his hand so she would get to the bottom step safely, and gave her a quick kiss.

"You look gorgeous, babe. I would have dressed up if I'd known. . ."

Lily took his hand. "You look fine."

"You got that right." Jodee said under her breath.

Lily smiled and introduced the two. To Jodee's credit, she was a perfect lady with him.

Jamie and Lily went out the stage door onto West 53rd Street, where throngs of fans were waiting patiently to get their Playbills autographed. As soon as they saw Lily and Jamie, the crowd called their names and pulled out their phones and cameras. Lily had to close her eyes because the flashes, against the dark night, temporarily blinded her.

Chapter 4

Still blindfolded, the prisoner lay unconscious on the dirt floor. His leg, which two days earlier had been brutally crushed, was now twisted in a grotesque position. A horde of rats swarmed over their lifeless host, gnawing at his face, arms, and legs until their own faces were drenched in his blood. Still, he did not move.

Two of the guards threw a bucket of ice water on him. The rats scurried to their hiding places and the prisoner was jarred back to reality. For a split second, before his nerves delivered the pain message to his brain, he couldn't remember where he was. Once his brain received the communication, it felt as if his leg was being sawed off. The prisoner remembered everything. He cried out, begging for the reprieve of darkness, where he did not have to feel, think, or remember.

He heard footsteps and the two guards returned. The prisoner braced himself for the torture that would surely follow. They each grabbed an arm and pulled him to his feet. His weakness and injuries would not allow him to remain upright and he fell hard to his knees. The guards dragged the prisoner across the room and out the door. He screamed with pain and protest, not knowing what fate awaited him outside that room.

The prisoner would never forget how he, Ivan, Frosty, and Simon were forced to their knees, guns to their heads, as they shivered in fear while their captors furiously circled them, their dark faces distorted with hate and anger. The thugs screamed at them in a language that none of them understood and pointed at the four accusingly.

In the middle of this chaos, one of the men walked slowly over to Frosty, calmly put a gun to his head, and shot once. The prisoner could still hear Ivan's and Simon's screams as Frosty's brains and blood splattered onto their clothes and over their faces. Next, they put the gun to Ivan's head laughing at him, tormenting him. Ivan closed his eyes and screamed. One pop to the head silenced his screams for eternity. Next was Simon. He looked the gunman straight in the eye and spit in his face. Simon was dead before the spit hit its target.

Then only the prisoner remained. His body convulsed with fear. He held his breath and closed his eyes, waiting for the one shot that would keep them closed forever. Nothing. They dragged the prisoner away from his friends' bodies, into the room where he was viciously beaten. Since then, that room had become, in some perverse way, his safe haven—a place where he may be brutalized but would not be killed.

He couldn't breathe. They dropped his arms. The prisoner could tell he was outside. Then one of the guards ripped off his blindfold and the prisoner knew instantly that he could barely open his eyes because they were so swollen. He looked around and saw that he was in a makeshift outdoor shower, with a hose that hung over the large muddy hole that his knees had sunk into.

One of the guards lifted the prisoner up, but again the prisoner could not stand on his own. The guard shouted to the other one and he came running over.

While the first guard held him upright, the second took off the remainder of the prisoner's tattered clothes and turned on the hose. The ice-cold water shocked his body, but then thankfully acted like an anesthetic and numbed some of the pain.

The guards put what looked like hospital scrubs on the prisoner and between the two of them carried him out of the area.

The prisoner passed a group of men seated around an outdoor stove. A kettle aroused his hunger. His stomach suddenly felt as if it were being sucked so far inward that it was fused against his spine. He couldn't remember the last time he had had even a morsel of food. He prayed that he would eat soon.

Chapter 5

"*I* may never eat again. I'm stuffed." Jamie pushed his plate away.

Lily laughed. "I highly doubt that, knowing the love affair you have with food."

"You know me so well."

Lily's phone rang and she took it out of her purse. A picture of her manager popped up on the screen.

"Hey, Franny, you're working late."

"No rest for the wicked. How are you doing, doll?" Franny's raspy smoker's voice seemed to be getting deeper and deeper each time Lily spoke with her.

"Good, everything's great."

"Well, exciting news here, I just got a call from Arthur Thomas." Lily's ears perked up and she put her wine glass back down on the table. Arthur Thomas was *the* hottest new director to come out of the hip-hop world. He had called himself Arty T when he'd been a hardcore rapper and a young protégé of Tupac Shakur during the east coast-west coast hip-hop rivalry era. After the deaths of Tupac and Biggie Smalls, Art was the one left standing and soon thereafter was propelled into stardom. Then, a couple of years later, he wrote and directed an extremely commercial, big-budget feature film called *After The Sun,* a post-apocalyptic story that showed genuine depth and talent. He and the film were both nominated for an Academy Award.

"So, he's written a screenplay and it looks like Paramount is the highest bidder. It's big, big, big budget—

"— I like the sound of that." Lily interjected

"You got that right, little sister," Franny laughed. But her laughter soon devolved into a ten-second coughing spell.

"Are you okay?"

"These damn cancer sticks are gonna be the death of me yet. So where was I? Oh yeah, so he contacted me, looking for you, for the starring role."

"No way." Lily mouthed 'Oh My God' to Jamie and pointed to the phone.

"Oh yes, way! Anyway, they've already messengered over the script to you; it should be in your doorman Mario's hot little hands as we speak. I've got mine right here and I'll read it tonight."

"Excellent! When and where does it shoot?"

"In LA, starting in six weeks. He wants to get the leads together a week before for bonding and rehearsal."

"Wait, what about *St Joes*, aren't we supposed to be considering my return to the show?" Lily finished her last drop of Cabernet and pointed to her glass. Jamie called the waitress over and ordered another.

"An Arthur Thomas film trumps a TV series any day. You know that. Let's wait and see what happens. So get reading and call me tomorrow."

Lily hung up and relayed the conversation to Jamie. He had looked a bit bored and even annoyed while she was on the phone, but as he got up to speed, his excitement level seemed to rise.

"So that's all I know. Sounds cool, huh?"

Jamie smiled. "Yeah it sounds awesome. First of all, it's going to breathe life back into your film career." Lily winced.

Jamie continued, "You'll be out in LA, which is where I need to be in the next couple of months. So we can be out there together and I can be with my two favorite girls. Now, here's the best part: I've been asked to audition for a part in Arty T's movie too."

Lily didn't know how to react, so she said nothing. Jamie didn't notice because he was doing enough talking for both of them.

"We can either move back into your Malibu house and make a nursery for the baby, or we could stay in an awesome house I just leased in the Hollywood Hills. It has four bedrooms, so there can be one for the nursery and the nanny. Or we can spend the week at my place in town and then head to Malibu on the weekends and during our time off. How does that sound?"

"You know, Jamie, it's a lot to think about. Let me see what's going on with both these projects and then we can talk about the logistics."

Jamie took Lily's hand and held it across the candlelit table. "You got it. I want you to know how lucky I feel to be sitting here with you and looking at your beautiful face. All I wanted, Lily, is to get back together with you and have the opportunity to be a real father to Daisy Rose."

Lily gently pulled her hand away from his. "I told you that we need to take things super slow. I can't be rushed, not after all that's happened. And whether we're together or not, you *are* a real father to Daisy Rose."

"I know, I know. I just mean that I want us to be together like a real family, living under the same roof."

Lily looked down. She folded and unfolded her napkin several times. Jamie put his hand under her chin and tilted it up so that she was forced to look into his eyes. "Babe, what's all this about?"

"Just don't push too fast. That's all I'm asking, okay?" she replied.

He looked hurt and she took his hand this time. "Let's just go with the flow, see how things progress, and try to be in the moment."

"Okay, you got it. I'll try to be in the moment—as long as you're in the moment *with* me."

The waitress walked over to the table and asked if they wanted any dessert.

Jamie winked at Lily. "Well, that all depends, if I'm getting dessert at home later, I'll pass. If not, bring on the damn menu."

Lily laughed. "Check please!" Jamie kissed her hand.

Later that evening, after the "dessert" was finished, Lily lay in Jamie's arms, drifting into a much-needed sleep. Suddenly, Daisy Rose let out a shriek and started to cry.

"Our daughter is very considerate. She was nice enough to wait until her Mommy and Daddy were all finished fucking before she made any noise." Jamie got out of bed and put on his shorts. "Unless all that noise her Mommy made earlier woke the poor child up."

Lily threw a pillow at him and said, "You stay. I'll go to her and we'll both meet you back in bed."

"Wow, years ago—before I met you, of course—when I waited for two beautiful girls to get into bed with me, it was a little different."

Lily shook her head. "You're an asshole."

Jamie laughed. "Babe, I'm joking, c'mon don't be that way."

Lily stood and went to get her nightie out of the closet. Jamie sat up in bed and watched her walk naked across the room. He jumped up, walked over to her, and put his arms around her. "I love you, babe, I really do."

Lily didn't say anything, she couldn't. Tears welled up in her eyes. Jamie saw them, smiled, and kissed her. "Don't worry, it's all gonna work out, I promise." The baby gave another insistent cry.

"I better go get her." Lily put on her nightgown and walked down the hall to the nursery. Once inside, she closed the door behind her.

"Ma, Ma, Ma," the toddler cried out and reached her hands up to her mother.

"Mama is here Daisy Rose. Lily picked her daughter up, held her close and rocked her. A wave of loneliness overcame Lily—she missed and needed her own mother. As she held her daughter tightly, Lily began to cry. She did so because, unlike the impression Jamie must have gotten, she wasn't moved to tears when he had told her he loved her. She cried then and she was crying now, because the man she truly loved and wanted to be with, was not in her bedroom and had not been anywhere near her bedroom for a very long time.

Chapter 6

*D*onna lifted the plastic top off the to-go tin that housed her Caesar salad, pushed aside the dreaded anchovy, and took a bite. It had started out as a beautiful June day when she and her goddaughter had made plans to meet for a lakeside picnic at Ladies Pavilion in Central Park. Only a half hour earlier, pitch-black clouds devoured the blue sky and within minutes erupted into an angry downpour. The charming blue and gray cast-iron structure—erected in 1871 and originally situated on the park's W. 59th Street and Eight Avenue entrance—provided shelter for passengers waiting for the trolley car. In the early years of the 20th century, the open-air structure with its many decorative columns and ornate details was moved inside the park, beside the scenic Hernshead Lake. Its slate roof protected Donna, Lily, and Daisy Rose from the rain, while the two benches inside provided them comfort as they watched soaking-wet row boaters furiously paddle back to the Boat House.

"Birdy. Birdy." Daisy Rose pointed to a baby sparrow happily splashing in the rain water that had gathered inside one of the many cup-shaped flowers sculptured on the posts. Lily picked up her daughter and brought her closer to the bird. "That's right, sweetie, it's a little birdy."

Daisy Rose squealed, clapped her chubby little hands, and the bird flew away. She waved and shouted. "Bye-bye birdy. All gone, Ma Ma." Lily gave her daughter a kiss and a cracker before putting her back on the bench.

Donna nodded to the empty spot where the sparrow had been. "Sometimes you have to let the one you love go and simply keep your fingers crossed they'll return."

"Seriously, the advice you're going to give me is 'if you love something set it free' bullshit?" Lily stuck her plastic fork into Donna's salad, and helped herself to it, then continued eating her Turkey Panini from Zabars.

"It's not bullshit, Pali, and I'm not minimizing your feelings. I know Robbie loved you. We were there. We all saw it. If it's meant to be, he'll find his way back to you. Meanwhile, what's going on with Jamie?"

"What do you mean?" Lily averted Auntie D.'s eyes and suddenly got very busy trying to locate a napkin in her Gucci black-and-white diaper bag.

"Don't hand me that Miss Innocent routine. A *little birdie* told me that he's been spotted very early in the morning, in his boxers, eating Captain Crunch at your breakfast table."

"Gladys has a big mouth. One day I'm gonna have to fire her disloyal ass." Lily chuckled.

"Don't bother. I think your mother once tried to do just that. She still showed up for work the next day *and* had the gall to ask for a raise." Donna smiled encouragingly. "Spill it. You know it's going to make you feel better."

Daisy Rose whimpered and raised her hands up to Donna, who proceeded to pick her up. The toddler yawned, rubbed her eyes, and dropped her sleepy head onto Donna's shoulder.

"Okay, so Jamie and I have been spending time together, no biggie. Because of the baby, I started feeling guilty that I was not seeing him, so I'm giving it another try."

"Is it going well?" Donna asked.

"Not so much. But I'm working on it. I just have to figure out a way to get Robbie out of my head."

"And your heart?"

Lily sighed, "Yeah, that's true. But I have to say, Jamie is being really great and trying so hard. We've been discussing going back to LA together."

"Oh?" Donna raised her perfectly shaped right eyebrow.

"Uh oh. You have that tone in your voice like Mom used to—you don't approve but you don't want to interfere."

"Listen, it's up to you. I certainly don't disapprove. But it would be hard for Robbie to come back to you if you're living with Jamie."

Lily stood up and started gathering the empty containers and paper bags left over from their picnic. "We're not going to be living together. Not at first."

Donna took Lily's hand. "Sit down; I have a story to tell you." By that time the sun had burst through the clouds and its brilliant light caught Donna's face in such a way that it made her shoulder-length, caramel-colored hair sparkle. She was a beauty, and even at 49 years old, still turned heads wherever she went.

"So do you remember when you were, oh, 11 or 12 years old, when I was dating an artist named Ken Richards?"

"Kind of." Lily thought for a second. "Wait. Was he the artist from Massachusetts?"

Donna nodded her head. "New Bedford, actually."

"Yeah I think so. Didn't Mom and I visit him in Greece when I was shooting *Aegean Paradise?*"

"Yes, he also has a home in Mykonos, where he spends a couple of months each year painting."

Whatever happened with you guys?"

"Nothing major. The timing wasn't right. However, I recently ran into him again." Donna's face turned crimson. "Well to be honest, I had a gig on the Cape with Carly and I read in the local paper that he was hosting an exhibit in New Bedford, which wasn't too far away. I decided to attend."

"How did it go?" Lily asked, intrigued.

"Great. I bought a colorful landscape that he'd painted of the island of Paros. The work is gorgeous and already hangs in my living room. You should come over and see it."

"No I mean, between you two. How did it go?

Well, so far, so good." She smiled. "Great, actually. The timing seems a lot better this go round. So Pali, even after fifteen years, it proves that if you love someone, then set them free." Donna stood up and brushed the crumbs of Daisy Rose's crackers from her lap.

"So do I get to spend some time with you and the artist?"

"Absolutely. He's got to meet you. After all, you're my family." Donna squeezed Lily's hand and smiled.

I'm glad for you, Auntie D., I really am. But I don't know if it's ever going to happen with Robbie. I think I better move on and try to forget him."

"Think about what I said. Follow your heart and I know you'll make the right decision.

Donna opened her burgundy tote and took out her cosmetics bag. Without even looking into the mirror, she expertly applied her wine-red Chanel lipstick.

"Mom used to do that—put on lipstick without looking at a mirror. How do you do that?

Donna smiled and her newly painted lips glistened. "It's like anything else: After you do it for so many years, you become a pro. It's the same thing with love and relationships. Experiences soon enough make you an expert. So be smart."

"Wow, you even turned makeup application into a teachable moment. Very impressive."

Donna put her makeup back into her purse and looked at Daisy Rose, peacefully asleep in her stroller. "I've been meaning to ask you if you're going to plan a big to-do for the baby's first birthday."

"Of course. I have to finalize a few details. The next couple of weeks are a bit hectic—my last performance is Saturday the 19th and I was thinking of having her party the following weekend, Sunday, on her actual birthday. Do you think Serendipity 3 is a good place to have it?"

Serendipity 3 is an Upper East Side New York City ice-cream restaurant that, since the 1950s, has catered to children. As soon as customers enter the front door, they are immediately propelled back in time. The front room resembles an old-fashioned ice-cream parlor, with vintage toys and penny candy for sale. The restaurant is located in the back room that you reach by walking through this nostalgic General Store. With its balloons and bright colors, the décor is eye-catching for both kids and adults. Over the years, the restaurant had been featured in movies and TV shows because of its unique ambience and wonderland quality. Their sundaes are huge and world-famous, and the frozen hot chocolate is the epitome of sweet decadence.

"Perfect. I'll be there with bells on. Who knows: I may just ask Ken to join us."

"Oh I get it. Sort of put him through trial by fire. If he can make it through the day with fifteen toddlers high on sugar, then maybe he's the perfect man for you."

Donna laughed. "Now you're catching on."

"Speaking about 'perfect men,' the guys are coming over in a little while for some family time. Want to join us? It's going to be only for an hour or two because Kristin, Jessica, and Jodee are coming over later for take-out and for what they call a *tribunal.*"

Lily spied a group of sparrows cautiously hopping toward the opposite bench and threw leftover pieces of her sandwich bread in their direction. Ten of them swooped down and quickly retrieved the ciabatini morsels.

"A *tribunal?* I'll bite, what's a tribunal?"

"How about we start walking back to the apartment and I'll fill you in on the details on the way," Lily said.

Lily stepped out of the Pavilion to throw her leftover wrappers in the trash-can on the other side of the flower-lined cobblestone path. She paused to watch a family pass by—a couple walking hand in hand on their way to the lake, their two young daughters skipping a few feet ahead of them. The adorable girls were dressed in matching polka-dotted dresses and each carried a large pink hula hoop. Their long, shiny, blonde curls bounced up and down as they skipped.

Lily looked wistfully at Donna. "Oh, see *that's* what I want for Daisy Rose. A mother and a father who love each other and a sister for Daisy Rose to play and share secrets with. I missed that growing up as an only child."

First of all, you didn't miss anything. Trust me it's not always so wonderful. You know I have an older sister?"

Lily nodded. "Cheryl Lynn, right?"

Auntie D. shook her head. "Yes, what you don't know is growing up she made my life miserable. She's a bitch now and she was twice the bitch back then. There was no sharing, hand holding, or skipping in our household."

"I'm sorry, I had no idea." Lily said as she gave the stroller an extra push up a small hill toward Central Park's West 72nd Street transverse, a place where pedestrians, joggers, bicyclists, and horses and carriages travel across the park to get to the East Side.

So, I'll bet when those perfect-looking sisters get back home after a long day in the park, they'll be fighting and calling each other names, instead of skipping and singing." Donna said.

Lily shook her head when she saw the sadness in her Aunt's face. She stopped and looked at the sky, eager to change the subject. "It turned out to be a beautiful day, didn't it?" Before Donna could reply, Lily added "And please don't make the analogy about sunshine appearing after stormy weather and how that applies to relationships, please."

"Wouldn't think of it. So, tell me about the tribunal the girls are holding at your apartment tonight." Donna stopped to take a breather. She was wearing black Ferragamo suede pumps that were not meant for the steep hills in Central Park and certainly not for dodging poop left behind by the horses as they went clop, clop through the park.

"First off, I'm positive it'll include lots of wine and laughter— both at my expense. The tribunal is Jessica's, Jodee's, and Kristin's way of judging whether Jamie and I ought to be back together or not. Because of all the conversations we've had over the last two years— where I totally trashed Jamie—they feel it is their earned right to judge, based on the hours they listened to me. If the evidence shows that he has redeemed himself, then they won't ever again say another negative word about him. If the decision is that he hasn't, they're allowed to remind me, once a week, what a big jerk he is," Lily explained.

"And what is Jodee going to be doing while this is going on?

"Oh, she's the attorney for the defense."

"She's *defending* the relationship?"

"Oh yeah—she thinks Jamie's hot." Lily winked. "So do I."

They walked past the two grand staircases leading down to Bethesda Terrace, a large fountain with the famous Angel of the Waters statue on top. The fountain's water cascades into the upper basin and surrounding pool. The beautiful angel symbolized the purification of water and is an artistic tribute to the time New York City finally got its first clean water supply from Croton Aqueduct in 1842. The Statue refers to chapter 5 of the *Gospel of John*, where an angel is blessing the Pool of Bethesda.

Lily and Donna stopped to look at the statue and its grounds. The latter was crowded with children who danced around a trumpet-playing musician, as well as with couples walking hand in hand and people seated all around the fountain, soaking up the sunshine.

"I've always loved that statue; it's one of my favorite places in Central Park."

"You *should* love it. Did Mom tell you the story of how she came up with your first name?" Lily shook her head, so Donna continued. "The next time you walk down there, take a look at what the statue is holding in her hand. You'll see that it's a lily, which symbolizes purity. Your mother and father met one summer afternoon right by the fountain. He was throwing a Frisbee on the grassy hill directly behind it. Your mom was waiting for me to meet her for a picnic and walk through the park. Anyway, the Frisbee hit her in the back of the head, which he *said* was an accident—I never believed it." Donna chuckled. "Anyway, by the time I arrived, they were deep in conversation. The fountain became their meeting place when they started to date. So after they were married and Mom got pregnant with you, she thought of the lily in the angel's hand."

"What a sweet story. How come my Mom never told me?"

Donna shrugged. "Hard to say. Could be that talking about your father was not a favorite topic of conversation for her.

A look of regret washed over Lily's face. "I often wonder about him. Why he never contacted me—how can a person do that? Leave a child and go have a life somewhere else, with a second family." Lily looked down at her sleeping angel and continued. "I couldn't imagine that."

Donna sighed, recalling the mess—financial and emotional—that Lily's father, Scott, had left behind for Daisy to deal with. Lily was only six months old at the time and the burden he had dumped on his young wife was unfathomable. It took her years of hard work to pull herself out of the mire he had left behind. "You know, Pali, I'm sure that your Mom never told you this, but Jamie reminded her of your dad, and not in a good way."

"Really?"

"Yes. His anger issues, his cheating, and even his looks. Your Mom never wanted you to make the same mistakes she had."

Lily looked puzzled. She stopped and turned and looked at her Aunt for a few seconds. "Wait a minute: Is this your way of telling me that Jamie isn't good for me?"

Donna feigned innocence. "*Moi?* I wouldn't do that."

They finally arrived at the East Side entrance to the park. Once they stepped out and on Fifth Avenue, Donna held up her hand and hailed a yellow cab.

"What are you doing—the apartment's only a few blocks away?"

"Tell that to my feet!" Donna said as she stepped into the taxi.

"Daisy Rose, come to Mommy!" Tommy, Fernando, and Donna were all seated on Lily's living-room floor. Recently, Daisy Rose had progressed from crawling to walking by holding on to chairs, sofas, table legs—anything she could grab that would get her from one place to the next on two feet.

Lily extended her arms, urging the baby to walk toward her. "Come on, Munchkin, you can do it."

"Day Ro do it!" The toddler declared proudly. She took one step and promptly fell on her bum. A stranger would have thought the adults in the room were blithering idiots, the way they reacted. They clapped, they cheered, they whistled, and they carried on as if the toddler had won the New York City Marathon.

Daisy Rose sat in the middle of the room full of her admirers—her minions. She laughed and clapped her hands, looking from one adult to another. When they stopped clapping, she would point her finger and command. "More, clap, more!"

When Daisy Rose became sleepy, she stretched out on the carpet. Her t-shirt lifted up, revealing her little round belly. Lily bent down and gave Daisy Rose a loud "raspberry" on her stomach. The "raspberry" tickled and Daisy Rose giggled until she began to hiccup. This sent the adults into another round of laughter.

"When the merriment slowed down, Lily stood up. "Well folks, playtime's over. I have to get Miss Daisy Rose ready for bed before her Mommy's friends come over for a play date."

"You sure know how to spoil a good time, don't you Mommy?" Fernando said as he handed the toddler over to her mother.

"Yeah I'm a regular buzzkill." Lily laughed and took the baby from him. "Oh my God. What did we feed this child today? She feels like she's gained a ton."

Donna walked over and pushed Daisy Rose's curly long hair out of her eyes. "The way she's been eating lately, I wouldn't be surprised if she's getting ready for a growth spurt."

"That, or she is carrying an extra load in her diaper." Fernando quipped. Lily lifted Daisy Rose over her head and smelled her bottom to see if she could detect a soiled diaper.

"No, smells as fresh as a Daisy," Lily joked and gave the baby a nibble on her chin.

"Okay little girl, it's time to say bye-bye to your Auntie and Uncles because it's sleepy time."

Daisy Rose waved bye-bye to her fans. The three adults circled the toddler and each took their turn kissing her rosy cheeks.

"I have to get back to the office, so I'd better run." Tommy turned to his partner, Fernando "Honey, do you want to share a cab downtown?"

"Sounds good, as long as you're paying."

Tommy shrugged and put his right arm around Fernando. "Don't I always?" Donna picked up her tote bag and put her arm through Tommy's free one. "I'm meeting Ken in the West Village, so I'm going to hitch a ride with you handsome gents and maybe *I'll* pay."

"Even better," Tommy and Fernando said in unison.

It was not until Lily bathed Daisy Rose, read her two nursery rhymes, and sang her four songs that the toddler finally drifted off to sleep. Lily tiptoed out of the nursery, walked into the dining room, and opened the antique credenza. She took out four Baccarat wine glasses and two bottles of Merlot produced by one of the local vineyards on the North Fork of Long Island. She opened the bottles to let them breathe and walked over to the window seat and stretched out. She was bone tired and could have used a hot bath and a long nap before the girls came over.

The night before they had gone to sleep later than usual and the morning had arrived way too early, when Daisy Rose cried for attention at 6:00 a.m. It was Margaret's day off so Lily brought Daisy Rose into her bed, hoping the toddler would go back to sleep. Instead, the infant had ended up entertaining her parents and keeping them awake.

Lily smiled when she thought of her beautiful baby and how precious she was first thing in the morning—her eyes half opened and her curly hair a messy tousle. Lily felt fortunate that she had a happy, healthy, and loving child.

Daisy Rose invented a game that morning in bed. She crawled over to Jamie, pushed Lily aside, and said, "My daddy," and kissed him. Then she turned around and crawled over to Lily and pushed Jamie aside and said, "My Ma Ma," whereupon she kissed Lily. Then she would end the game by spreading out her arms so she could touch both parents and proudly declare, "Mine."

Lily and Jamie laughed and clapped, which motivated Daisy Rose to start the game over and over again. This went on until almost 8:30 a.m. when Jamie had to take a shower so he could get cross town for his 10:00 a.m. call time.

Jamie had recently landed a lead role in the new Clarence Howard movie, *Henry's Hammock.* The plotline that Lily had gathered, from what Jamie had told her and from the bits and pieces of the script that she'd read while running lines with him, was that the character Henry discovers, when he gets on his hammock, that it mysteriously transports him back to another place in time. When Henry is ready to return to modern day, he has only to get back onto the hammock and have it rock the opposite way.

Lily made a concerted effort not to roll her eyes when Jamie told her the premise of the film. He was excited about starring in it and she didn't want to appear condescending.

She poured the Merlot into the cut-crystal stemware and sat back down on the window seat to stretch out. She held the glass up to the window and turned it around slowly until she found the perfect angle that projected a prism bouquet of colors against the adjoining wall.

She recalled how much her Mom had adored prisms. One summer she had asked Lily to help string twenty of them on wires and hang them in front of one of the kitchen windows at the farm. Daisy would eat her lunch and watch the sun hit the prisms, splashing red, green, blue, purple, and yellow circles and diamonds across the entire kitchen.

She thought of Daisy and of the story Donna had told her about how her parents had met. It was hard to imagine Daisy as a young woman. As long as Lily could remember, her mother had always been in control and definite about all the decisions she made in life. From what Donna had told her, Daisy's choice in men was questionable—at least when she was younger.

Lily knew that if Daisy were alive, she would have weighed in as soon as Lily and Jamie had gotten back together. Lily could hear her mother's voice now:

"Darling, the man lied to you, cheated on you, borrowed money from you, and never paid you back. He even punched holes in your walls. What are you doing?"

Lily smiled, took a sip of wine and counted herself lucky that Daisy was not part of the upcoming tribunal. With her gift of persuasion and legendary "Daisyisms," Lily would not have a fighting chance and Jamie would be out the door in no time at all.

But Lily felt there had been a major shift in the way Jamie acted and treated her. He was thoughtful and generous—two things he had not been years earlier. And now he was so adorable with Daisy Rose that it melted Lily's heart.

The truth of the matter was that Daisy was no longer there to give her opinions. Lily was now a grown woman with a child. It was her responsibility to do whatever she felt was right for her and the baby. In this case, it meant trying to make the situation with Jamie work.

The only thing standing in her way was the strong pull she had toward Robbie. She was annoyed with herself because she kept hanging on to this feeling of connection with him, yet she did not even know where he was or what he was up to. Something inside told her that he was *the one* she was intended to be with. Her soul felt at peace when they were together. The nights she had lain in his arms, it felt as though her whole being breathed a sigh of relief. She had never felt that way before or since.

Why could she not get him out of her head, or, as Donna said, out of her heart? When she'd been with Robbie, she'd felt almost as though they were connected by fate.

She sighed and jumped off the window seat. Any relationship with Robbie was out of her power since: (a) he had left her; and (b) she had no idea where he was. So that was that. She needed to stop thinking about the past and start concentrating on the present and the future.

The intercom connected to the lobby rang. It was Mario, informing her that the girls were on the way up.

The energy in the room kicked up ten notches as soon as Kristin, Jodee, and Jessica burst into the apartment. They came bearing gifts: three shopping bags of Chinese food and two bottles of wine.

The women began talking at once, laughing, pouring wine, and then clinking their full glasses. Jessica and Jodee opened the bags and unpacked the containers of food.

When they finally settled down, Lily and Jodee sat on the couch while Kristin and Jessica sat across from them on the floor. They used the coffee table as a tabletop.

"Just how many people were you planning to feed?" Lily said and counted twelve different carry-out cartons.

"You know what I say: variety is the spice of life. And I make sure to live a very *spicy* life," Jodee said and waved her chopsticks around for added emphasis. They all laughed.

"You, honey, make living spicy an art form, that's for damn sure." Jessica said. Okay now, girls, I think we need to discuss the rules of the tribunal.

"Wait, wait. Don't start yet, I have to pee." Jodee looked at Jessica. "Promise you won't start until I get back."

"I don't know if we can make that commitment." Kristin teased "How long does it usually take you to tinkle?"

"No worries. If you can't wait for me, I'll just go to the bathroom right here—so start talking." Jodee stood up in the middle of the living room and pantomimed like she was going to pull her jeans down.

Lily tossed a pillow at her friend. "Hurry up and go to the bathroom *in* the bathroom and I promise we'll wait for you." Jodee raced out of the room.

"I'm warning you, you three better cut me a break during this tribunal, remember I'm in a delicate condition, being postpartum and all." Lily took a bite of her spring roll.

Kristin reached over the table to grab a packet of duck sauce. "I so hate to be the one to burst your maternal bubble, but you cannot play the postpartum card when your daughter is days away from her first birthday. Better think of something else."

Jodee came back into the room and plopped down on the floor. Lily took a spare rib and contemplated her next "pull at their heartstrings" move. She used all her abilities as an award- winning actress to conjure up tears. "Please be kind to me, I am a poor motherless child who has no one to defend me."

Jodee turned to Lily "Gonna have to do much better than that, girlfriend."

Once they had finished most of the food, Jessica stood up on the couch and proclaimed

"Here Ye, Here Ye, the tribunal will now commence in the case of the Whole World VS. Jamie Fleming—"

Lily stood and turned to the group? "The *whole world?*"

"Sit down, you will have your day in court, Miss Lockwood." Jessica took off her boot and used it as a gavel "The court calls upon Miss Lockwood to come forward."

"Wait one minute." Jodee ran into the kitchen and fetched a backless stool and set it down in the middle of the living room. "Let the records show the witness for the defense will now be seated."

Lily climbed up and sat on the stool. Jodee took the shade off a nearby gooseneck floor lamp and bent it so it was directly over Lily's head. The glare of the lamp made it impossible for Lily to see her interrogators.

Kristin stood and announced. "Before the witness is asked to state her name, everyone in this high court must take the obligatory shot of Tequila. Jessica, since you are the judge, won't you please do the "honors."

Jessica handed each one a shot of Patron and on the count of three, they all downed it. There were talking so loud and laughing so hard, they didn't notice that Jamie had walked into the room. "Hey Babe whatcha got here?"

Lily swiveled around so fast that the momentum of the stool, in concert with the wine and tequila she imbibed, sent her flying to the floor. Laughing so hard Lily ended up rolling around. Every time she attempted to stand she'd fall right back down on the floor. Finally Jamie chuckled, extended his hand, pulled her up and kissed her. The girls whooped and hollered like a bunch of twelve year olds. Lily put her arm around Jamie's waist, turned to her three friends, and introduced him to Jessica and Kristin, who still had never met him.

It was an unspoken understanding that due to the untimely appearance of the defendant, the tribunal had to be adjourned for another night.

Jamie ended up having drinks, talking and laughing with the girls for the next few hours. Lily sat back and watched Jamie turn on the charisma, full force. Sometimes when they were in a social setting—a party or industry event—she would hold her breath to see which Jamie would emerge. He could be outgoing and captivating, as he was tonight or he could be moody and withdrawn. At times, she felt like Jamie's personality was like an expensive Armani suit that he kept in the back of his closet and only took out for special occasions.

From the way her friends were hanging on to her boyfriend's every charming word, and laughing at all his jokes, Lily was quite certain a second tribunal would not be necessary.

Chapter 7

*L*ily bolted straight up in bed, her heart pounding, her hair drenched in sweat, with tears streaming down her face. She looked at the clock and saw it was only 3:30 a.m. She thought of the dream she'd just had—more of a terrifying nightmare, actually.

Robbie was living in this big house on a hill, surrounded by water. He opened the window and waved to her.

"Come on up," Robbie called down to her. She remembered how elated she had felt in the dream—that after all the years apart, they would finally be together again soon. She stood outside the house, by the front gate, waiting for someone to open it for her. The guard at the gate looked a Lily, shook his head, and refused to grant her entrance. She felt annoyed and then angry. She looked at the cement wall that surrounded the home, much like the privacy walls her friends in Beverly Hills have encompassing their mansions. She tried but was unable to climb the barrier.

Robbie, still at the window, kept calling down to her, urging her to hurry. Lily heard a clap of thunder and looked up at the sky. A large white-blue lightning bolt zigzagged and hit the top of the roof, right above Robbie's window. Within seconds there was an explosion and the house caught fire. The fire spread rapidly until it consumed the whole structure. She heard Robbie calling her name. Then everything went still and Lily fell to the ground crying.

That was all Lily could remember of the dream. She took a deep breath and quietly swung her legs around the side of the bed, looked over her shoulder to make sure she had not disturbed Jamie, and stood up.

She walked into the kitchen and took out a small saucepan from under the sink. Lily remembered the times growing up when she had had horrible nightmares and her mother would pick her up from her bed, bring her into the kitchen, and lift her up onto one of the kitchen stools. Daisy would keep a stream of conversation going to distract Lily from the memory of the nightmare that had woken her.

Daisy poured milk into the same saucepan Lily now held in her hand, and waited until it was heated to just the right temperature. She would lower the heat and very slowly stir in the chocolate until the powder completely dissolved. She would present it to Lily with a dollop of whipped cream on top. While Lily drank her hot cocoa, she and her mother would chat and laugh together. By the time she'd finished the last drop, she had forgotten the nightmare and she would be ready to go back to sleep.

Lily poured the milk into the saucepan and put it on the stove. Because her mother was not there to distract her, she thought of the heart-pounding nightmare that had caused her to awaken in such distress and in a pool of sweat. It seemed as if she had been thinking and dreaming about Robbie more often than she had in the past. She felt a bond—a connection—that she had never felt with any other man.

Was it because Jamie was in her life again and the comparison she found herself making between the two men, always had Jamie coming up on the short end of the stick?

Lily lowered the heat, poured the chocolate into the warm milk, took a wooden spoon, and slowly stirred. Lately she felt that the connection she had with Robbie was becoming stronger instead of weaker, with the passage of time. Lily poured the chocolate into one of Daisy's favorite mugs and sat on the stool in front of the breakfast bar.

She recalled a story Robbie had told her when they were out at the farm. It was an autumn day and they made plans early in the morning to take the sailboat out in the afternoon and spend the day on the water. By the time they had finished breakfast, made love and spent hours talking in bed, black clouds covered the sky, the wind picked up, and the waves became angry and choppy. They decided to forego the sail, stay indoors, light a fire, and cook a hearty dinner. Robbie actually did all the cooking and Lily's job was to pour the wine, sit on the counter beside him, and watch Robbie perform his culinary magic. That afternoon, he decided to make a dish called Glazed Brisket that his grandmother used to cook for him and David when they were growing up.

Robbie opened the refrigerator and pulled out an onion and garlic from the vegetable bin. He placed them on the wooden cutting board he had prepared on the counter. Suddenly a look Lily did not recognize came over his face and he smiled.

"What are you smiling about? Lily asked.

"I was just thinking about my Grandmother and about a story she told me a long time ago when I was sitting and watching her prepare this dish. Wow, I haven't thought of that story in years." Robbie began cutting the onion into very thin slices.

"Tell me, I'd love to hear."

"Well, when I was growing up my grandmother, my father's mother, we called her Bubby, lived in a small house on my family's property, very close to us. My grandfather had died long before David was adopted and I was born. As a matter of fact David is named after him.

"As you know, my Dad is a doctor and his office is actually attached to our house. All day long patients would come and go using the side entrance that led to the waiting room." Robbie took out three cloves of garlic and crushed them.

"When David and I got older, my mother, who had been a nurse when she met my father, started helping out in the office. You know my mother, she has this great personality and the patients love her."

Lily nodded, imagining Hannah, with her big heart and soft voice, talking to the patients and making them feel comfortable and safe.

David put the brisket into a large ovenproof casserole dish, added water, sliced onions and crushed garlic, and placed it on the stove. "It needs to simmer for an hour and a half, then I'll add the apricots and brown sugar and get it into the oven. So I'll put the timer on and we can go in and sit by the fire."

Robbie picked Lily up off the counter and carried her into the living room and gently placed her on the couch. He picked up the afghan that her Grams had crocheted and handed it to her. He went back into the kitchen to retrieve the wine. He brought the bottle and glasses back into the living room and sat down on the couch next to her. She covered herself with the afghan, put her legs over his lap and wiggled her toes. As was their routine, he started rubbing her feet.

"So where was I?"

"Your Mom helping your Dad in the office." Lily took a sip of wine.

"My Dad is an excellent doctor, but is not a people-person. So my mother, even now, is a big asset to his practice. On the days my mother worked with him, the bus would pull up in front of our house and Bubby would be standing there waiting to envelop her boys with a hug. She took us to her house and fixed us snacks before we went back out to play.

One day, I must have been ten or eleven years old and the school was closed because it was teacher's conference day. David had slept over at a friend's house so I was by myself and bored. I walked over to Bubby's house to see if she happened to be baking cookies.

When I got there, she had just begun to prepare the meal for dinner later on. As was our family tradition every Friday night my parents, brother, and I would walk down the hill, to my Grandmother's house for Sabbath dinner. On those nights, when we were halfway down the hill, we could already smell the aroma of the food she had prepared and our mouths would begin to water before we even got to her front door. And when we walked into her house, the old wooden table that I did my homework on every afternoon was transformed. There would always be a white, lace tablecloth covering the worn table. She once told us it was the first thing she purchased when she married my grandfather. Her best china would magically appear on the table, and the bronze candlesticks that she polished earlier in the day found a proud place of honor in the middle of the table."

Lily shivered and wrapped the blanket around her shoulders. Robbie stopped talking and walked over to the fireplace and threw in a large chunk of wood and sat back down.

"So go on—Sabbath dinner," Lily urged.

"Anyway, the day I went over there, the day I was off from school, she had just started the brisket. She gave me milk and cookies and told me stories about how she used to sit and watch her Mama cook in the 'Old Country.' I asked her if her husband, my Grandpa, was also from the 'Old Country.' She smiled and wiped her eyes that always filled with tears whenever she spoke of him.

"'Yes *Tatela*. I knew him since we were children, but then we were separated, lost from each other for many years.'

"I asked, 'Bubby, why were you lost from each other?' I saw a look of sadness come over her face and I felt bad, as if I'd said something wrong to make her look like that. After she put the brisket on the stove, she sat at the table next to me and told me the story.

"'Your grandfather and I lived in a city in Poland, not far from Warsaw, called Lodz. I lived in a building where each apartment was as big as a house. David, your Grandfather, lived a few streets away, in a part of the city that was not as grand. One morning, when I was a little older than you, your Grandfather knocked on my front door. I was in my bedroom curling my long hair. I heard him say to my Father, 'Sir, may I walk Chaya Ruchel to school?' My Papa, who was a big-shot banker and one of the wealthiest men in the city, could at times be somewhat arrogant. He wanted us to play only with children whose parents were in the same social stratus as our family. What he didn't know is how very much I liked David Rosen from the moment I had met him on the playground. There was something about his eyes. . .'

Then Bubby moved closer to me and peered into my eyes over her bifocals.

"'They were as blue as yours, *Tatela*!'

Robbie smiled at Lily. "Bubby, stood up, put her hands on her hips and Lily, in that moment, I could see in her face, the strong little girl that she must have been. She continued telling me her story:

"'I finally walked into the living room where Papa was talking to David and said, 'Papa, please let David walk me to school.' My Papa finally gave in. From that day on, every morning at 7:30 a.m. sharp, David would walk me to school. Every day, after school, he carried my books and walked me back home.'

Robbie leaned back and closed his eyes. "I remember Bubby's face started to glow, as though she was that young girl in love again.

"'*Tatela*, Lodz was a city that had many rivers and woods. One day after school, David and I sat by one of the rivers and skipped stones. He turned to me, looked into my eyes, and said, 'Chaya Ruchel, one day I am going to make so much money and put it all in your father's bank. Then he will know I am good enough to marry his only daughter.' I smiled and kissed him on the cheek. I remember his face turned as red as the borscht that my Mama always made for Shabbat dinner. Then he took my hand and kissed it and said 'Chaya Ruchel, you are my *bashert*!'".

"I interrupted Bubby to ask her what a *bashert* is," Robbie said.

'*Tatela*, your *bashert* is your intended—someone who you are intended to be with and love forever. They say the match is made in heaven. Many people nowadays call it soul mates. And when you meet the one, the bond is so strong that even if you are apart, you will always find your way back to one another.

Then David said something I would never forget: 'There is a silver cord tied from my heart to yours that can never be severed. Chaya Ruchel you are the love of my life.'

"Before she continued her story, my Bubby put her hand to her heart and closed her eyes, as if she was again hearing those words of love and commitment that my Grandfather had spoken so many years ago.

"'Later on that year, there were terrible things happening in Poland. And, *Tatela*, do you remember when you read all about that little girl Anne Frank? German men, called Nazis, with guns, burst into our home early one morning and took my Mama and Papa and me. They pointed to the Stars of David that we had been forced to sew on all our clothes, grabbed us, and pushed us out on to the street. Our neighbors were all gathered together and the Nazis forced us to walk all the way to the railroad train. I remember looking up and down the street to see if my David was close-by. But I never saw him.

'When the train finally arrived, the men pushed us all into a railroad car. It was so crowded, with hundreds of men, women, and children cramped together in a small space.

They locked us in and there was no food or water or air. The smell became so bad—there was no bathroom so people ended up soiling themselves. It was extremely hot and I felt sick to my stomach. I could not stop weeping and my Papa held me close and said,

'My *Shana Maidela*, my Chaya Ruchel, Papa is with you. I will take care of you always.' We sat like that for what seemed to be an eternity. The train finally stopped and we all got out. There was a big sign on the entrance gate that said *Arbeit Macht Frei*, a lie which means *Work Makes You Free*. We had arrived at Aushwitz.

They separated the men and women into two lines. I screamed 'Papa don't leave me. Papa stay with me.' I was shocked to see that my big, strong Papa was weeping. I had never seen Papa cry in my whole life. That was the last time my Mama and I saw him.'

Robbie smiled and wiped his eyes, "By this time, tears were streaming down my Bubby's face. She took a deep breath and continued her story.

"'During the years I was in the camp it was a horrible place, where we worked very hard and had almost no food to eat. Everyone was hungry and thirsty; we had lice; and many became ill and died. Oy, so many of our friends were killed, you shouldn't know from such things.

Every day I thought of the young boy David who had called himself my *bashert*. Every night, after I said my prayers, I would try to remember how it felt when David kissed my hand and walked me to school every morning. Then I would put my hand on my heart as if to touch the silver cord that was still tied to it. I imagined that David—far, far, away and safe from the Nazis— had the other end of the silver cord tied securely to his heart. I never felt the bond was severed. I always felt connected. Before I closed my eyes every night, I would imagine I was able to follow the silver cord for miles and miles until I came to the other end, which was firmly tied to David's heart. I would then whisper into the darkness, 'My *bashert*, my *bashert*, where are you? Please find me, please save me.'

Robbie leaned over and wiped away the tears that were dripping down Lily's face,

"Bubby covered her eyes with her hands as if to block out the horrible events that were forever burned into her memory and, like the numbers that had been branded on to her arm, could never be erased. With her hands still covering her eyes she continued telling me her story.

"'One day they took my Mama away from me and I never saw her again. So there I was, *Tatela*, all alone, an orphan in hell. Not long after, the Americans came and set us free. So with nowhere to go, no family at all, hundreds of us walked.

One day we stopped by a small river to wash our faces and dip our hands into the clean water and drink. It was then that I heard 'Chaya Ruchel, Chaya Ruchel.' I turned around, wondering who was calling my name. I saw a very tall teenage boy, his head was shaved just like mine and he was so skinny he looked like a lanky bag of bones.

He said 'Chaya Ruchel, don't you know who I am? It's me, David Rosen. I have been searching for you, for so long.' He took my hand—no longer smooth and pretty—and placed it on his chest. 'There is a silver cord tied from my heart to yours that can never be severed. Chaya Ruchel you are the love of my life.'

Later that night, I remember thanking God, The Almighty, for allowing the silver cord to remain intact and for helping my *bashert* find me once again. And, *Tatela*, my *bashert* and I were together for the rest of his life.'

Robbie got up and stoked the fire, "I looked at my Grandmother and asked if the silver cord was still tied, even though my Grandpa had died so many years ago. She wiped her eyes and smiled at me."

'Yes, it is still tied. But now that your Grandpa is in heaven, the silver cord has had to stretch many more miles then it ever had to before. When I join my *bashert* in heaven, and we are once again side-by side, the silver cord will become small once again.'"

Robbie walked over to Lily, wiped away her tears, and leaned in to kiss her, "So that is the love story of Chaya Ruchel and David."

The timer rang and Robbie left the living room to put his Bubby's brisket into the oven.

Even years later, as she sat alone in her darkened kitchen, the story brought tears to Lily's eyes and hope to her heart. She drank the last of her cocoa, closed her eyes and thought of Robbie. Lily put her hand over her heart, where she knew one side of the silver cord was tied; she imagined following it, for miles and miles, until she found the other end of the cord—firmly tied to Robbie's heart.

Lily whispered, "My *bashert*, my *bashert*, where are you? Please find me, please save me."

Chapter 8

The next few weeks flew by as Lily made a conscious effort to leave Robbie where he belonged—in the past. She and Jamie saw much of each other and had fallen into a new routine. On days when the theater was dark and Lily had time off, they would pack their bags and head east to her farmhouse in the quaint town of Southold, on the North Fork of Long Island.

The farmhouse is a waterfront property on the beautiful Long Island Sound, a 110-mile-long estuary of the Atlantic Ocean. Only twenty-one miles of its waters separate Long Island on the south and Connecticut to the north. The 1897 farmhouse once proudly sat on a thirty-acre parcel of land. In the late 1940's, Lily's Grandparents, Samuel and Rose Edwards, had purchased it and turned it into one of the many potato farms on the North Fork. But little by little, over the years, Grandpa had sold off all the acreage to land developers— except for three acres of beautiful waterfront property. Even though most of the original farmland no longer belonged to the family, everyone still referred to the home as the "farmhouse." Daisy, who was Sam and Rose's only child, had inherited it from them, and when Daisy passed away, the three waterfront acres, farmhouse, and a large barn were passed down to Lily.

Sometimes Daisy Rose's nanny, Margaret, would accompany them out to the farmhouse, but more often than not, Lily and Jamie wanted privacy and time alone with their daughter. It was during those lazy summer days, while sailing on her boat and swimming in the Sound that the little family bonded. Daisy Rose came to love the water and would whoop and holler and splash about while her parents held her.

She would lift her arms up to her daddy and scream, "Up, up, Da!" and Jamie would do as the princess commanded and lift her high up on his shoulders. That gesture melted Lily's heart and was confirmation that she had done the right thing by deciding to allow Jamie back into her life.

However, it was the times after Daisy Rose fell asleep for the night and Lily and Jamie were alone that the remnants of doubt buzzed around her head, like an annoying house fly that could not be quieted.

One night, the baby was fast asleep and Jamie and Lily lay naked, making love in the hammock in the back yard. Lily struggled to keep her mind focused on Jamie as his hands caressed her body. She willed herself not to drift off and think of another set of hands—hands that instinctively knew better than anyone where to touch her and how to awaken sensations that had lain dormant before he had entered her life. Frustration and sadness overcame Lily and she gently pushed Jamie away and got up off the hammock.

"What the hell, Babe? What happened?"

For a second she thought she might tell him, but she knew that would be unwise. It would open a floodgate that she might never again be able to close. She had to decide either to forget Robbie or make this work with Jamie, or to move on without Jamie. Could anyone ever make her feel the way that Robbie had? What if her time with Robbie was the apex and nothing else—no one else—could ever come close? What kind of life would that be?

"I'm sorry, I'm just tired. Must be from all the sun today." Lily lied. Before Jamie could respond, she got dressed, walked down toward the water, and sat down on one of the Adirondack chairs. Jamie sighed and went inside the house. Twenty minutes later he came back, having showered and dressed, holding a bottle of Cabernet and two wine glasses. He sat on the chair next to Lily and handed her a glass. She accepted it and he poured. They sat in silence, listening to the waves and looking up at the star-filled sky.

Jamie finished his first glass of wine, poured himself another, and while still looking straight ahead toward the water, said, "I was just thinking about the night you held that memorial service after your mother died. The tent was over there, right?" He pointed to the field left of where they were seated.

After the terrible car crash, her mother had passed away from the results of a traumatic brain injury. Lily, Donna, and her mother's friend Theresa had decided that instead of having a traditional funeral, they would honor Daisy by having a black-tie memorial fundraiser with proceeds to benefit the Brain Injury Association. The guest list read like a Who's Who of both the literary and entertainment industries. Daisy's dear friends paid tribute to her as one after another walked onstage and told heartfelt, emotional, and often funny stories about their beloved friend.

The guests danced the night away beneath the crystal chandeliers that hung from the ceiling of the draped, tufted-silk tent that had been handcrafted by sixth-generation New England sail makers. Daisy would have been proud and honored to know they had raised more than $100,000 in her name for the worthy organization.

Lily and Jamie were already broken up by that time. However, since Harvey, the producer of the movie Jamie was currently filming, and his wife Mitzi had bought a table at the event, which cost them over $5,000, they invited Jamie. They were smart enough not to invite Natalie, Jamie's curvaceous co-star.

"Whatever happened to that guy you introduced everyone to, that night, as your brother. You know the one who was in the accident with Daisy. The guy she gave up for adoption when she was a teenager? What was his name again?"

Lily shrugged nonchalantly and closed her eyes. "His name is David and I haven't seen him since that night." Lily thought about David and the terrible events that resulted in his and his brother, Robbie, coming to fisticuffs that night. It was the last time she had seen either one of them.

She sighed and tears welled up in her eyes. She wiped them before Jamie could notice, "I don't know what happened to him." She hoped Jamie wouldn't push for any more information. But, of course, he did.

"So tell me again, how did you find out that he was your brother?"

Lily understood, at that moment, where Jamie was headed with this line of questioning.

"Jamie, we've gone through this before. I already told you everything, way before the baby was born. Don't you remember" Lily held on to her chair's wooden armrests so that she wouldn't give in to the temptation to run far away from Jamie and this conversation.

"Not really, tell me again." He turned his chair, ever so slightly, just enough to be able to see Lily's profile, gently illuminated by the moonlight. "By the way, you knew you were pregnant by that time, right?"

She tensed up. "Yes, I had just found out. It was a few days after my mother's accident."

"And you didn't think to call me to let me know I was going to be a father, right?"

Lily's cheeks blazed and her heart pounded. "Jamie, is this about before, when we were on the hammock? I told you, I'm just tired. . ."

He poured himself another glass of wine and smiled. "Not at all, Babe. Finish the story, it's getting interesting." He reminded Lily of that mean boy in the playground—the one who caught spiders to torture them by pulling off their legs, one by one, to see how they would react.

So remind me again, why didn't you tell me you were pregnant?"

Lily had had enough. "You seriously want me to go there, Jamie? Huh? Okay, let's go there."

Lily moved to the edge of her seat and got ready for what was to come. "I didn't tell you because you were screwing your co-star at the time. I didn't think you had the urge to climb off her body to talk to your pregnant girlfriend."

Jamie laughed. "God, Lily, how many times do I have to tell you that never happened?"

"Jamie, why do you need to lie about this?" Lily's face was beet red, "She told me at the party that you and she were planning to fuck around. Then, when you came to visit me, I read the text she sent saying her bed was empty and she missed you."

Jamie jumped out of his chair. He was no longer smiling. "And who was in *your* bed at that time?"

"In my bed at that time? No one. No one was in my bed." She sat back down, took a calming breath, and closed her eyes.

"Bullshit," Jamie said and stormed into the house.

Lily was happy to be alone. She thought of her brother David and of the day she first met him. She didn't know there had been another person in the car at the time of the accident, until she read about it in the news. She found out the ambulance had transported someone named David Rosen to University Hospital. He was badly injured; his arms were broken, his spleen shattered, and his kidneys damaged.

She was shocked when he told her Daisy had been the mother who had given him up for adoption. For years they had looked for each other. They finally found one another and he flew in from Texas to visit with her. They had a wonderful time together and planned another visit the following month. The accident occurred while she was driving David back to the airport and would ultimately prove fatal for Daisy.

Lily sat in the dark and thought about her own daughter, asleep in the house. Tears streamed down her face when she thought of what her mother must have gone through having to give up her son. And all those years she searched for him, to no avail.

Jamie emerged from the house, sat next to Lily, and touched her face.

"Babe, please don't cry. I don't want to fight with you. After you got up out of the hammock, I was upset. I don't know, I had this feeling that something else—someone else—was on your mind. Then I remembered the night of the memorial gala and the guy you were dancing with all night. You know, the tall guy who walked in with your brother. What was his name? Who was he again?"

"His name is Robbie. He's David's brother—the natural son of David's adoptive parents.

"I just got jealous thinking about you dancing with that guy all night. He seemed to be holding you a little too close. You really looked as if you were into each other." Jamie kneeled in front of Lily's chair and took her hand. "We've been doing good, you and me. And having so much fun just being a family. I don't want to ruin it by being a jerk. I'm really sorry." He kissed her hand. "Please let's start again and forget what happened tonight. She nodded and smiled. Jamie kissed Lily and pulled her up to her feet.

"Come on, let's get to sleep. We have to get up early in the morning to drive back to the city. Also, remember you told Tommy you were going to deliver the next few chapters of your manuscript to him by end of day tomorrow." Lily groaned.

They walked hand in hand, back into the house, where their daughter soundly slept.

In bed, later that night, Lilly tossed and turned. She had come dangerously close to telling Jamie about her feelings for Robbie. She finally drifted off to sleep, knowing that at least for the time being, she had dodged a bullet.

Chapter 9

The bullet whizzed by The Prisoner's left earlobe. He ducked and the shell barely missed him. The Prisoner didn't need to look up to see the perpetrator because it no longer mattered to him. A burst of laughter caused him to finally lift his head. He saw that it was a mere child holding the pistol. The little boy had pulled the trigger hoping to prove to the older boys in the group that he too could hit a moving target. When the little boy failed, the older ones mocked him. One of the guards walked over to the boy, grabbed the gun from his hand and chastised him in front of the others. Humiliated, the boy sat on the ground and cried.

The Prisoner shook his head. The ringing in his ear became a residual by-product which remained with him the rest of the day— a physical reminder of how little regard there was for life. The Prisoner understood, all too well, that any moment could very well be his last. After all these months The Prisoner had grown accustomed to it and felt strangely comforted to know that by some twist of fate, he had, at least momentarily, cheated death.

The Prisoner could not have known he was being kept alive for a specific goal, which soon enough would be revealed. He was oblivious to the fact that the ambush and brutal murder of each of his colleagues were simply ways to capture his attention, heighten his fear, and elicit his gratitude. The men who were holding him captive knew The Prisoner would eventually be so profoundly indebted to them, that he would renounce all that he had known to be ethical and moral—that The Prisoner would, without a moment's hesitation, relinquish the Hippocratic Oath which he had so proudly sworn to uphold.

One night, when the guard who called himself Max presented The Prisoner with a wafer thin mattress and box spring, it almost brought him to tears. The following evening when Max returned, he brought with him another gift that helped The Prisoner to forget everything. He felt as if he was floating upon a cloud. The Prisoner had never felt such intense euphoria. From that night on, he lay on his bed, closed his eyes, and waited for Max to appear with another fix. For the next three weeks Max visited, bringing with him the drug that had become The Prisoner's nightly escape.

Abruptly Max's visits stopped and for two days and nights The Prisoner waited for Max and his syringe filled with magic. On the third night, when the hot and cold tremors of withdrawal had rapidly elevated and the core of every muscle in The Prisoner's body began to ache, the door finally opened and Max walked into the room. He stood for a few moments and looked at The Prisoner who was on the floor in a fetal position, rocking side to side, and moaning in pain.

Max walked up to The Prisoner, knelt down beside him, and patted him on the leg. The Prisoner, who was bathed in sweat and shivering, weakly held out his left arm. Max took it in his hands, tied an elastic strap around The Prisoner's bicep, and pulled tight. Then Max ran his finger up and down The Prisoner's arm, looking for a bulging vein. Max lifted the syringe, punctured The Prisoner's vein and released its contents into his arm. All pain immediately vanished.

That evening, he did not miss her, nor did The Prisoner even think of her. He floated away from his tiny cell of a room, across the rooftops, above the trees, and straight into the billowing clouds.

Chapter 10

*D*avid looked past his sleeping mother, her head resting on the small window. He glanced past her to the clouds, which resembled layers of wispy fog as they engulfed the Boeing 747. He touched her shoulder to gently wake her, just as the stewardess's announcement came over the intercom:

"Ladies and gentlemen, we have started our descent in preparation for landing. Please make sure your seat backs and tray tables are in their full upright position. Make sure your seat belt is securely fastened and that all carry-on luggage is stowed beneath the seat in front of you or in the overhead bins. Please turn off all electronic devices until we have safely arrived at the gate and the captain gives you the go-ahead to turn them on again. The flight attendants are currently passing around the cabin to pick up any remaining cups and glasses. We will be arriving at terminal 8 our gate is C34. The weather in New York City is a sizzling 91 degrees and local time is 4:40 p.m. On behalf of our pilot, Captain Jose Santiago, and my fellow flight attendants, we thank you for choosing American Airlines."

Hannah smiled at her son, and, as instructed, adjusted her seatback and grabbed both ends of her seatbelt and clicked them together.

"Were you able to sleep at all?"

"Not a wink." David threw his plastic cup into the open garbage bag that the flight attendant held out to him.

Hannah looked at her watch and saw they were ahead of schedule. Since they had not checked their bags, they should be in a cab heading into the city within 45 minutes if there were no delays on the tarmac.

"We should be on time. Should we check into the hotel first? Curtain time isn't until 8:00 p.m. But then again, maybe we shouldn't, because if we get caught in traffic, who knows how long it will take us to get to the theater."

David smiled at his mother. During his childhood, he and his brother, Robbie, had called her Nervous Nellie because she fretted over everything. At times, it drove the guys crazy. But she was married to the right man; his father had had the patience of a saint when it came to his wife. He would smile, pat her hand, kiss her cheek, and tell her there was no need to worry. Like a tranquilizer, it would immediately calm her down and she would be relaxed until the next anxious incident. Now that his father was gone, it was up to him to be the one to quell her nerves, which had become a massive undertaking since the day they received the phone call about his brother, Robbie.

"Do you think we'll get a chance to speak with Lily tonight?" Hannah asked.

"All we can do is give someone at the theater a note telling Lily we're in the audience and that we'd like to see her after the show. The rest is up to her."

Hannah sighed. She wanted to make sure Lily understood that they had exhausted every possibility before flying 1400 miles from Dallas to see the actress and ask for her assistance. She looked at her handsome son and smiled because he closed his eyes. It was something David did every flight he had taken since he had been a child. She supposed that it made the landing experience easier for him.

David kept his eyes closed and thought of the last time he had seen Lily. His stomach did a small flip. He and Robbie, who hadn't argued since they were kids, got into a knock-down, drag-out brawl at Daisy's memorial service. Lily was the reason the brothers had fought. They had acted like imbeciles in front of her. Truth was, they were always competitive—ever since they'd been young—but it had always been a friendly competition. Until that night.

David's face grew flush with embarrassment when he thought about the events of the evening. How horribly he had reacted and the hurtful things he had said to Lily before they left. Ghastly things—words that can permanently alter a relationship. He wondered if he and Lily could ever get back on track, where they had once been. Would she even be open to speaking to him again?

David opened his eyes after the four wheels touched the ground. "I think it best if the note comes from you."

Hannah had heard bits and pieces of what had happened with her sons and Lily. She figured it must have been worse than either one of her sons had told her. After the incident there was a coldness and separation between her two boys that had never existed before. No matter how many times she'd tried to discuss it, David made it clear that the subject was off-limits.

She reached for David's hand. Whatever had happened that night, now had to be put aside. They were family and in times like these, families must stick together.

Chapter 11

During the intermission, Jodee put the back of her hand up to her forehead in a dramatic gesture of woe. "So this is it—our final performance—our beautiful swan song." Lily, seated at her dressing-room mirror, fixed her mascara, and rolled her thickly lashed eyes at her co-star.

"That might be so, Sarah Bernhardt, except this morning I spoke to Arty T., I mean Arthur Thomas, about you. His casting director should be calling your agent tomorrow to set up an audition. If it goes the way I think it will, you and I will be spending the next two months together in LA, shooting his new movie, *Seventh Sister*."

Jodee rushed over and hugged Lily. "You are *the* best friend ever! Oh my God, how great would that be? I can see it now, you and me having cocktails in Malibu, on the deck of *Moonshadows*, after a day of sun and surfing."

"First of all, we don't surf. Second, as I hear it, days off are hard to come by on Arthur Thomas's movies. So be prepared to work your little butt off."

"Oh I will. And that Arty T. is one *fine* brother. Maybe I'll become a big Hollywood star *and* catch me a man." The friends laughed.

There was a knock at the door and Lily nodded to Jodee to open it. Timmy, the stage manager's assistant, was standing on the other side.

"Sorry to bother you, Miss Lockwood, but I was at the stage door and a man and woman asked me to give you this note." He held up the folded piece of paper.

Jodee grabbed it out of his hands. "I'll take that. Let's see who your secret admirers are this evening." Jodee opened the note and read aloud:

My dearest Lily,

We are here and would like to see you for a short visit at the end of the play. Please let us know if it's possible.

Best wishes

Hannah Rosen.

Lily, stunned, stopped in mid-curl and put the mascara wand down. Her heart pounded as she turned to Timmy. "Did you say a man and a woman? Was the man younger than the woman?

Timmy shook his head. "Yeah, like he could be her son or something."

Lily looked into the mirror and even through the heavy layers of stage make-up she could see that she had gone pale. She covered her mouth and took a breath to steady her nerves.

She turned to Jodee who looked confused. "The note is from Robbie's mother."

With that, the chimes rang three times, indicating that intermission was coming to an end. Lily wondered if Robbie was, at that very moment, in the audience, taking his seat. This was the moment she'd been waiting for since the night of the memorial gala. She wondered how he would look. What would they say to one another? She smiled because she would make sure, before the evening was over, that Robbie knew she was still in love with him. Her heart soared as she and Jodee walked out of the dressing room, down the stairs. The women took their places on stage. The curtain rose, the audience clapped, and the final act began.

Chapter 12

Lily looked around. The other passengers in Business Class—all members of her group—were fast asleep. Hours earlier their seats had been converted into long private beds; thick woolen blankets protected them against the chill of the cabin, while down-filled pillows gently cradled their heads.

Lily turned her overhead light on and quickly looked around to make sure it did not disturb anyone. Once again, she took out the news article, the one she had read and reread over the last ten days. She stared at his photo. The camera captured his essence—amused expression, twinkling blue eyes, and a slightly lopsided grin. He appeared to be on the verge of revealing a secret, one that he found too entertaining not to share. And in life, if you were the recipient of his stories, his attention, his warmth, his love—that was all the sustenance that a person would ever need.

Lily took a deep sigh to calm her nerves. She had been crying almost non-stop since that first night, the night they visited her in the theater.

She had practically run off stage after the last curtain call. It was the final performance of the play's Broadway run and the audience refused to let them leave. They went ballistic—on their feet, clapping and shouting, demanding the actors take another bow, then another. The curtain ultimately fell for the last time and the reluctant audience left the theater.

Ever since intermission, when Lily had received Hannah's note, the end of the play couldn't come fast enough. By tradition, actors savor every moment of their final show, knowing they will never again deliver those lines or interact with the other actors in the same way. Lily had only one thing on her mind— seeing Robbie. She raced up the stairs and waited.

Finally there was a knock and her heart felt as if it was going to catapult out of her chest. When she opened the door, it took all her skills as a seasoned actress to hide her naked disappointment. It was not Robbie on the other side, but his brother David.

"David, come on in. What a wonderful surprise." David entered and looked genuinely happy to see her. The moment was awkward, as neither one of them knew what the appropriate greeting should be. The last time they had been together, David's remarks to her were brutal, even devastating.

She initiated a hug. She looked into his eyes—eyes that were so like her mother's—and she saw his relief. Lily offered him a seat.

"Would you like a glass of champagne? The cast was celebrating earlier. I'm sure there's some left." She walked over to the table in the sitting area of the room.

"No don't bother, Lily, I've been sober now for 21 months and 3 days."

"Good for you." Lily said and truly meant it. "David, where's your mother?"

"She's waiting in the coffee shop, around the corner. I told her I wanted to talk to you first. If you have time, can you walk over with me and see her?"

"You know I normally would, but the cast is meeting tonight at a restaurant uptown to celebrate. You know, end of the play and all."

He looked disappointed, which made Lily feel guilty. "But I can always get there a little late. I have to get out of my wardrobe. So why don't you go down, keep Hannah company, and I'll meet you both in ten minutes."

David stood up. "Uh, before I leave, I want to apologize. The things I said to you were unforgiveable. I was drunk. I didn't mean any of it. I've missed you, I really have."

Lily kissed him on the cheek, "No worries, it's in the past. And I've missed you too."

After he left, Lily collapsed on the couch, sighed, and thought about the last time she, Robbie, and David had been together, at Daisy's Memorial Fundraiser. By then, she and Robbie had become involved romantically but had decided to wait to tell David until after the event. Hadn't he gone through enough already? He had just been released that day from the hospital. He was recovering from the injuries he had sustained in the car crash and from the kidney transplant he had received. The kidney that he had gotten because the woman he had been searching for his entire life, Daisy—his biological mother—had lost her life. But through the gift of her kidney, she'd been able to save his.

Still reeling from Daisy's death, David had consumed far too much alcohol that night.

"Hey, slow down there, cowboy," Robbie had said, pointing to the newest martini that the waitress just slammed down in front of his brother.

"I'm fine, you worry about yourself," David downed his drink and stumbled against a chair.

Robbie lowered his voice. "Bro, you can't drink with the Cyclosporine A you're taking. It'll potentiate the side effects into high gear. You don't want to mess up that brand- new kidney, do you?"

David glared at his brother. "Take care of your own business, *bro*. You're off duty and I'm not your damn patient. It's my fucking kidney now and I'll do whatever I want with it."

Robbie's face turned deep red. Lily excused herself—she needed to get some fresh air and clear her head. She walked down the hill and sat by the edge of the water.

A few minutes later, she jumped when she felt a hand on her shoulder. She turned and smiled at Robbie. He sat and put his arm around her. "How are you doing, kiddo?"

"Better now."

He tenderly kissed her cheek and forehead, then pulled back a little so that he could look into her eyes. He softly kissed the tip of her nose and her lips as Lily put her arms around him and pulled him closer. Their tongues found one another.

"Are you fucking kidding me?" They both jumped and turned.

Standing there was an inebriated David looking down on them. "Again! You're doing this to me again!"

Robbie jumped up and put his hand on David's arm. Lily was frozen.

"Slow down, David, chill out—"

"Get your hands off me." He pushed Robbie back. "You never surprise me. Ever since high school, you've broken me down bit by bit, so I'm always less than you. You always get everything. Every girl I tried to date ended up with my brother; every friend I had, you took away. Hell, Mom and Dad always had to love you just a little bit more than their fake son."

Robbie tried to calm him. "Slow down. No one's out to take anything away from you, David. You're drunk; you don't know what you're saying."

"Oh, I don't? Every opportunity you get, you take out your fucking scalpel, and like the quote unquote *brilliant* surgeon you claim to be, you keep cutting me until you've dissected everything and there's nothing left. And you…." He pointed his finger at Lily. "you're the only blood relative I have in the world. There aren't enough guys around? You have to screw my brother? My fuckin' brother! Shit, this is priceless." He moved closer to Lily. Robbie stood protectively in front of her.

David shouted, "You had Daisy all to yourself, your whole life. She kept you instead of putting you up for adoption. Daisy didn't throw *you* away like a piece of shit garbage. You were worth keeping. And look at you, you turned out to be a spoiled brat and a slut."

Robbie held on to his brother's shoulders and looked into his eyes and through clenched teeth said, "I'm warning you, that's enough,"

"You're warning me? Who the hell do you think you are? Get your fucking hands off me." David took a swing, and his fist connected with his younger brother's face. Robbie instinctively punched him back; his right hook sent David to the ground. Lily screamed and ran over to him. David was out cold.

When he finally came to, he tried to stand up but his legs could not support him. He looked green and said "I'm gonna be sick."

Robbie helped him up, walked him inside the house and into the guest room, so he could rest. A little while later, there was a knock at Lily's bedroom door and Robbie walked in. He looked pale.

"How is David?" Lily motioned for Robbie to sit next to her on the bed.

"Not too good. I should have stopped him from drinking so much."

"What were you supposed to do, cut him off?"

"Yeah, that's exactly what I should have done. I'm a doctor. I should have known better." Robbie shook his head. "I punched him, Lil. After all he's been through, I knocked him out."

He stood up, walked over to the window, turned his back on Lily, and looked outside. A few minutes later, Robbie turned and looked into Lily's eyes. "I almost lost my brother a couple of weeks ago in the accident, and now, because I'm being selfish, I'm pushing him away and I'm going to lose him for real. I never thought he would take it like this. He's got this thing, I don't know why. He feels that I'm better than him. Has since we were kids. I've told him over and over again that it's bullshit. Maybe it's cause he was adopted, I don't know. I never play into it. I'm careful. But this, you and me—I can't do this to him, it's not fair. I'm sorry."

So now what? We end it? That's it?"

"For now, yeah. I'm sorry, I really am. I care about you, Lil, I do—really. But it's all way too much." Robbie hugged her tightly, "I wish…"

Lily brushed her tears from her eyes and kissed him. In less than twelve hours he boarded a plane headed to Africa.

Thirty minutes later, Lily walked into the coffee shop, looked around, and saw David and Hannah. She waved to them.

On the way over to the table Lily was stopped by three young women who asked her to sign their Playbills. She spoke to them briefly, then sat down at the table with Hannah and David.

Hannah gave her a heartfelt hug and Lily was once again struck by the warmth of her smile. She was a beautiful woman whose dark, wavy hair that had softly fallen upon her shoulders the last time Lily saw her was now cut very short. Lily noticed there were dark circles under her eyes that had not been there a couple of years before.

"It is so wonderful to see you both."

"Darlin' we have missed you terribly." Her Southern drawl was charming and made Lily smile.

For the next ten minutes the three chatted up a storm, though Lily actually did most of the talking. She filled them in on what was happening in her life and made them feel welcome as her guests, even if it was in a side-street luncheonette and not backstage at the theater. They congratulated her on winning the Tony Award. Lily was pleased when they told her they'd been glued to the television the night of the awards show.

She showed them photos of Daisy Rose and both agreed she was just about the prettiest child they had ever seen. Finally she nonchalantly asked about Robbie.

Hannah's mouth tightened and her eyes became watery. She touched Lily's hand and looked into her eyes.

"You see, my darlin', that's the reason we're here, to tell you about my boy." Lily looked from one to another, confused and terrified. Hannah tried to talk, but soon dissolved into distress.

David spoke up. "You knew Robbie was part of MSF, Doctors Without Borders, right? Well he was sent on a mission to Africa. Did you know that?" Lily nodded.

"Actually he was sent to the capital of Somalia, Mogadishu, to work at Daynile Hospital. The area is horrendous—filthy, dangerous, and war-torn. It's a mess, with thousands of people displaced. David swallowed hard and said, "Nine months ago, four doctors were abducted. Three of them were executed at point-blank range, their bodies dumped on the roadside." David cleared his throat. "Robbie was one of the ones taken."

The room spun and Lily grabbed the edge of the table. "Oh my God," she began to cry. People at the neighboring tables fell silent and stared. David stood and comforted his sister.

"He's missing, Lily. So far they haven't found his body, so we have to believe he's still alive."

Hannah took a piece of paper from her purse and handed it to Lily. Lily took a deep breath and read the press release:

MOGADISHU/ NAIROBI/ BRUSSELS, September 29, 2012 - It is with great sadness that the international medical humanitarian organization Doctors Without Borders/Médecins Sans Frontières (MSF) confirms that three bodies of its four staff members who were abducted last week were discovered this morning on a roadside close to the MSF compound in Mogadishu, Somalia. They are thought to have perished less than one week ago.

Simon Janssens, a 43-year-old surgeon from Belgium, an experienced medical doctor who had been working with MSF since 2000 in many countries, including Angola, the Democratic Republic of Congo, Indonesia, Lebanon, Sierra Leone, South Africa, and Somalia, was well known throughout the international medical community as one of the finest in his field.

John Frost, better known as "Frosty," was a 44-year-old medical doctor who has worked with MSF since 1998 in Ethiopia, Thailand, and Somalia.

Ivan Adem was a 35-year-old medical coordinator from the Czech Republic who began working with MSF only three months ago.

Details of the shootings are not yet clear. MSF's immediate priority is to take care of those most affected by this tragedy, in particular the families and colleagues of the victims.

The body of the remaining abductee, Robert Rosen, a 32-year-old medical doctor and surgeon from the United States, has not yet been discovered. It is the hope of MSF that he is alive and will return unharmed. At present, he is considered "missing" and not a "casualty."

MSF will be relocating some staff from Somalia for security reasons but remains committed to continuing its humanitarian work in Mogadishu and elsewhere in Somalia.

All four men were in Mogadishu working with the MSF teams to provide emergency medical assistance to displaced persons and residents of the city.

We are shocked by these tragic events and will greatly miss Ivan, Frosty, and Simon. We continue to pray for the safe return of Robert Rosen. We extend our heartfelt sympathy and condolences to their families and friends.

Lily stared at Robbie's smiling photo at the bottom of the press release. "This cannot be happening, David. Please tell me that this is a misunderstanding."

Lily gasped when David showed her a photo of Robbie on his knees, blindfolded and bloody, his hands in the air and a gun pointed to his head.

"MSF received this proof of life photo soon after Robbie was abducted. Usually there's contact after the proof is sent, discussing the kidnapper's demands, but to date we've heard nothing from them."

As Lily collapsed onto the table, sobbing in despair, David quietly put his arm around her in a genuinely loving attempt to console her. She had not felt such sorrow since her mother had passed away—and at that time it was Robbie's arms that had held her.

Within minutes, camera phones began to flash. The diners at surrounding tables took countless photos that they rushed to upload to their Twitter and Facebook accounts, ghoulishly capturing Lily in one of her most vulnerable, devastating moments.

Chapter 13

$\mathcal{L}$ily stared at Robbie's photo on the MSF press release before she put it back into her purse. Would those eyes ever gaze into hers again? Her eyelids closed as she silently willed herself to remember the feeling of the weight of his body on top of her, holding her to the man she knew was the great love of her life. What if his body—the body that had given her a lifetime of pleasure in such a short period of time—now lay abandoned on an isolated road somewhere? The horror of this thought threw shivers throughout her body.

She could not allow herself to enter that dark place again and thus looked around the cabin and saw that Maniadakis was the only other passenger still awake. The overhead light illuminated his profile as he scribbled furiously on a legal pad—his fleshy jowls bouncing to the rhythm of his pen. She had vested all her faith and a great sum of money in this man's ability to help her find Robbie, even though a mere two weeks earlier she'd never heard of Maniadakis. A man whom Aunt Donna had not seen in more than fifteen years had recommended Maniadakis to her and in a moment of stark lucidity, Lily wondered if she had lost her mind embarking on such a precarious adventure.

After Hannah and David had revealed the distressing details about Robbie's abduction and the deaths of his co-workers, Lily promised to do everything in her power to support their efforts to find him.

After she said goodbye to the Rosens, she headed to Paola's Restaurant on E 92nd Street and Madison Avenue, one of Manhattan's most beloved and respected uptown eateries. Her friends and fellow castmates had gathered there to celebrate the successful run and closing of *A Small Life*. She was more than an hour late and did not feel like talking to anyone, much less joining the festivities that she was certain would, by then, be in full swing.

She walked into the restaurant, its tables always set with crisp white linen, sparkling silver, and fresh flowers in crystal vases. Each time she had visited the restaurant, she found her senses teased by its tantalizing aromas of authentic Italian cuisine. Tonight, in her agitated and distracted state of mind, she experienced none of this. She hurried past the hostess and over to a bank of tables that had been pushed together to accommodate the large party.

"I'm sorry for being so late." She feigned a smile and slid into the empty chair at the head of the table. Jamie was on one side and Donna on the other. She gave Jamie a peck on the cheek and looked at her dearest friends: Tommy, Fernando, Jodee, Jessica, Kristin, Paul, Theresa, and her fellow castmates and members of the stage crew and wardrobe department. She smiled and felt a rush of comfort. Seated next to Donna was an attractive man whom Lily vaguely remembered as Auntie D.'s old flame, Ken. His tweed beret, jauntily perched atop his shoulder-length, salt-and-pepper hair, along with his trimmed goatee, gave him downtown artisan flair. He smiled warmly at Lily, who extended her hand in greeting.

"One thing you learned from Daisy is how to make a grand entrance!" Theresa laughed.

"I know and I'm sorry everyone. Something came up that I had to take care of." Jamie poured her a glass of champagne, which she then raised and said, "Thanks for coming tonight."

Jodee stood up. "Quiet, please. I'd like to make a toast. Getting to work with you, Lily, has been a dream come true. And even though I was not nominated for a Tony Award like *some* people we know....." she pointed her champagne glass in Lily's direction and everyone laughed, "the experience was one I will always remember. I love you, girl." She blew Lily a kiss across the table and sat down. Everyone began to talk at once.

Lily felt as if she were in a dream. She didn't tell anyone where she had been or what David had told her. Sadly, there would be plenty of time for that tomorrow.

Jamie had ordered her Paola's specialty dish— Pappardelle with marinara. Lily had no appetite and pushed the food around her plate, hoping no one would notice. Her thoughts returned endlessly to the conversation she'd had earlier in the evening with Hannah and David.

Donna leaned close to Lily and whispered. "Pali, are you okay? You seem distracted." Before Lily could reply, Jamie stood up.

"If you don't mind, now I'd like to make a toast." He lifted his glass of champagne, as did everyone else. "Um, I know that, in recent months—okay, years—I may not have been your favorite person in the world. I certainly understand why." He looked at Lily and continued. "But I want to say, in front of all the people you love most in the world, Lily, how very proud I am of you and how much I love you." Lily looked around the table and smiled nervously.

Jamie moved his chair back to give himself room, then took Lily's hand and kissed it. Still holding her hand, he went down on one knee.

"Babe, I love you so much. I want to spend the rest of my life loving you and taking care of you and our daughter. If you'll have me, I would be honored if you would be my wife."

He went into his pocket and pulled out a Tiffany box and opened it. Everyone at their table as well as at the surrounding tables stopped talking and watched. Inside the peacock-blue box was the most perfect 5-karat, emerald-cut, yellow diamond ring with a double row of white round diamonds in a platinum and 18-karat gold setting.

Everyone at the table began to clap and talk. Then the diners at the other tables joined in. Many took out their smart phones and snapped photos. Lily was dumbstruck. Seeing Jamie on his knee brought back the recent memory of the proof of life photo of Robbie on his knees, that David had shown her just a few hours earlier.

Lily was shocked. She covered her mouth with her hand, began to cry, and ran to the Ladies Room.

At 1:00 a.m. Lily, seated in her living room, surrounded by her dear friends and a brooding Jamie, repeated the story that David had told her hours before. No

one spoke a word until she finished talking. After telling them the entire story and showing the MSF press release, she was emotionally drained.

They began to talk at once, each one bombarding her with questions—questions that Lily had no idea how to answer. Why had he been abducted? Were they looking for a ransom? Are you sure he's still alive?

All of a sudden Ken, who barely spoke a word the entire evening, said, "I know someone who may be able to shine some light on the situation." He had their attention. "I have a home in Mykonos where I go to paint a few times a year. I also have regular gigs in many of the clubs, where I sing and play guitar.

"He has a wonderful voice." Donna added.

"Thanks, honey" He smiled at the group. "Anyway, a few years ago, I was playing one of my regular gigs in a club called *Notorious*." He looked from Fernando to Lily. "It wasn't open yet when you were there shooting your movie. I don't know if you remember the area. It's one street back from the *limani*—the waterfront, located off an alley, that can't be, I don't know, more than 12 feet wide. Anyway, there are about seven or eight tables out front. Customers gather there nightly—some at the tables, others sit on the stone steps in front. They hang out and shoot the shit. Last year, I noticed this one guy, a funny-looking dude, who would sit each night at the same table outside. No one ever sat with him and no one ever spoke to him. But you could set your clock by him. Every night 9:00 p.m. he would sit there and would smoke a Montecristo, eat a little, drink a lot, and listen to the music from inside the bar. At 1:00 a.m. he'd get up and leave until the next evening.

I asked the owners, Susan and Andreas, who the guy was. Andreas told me his name was Nikos Maniadakis—an American expatriate, from Texas, whose grandparents were from Athens. When he retired, he moved to Mykonos. Andreas said the guy was quiet at first, a bit of an "aw shucks" cowboy type, but that if you gave him one too many Retsinas, he'd tell some amazing stories.

I was intrigued, so between sets I went over and talked to him. It became a nightly thing. It seems that the guy had been some sort of Government Special Op—C.I.A.—who had spent a lot of time in Somalia. From what I hear, he understands the ins and outs of the place and supposedly knows everyone there. Maybe he can be of some help to you in finding out about your friend."

"Oh my God, that would be great. Can you reach out to him for me?" For the first time that evening Lily felt a tiny spark of optimism. Ken checked his watch.

"It's around 9:00 a.m. in Greece, so I guess I could call him. Give me a second and I'll try."

Ken walked out of the room.

"I don't understand why you're doing this, Lily. Why are you getting so involved?" Jamie stood up and walked over to Lily who was seated on the couch. "Babe, he's got family, let them figure this out."

"Let's see what this guy Nikos has to say. If he can help, I'll put him and David together."

That seemed to settle Jamie down for a few minutes. When he left the room to get more refreshments for everyone, Donna gave Theresa a look and nodded her head toward Lily. They stood in unison and sat down on either side of her.

"How are you doing, honey?" Donna took her hand.

"Not good, Auntie D. When I heard about Robbie—well you could just imagine. And then Jamie's proposal on top of it. Holy crap, who saw that coming?"

"Well, I'm not surprised," Theresa said. "He's wanted to get back in the fold since that whole Natalie debacle." Theresa's husband Paul was the director on the movie where Jamie had met and had the affair with Natalie. Unbeknown to Paul, his wife Theresa—who was a good friend of Daisy and who was on the movie set with Jamie—had called and reported back to Lily almost daily.

Theresa continued. "He hasn't talked much about anything else, right Paul?"

"Right. Except to talk about the movie and ask when the sequel to *Standoff in Sante Fe* was going into pre-production," Paul replied.

"I don't trust him for a minute." Fernando looked toward the kitchen to make sure Jamie wasn't walking toward them. "He's a weasel."

"I don't think she needs to hear that now, dear," Tommy patted his partner's hand. "She's got enough on her plate.

Ken walked back into the room, iPhone in hand. I've got Nikos on the line. He said he's going to make some calls in the next few hours. If you want, we can set up a video chat with him around 1:00 p.m. our time."

"Yes, absolutely. I'll call David and ask him to join us." Lily replied.

When Ken walked back out the door, Lily squeezed Donna's hand. "So glad you got back together with Ken."

Donna smiled. She had no doubt that God and their guardian angel in heaven, Daisy Lockwood, worked in mysterious ways.

Chapter 14

Fewer than 14 hours later, David and Hannah joined Donna, Jamie, and Ken in Lily's living room for their video conference with Nikos Maniadakis. Earlier that day, Ken had warned them that there were connection and server problems in Mykonos, but assured them he had heard from Maniadakis and that the conference would happen as scheduled.

Finally they made the connection—a bit pixelated at first—but within a few minutes Maniadakis was on screen. Ken made the introductions and without further pleasantries, Maniadakis started talking. He was a heavy-set man with thinning hair and a pocked complexion. Lily thought he looked as unlike a C.I.A. Operative as one might imagine, based on the ones she'd seen on TV and in the movies.

"Before I begin, I must know who you have spoken to and what you were told."

"When Robbie first went missing we were contacted by one of the members of the International board of *Médecins Sans Frontières*," Hannah looked down at her notes. "His name was Dr. Juan Reseda. He told us that Robbie, along with three other staff members, had been abducted. Armed men came into the compound in the middle of the night and grabbed them out of their beds. A few days later they found the other three men's bodies about fifteen miles away."

David added, "That's right. And two days after my brother was taken, they received a 'Proof of Life' photo showing that he was alive. A newspaper indicated the date. I can scan or fax it over to you if you want."

Maniadakis held up a duplicate of the paper David had shown Lily at the coffee shop. "No need. I received it this morning. Who else you spoken to?"

Hannah said, "Beside the director and representatives of MSF, we've been in touch with our Congressman Frank Whitehall and Senator Tom Frankel, who were both very understanding and sympathetic—"

"— and haven't done jack shit." David interrupted.

"David!"

"Sorry, Mom. But it's true, no one has, not our government, not the MSF— no one. Meanwhile my brother may be in grave danger while everyone sits on their asses. Hannah put her hand on her son's arm. "What David is saying is true. Our next step was to go to CNN and other news channels and papers to get it out to the media. But first we came to New York to talk to Lily. She and my son had a very special relationship and we knew we could count on her— and we were right." She smiled at Lily.

Jamie shot Lily a questioning look, but Lily ignored it and turned her attention back to the screen.

Maniadakis folded his hands and sighed. "First off, let me tell you about the Baanadir coast. It is worse than any hell you can imagine. There are the different tribes—clans—and sub-clans at war with one another for land, goods, and food. They're led by tribal warlords who will do anything to get what they need. They treat murder as an everyday activity. When people walk down the street and hear a gun cock, they automatically hit the ground. It's a reflex and everyone in Somalia has it, especially in Mogadishu. So with no government in place, you got complete anarchy. Murder in the streets, piracy, you name it—if you find it in hell, you'll find it in Mogadishu. So then, in comes Al Shabaab to make things even more interesting."

"You mean al-Qaeda?" Jamie asked

"Correct, it's a Somalia-based cell of the militant Islamic group. It's an off-shoot of ICU—Islamic Courts Union—which splintered into several small factions after its defeat against Tradition Federal Government." Maniadakis looked down and shuffled several papers on the desk in front of him. "In 2006, they described themselves as waging jihad—war— against enemies of Islam. These included TFG and the African Union Mission to Somalia—and, by extension, it goes without saying, Americans and their allies. They've been killing, kidnapping, and intimidating members of any organization that seems even remotely connected to a humanitarian effort. So there you have it—the world's worst shit stew."

"Anything you can do to help?" Ken asked.

"Well, I have feelers out, as we speak. Since we don't know who's behind this, it's gonna take some digging. And bucks. Who's got the money?"

"We can mortgage our home." Hannah said. My husband died three months ago, so we're still going through probate—he shared his medical practice with his partner; I can talk to him about a loan until it's resolved."

"How much money are we talking about?" David asked.

Maniadakis looked back down at his papers. "A boatload. You got security—big time— that's something we need to talk more about. If we have to go in and get him, I have to put together a rock-solid group of military contractors—most of them ex-Navy SEALs. The best get big bucks and I would only get the best for you. Plus you gotta fly them in and put them up. Then you got guns, ammunition, and bribes. I'd say upward of $300,000, maybe more. If we find out there's a ransom—I fly in a special negotiator I know from Colombia— you're talking millions.

Hannah gasped. "I... I don't know if I can get that kind of money."

"I don't want to sound heartless, Ma'am, but the clock is ticking on your boy, and if you want to make a move, it's got to be now."

"I'll give you the money." Lily said. It'll take me a few days to get it together, but whatever you need..."

Hannah hugged Lily and started crying. "Whatever we have to do, darlin', we will get that money back to you. I promise."

"Whoever's got the bucks needs to be there. We're gonna need cash, can't tell how much 'til we get down there. Things change on a whim in a situation like this. I can't be on the phone every time looking for more money. It won't work unless you're there."

Lily swallowed hard. "I'll go."

Jamie jumped to his feet. "What are you talking about? You can't go there, Babe, it's worse than a war zone. You're gonna get killed."

Maniadakis shook his head. "Better decide fast and let me know."

Lily looked at Jamie "I *said* I will go. No need to decide."

"I'll go too." David took his sister's hand.

"That's good enough for me. I'll start putting this together. Get your shots, it's a hotbed down there." Jamie got up and stormed out of the room.

"Make sure to bring some head scarves, since you're going to be the only white woman there. The more covered you are, the better. And whatever you do, don't speak with the press. If they get hold of this venture, especially if they know that Lily Lockwood is involved, it'll become a three-ring circus. Let's talk tomorrow morning, your time 9:00 a.m. By then I should have more info."

"Thanks, pal, I appreciate it," Ken said.

"Don't thank me until your boy's back home safe." With that, the screen went dead.

After everyone else had left Lily's apartment, Donna sat at the kitchen table feeding Daisy Rose strained peas. The toddler thought it was the funniest thing ever to spit out the baby food all over herself, onto the floor, and also onto her great aunt. She squealed with delight and went into fits of giggles when Donna reacted to being sprayed with the half-eaten peas.

Donna struggled to look as stern as she could, while trying not to burst into laughter over the toddler's antics.

"Daisy Rose, now you stop that. You have to eat your food so you can grow big and strong." Lily walked into the kitchen just in time to see Donna cover her face against the newest incoming green attack.

"The next time I feed your daughter, I'll make sure to wear a raincoat."

Lily grabbed a napkin, and wiped the vegetable out of Donna's hair. "Make sure it's got a hood."

"Pali, can you sit with me a second? There's something I want to talk to you about."

Donna took her hand and said, "Listen, I don't want to tell you what to do, but I am really concerned about this whole thing. I'm worried about you going to Somalia. It's a grand gesture, I understand that. But it scares the hell out of me.

"I have no choice, Auntie D. Trust me, I'm scared too. But I'm already committed. And if I don't do this, how could I live with myself if he—you know—if something happens to Robbie." Tears welled up in Lily's eyes. "I've lost my Mom. I can't lose him, too."

"Oh honey," Donna hugged her, "you can't put this whole thing on yourself." She looked at the beautiful young woman in front of her—the closest to a child she would ever have—and wished that Daisy were there with them. Daisy always knew, without hesitation, the right thing to do or say when advising her daughter. Donna took a deep breath and tried to channel her oldest and dearest friend. "I cannot tell you what to do, sweetheart, but all I want to say is that I would like you to take however much time you need to think long and hard about the implications. Whatever you decide, I'll be there for you—100%."

Before Lily could reply Jamie burst into the room. "Are you insane? What do you think you're doing?"

Lily did not look up at him but slowly and deliberately put the miniature spoon into an open jar of banana-apple mixture and fed it to Daisy Rose. "Feeding the baby."

"Lily this is no joke, you could be killed. Why would you do this?"

"First of all, don't raise your voice in front of Daisy Rose. Second, I am helping my brother and his family out. Oh, and saving a life."

Jamie looked at Donna. "Can't you talk some sense into her?"

Donna stood, shook her head, and kissed her goddaughter on the cheek. "I have to run, honey. I told my agent I would meet him downtown. Think about what we talked about and call me later." She nodded to Jamie and left the room.

Jamie walked to the intercom that was on the wall next to the breakfast area and pressed the button that had NURSERY written beside it. The intercom beeped twice and Margaret answered.

"Margaret, can you come into the kitchen and finish feeding Daisy Rose?"

Lily looked at Jamie and shook her head. "Since when did you take over my household? I am feeding my child in my kitchen, in my house!"

Jamie crossed his arms, "Now who's raising their voice?"

Margaret walked into the kitchen and without saying a word, reached for her apron in the pantry closet and took the spoon out of Lily's hand.

A few minutes later, Jamie and Lily were in her bedroom on the opposite wing of the apartment and out of earshot.

"You can't go, babe. I'm worried for you."

Lily sighed. "Listen, I know and I understand, I really do. It's scary, but I have no choice."

"Of course you have a choice. Tell them no. You want to shell out all your money, that's your deal. Give them the money and stay home. Trust me: Maniadakis will take it in a heartbeat. Also, how do you even know the guy is for real? This whole thing may be a scam."

"He is for real, he's Ken's friend."

Jamie laughed. "You're so naïve, you have no idea who he is. Let's say he's for real, of which I have my doubts. You're gonna follow him into the shit-hole capital of the world? For what?"

Lily averted his eyes. "I told you: to help my brother and his family."

Jamie paused and thought of something that had been bothering him since Hannah had said it. "Wait a second. What did Hannah mean that you had a *special* relationship with her son?"

Before Lily could speak, Jamie threw his hands in the air. "Holy crap, now I get it. He's the guy you were dancing with at your mother's memorial, right?"

Lily nodded. Jamie laughed. "This is precious. You're gonna risk your life and throw away all your money for a guy you only saw a few times? You've gotta be kidding!"

Lily looked blankly at him. "It was more than that."

"More than that? Tell me what you mean," Jamie challenged her.

"Trust me, you won't want to hear it."

"Tell me," Jamie demanded.

She and Jamie had gone through too many things in the last few years and they were long past pretending or sugar-coating reality. Lily took a deep breath to steady her nerves, then said with courage, "I love him. I'm in love with Robbie."

Jamie took a step back as if he'd been punched. "In love with him? When were you going tell me?"

Lily took a step toward him and Jamie put his hands up to prevent her from coming any closer.

He shook his head, "Now I get it, it makes perfect sense. I knew there was a change in you. I thought that with everything we'd gone through, it would take you time. Time to get back to where we used to be."

"Listen Jamie——"

"Let me finish. So here I was thinking if I did the best I could, be the best boyfriend I could, the best father, then it would all be good. It would all work out." He sat on the bed and shook his head.

"You have to believe me; I was trying to figure it out." Lily sat next to him and put her hand on his shoulder. Jamie shrugged it off.

"I got down on my knee, in front of everyone," he said softly. He looked into her eyes. "I gave you a ring and all you did was run away crying in front of your friends, in front of the whole fucking restaurant. Everyone saw it—it was even trending on Facebook and Twitter. Do you know how that makes me look? God I feel like an ass."

Lily was close to tears. "You have to believe me. I am trying hard to make it work between us."

He looked up and glared at her, "Do you think I need anyone to *try* to make it work? I'm not a fucking charity case, Lily. I can have anyone I want, whenever I want."

"You have to hear me. I have not seen Robbie or spoken to him in two years. It's over."

"I'll tell you what's over." Jamie shouted. "If you go there and risk your life, then it's over between us!"

"Don't give me an ultimatum, Jamie. You'll lose, trust me," Lily warned.

"You know what? You go, Lily. Go get killed. Who's gonna lose then? You willing to leave your child without a mother?" Jamie shook his head as he walked toward the bedroom door and opened it. "After this stunt, you don't have to worry about winning Mother of the Year award, that's for damn sure. At least

Daisy Rose has a father who'll take care of her." He stormed out of the room, slamming the door behind him.

Shaken by their conversation, Lily took a good fifteen minutes to compose herself before emerging from the bedroom. She walked down the hallway and saw Gladys perched atop a ladder in the circular foyer, cleaning the crystal chandelier that gracefully hung from the sculptured dome in the middle of the 12 foot-high ceiling. One by one, she meticulously removed each oblong droplet and carefully released them into a small bucket situated on the ladder's platform.

Lily did not have to look into the pail to know that it contained equal parts white vinegar and warm water. And when the crystals hit the mixture, they would make a soft plop before quickly sinking to the bottom. When Lily was young, she adored assisting Gladys with this monthly task that took an entire afternoon to complete. She would proudly stand next to the ladder, red bucket in hand, waiting for the housekeeper to hand her each precious piece. After all the crystal pieces were taken off the heavy arms of the chandelier and immersed into the vinegar-water, she and Gladys would carry the heavy pail and its precious contents into the butler's pantry, which was a small room off the kitchen. They would remove the crystal pendants from the bucket, carefully rinse each one under cold running water and place them neatly, side by side in rows of six across, on an over-sized towel to dry.

The sun would shine down on the crystals from the skylight in the vaulted ceiling. Lily would watch for hours, marveling at the multitude of rainbows the tiny prisms sprayed across the opposite wall, when the sun hit them at the perfect angle.

For a moment, Lily stopped and watched Gladys perform the familiar task, it made Lily yearn for a simpler time when decisions were left for others to make—a time when her choices would never result in life or death consequences.

"He's way gone. The actor flew the coop. Couldn't get outta here fast enough." Gladys slowly descended the rungs, until she again had both feet firmly on the ground. "Not too pleased with your going across the world to help that doctor, right?"

Lily shook her head, stepped up on the ladder and lifted the bucket from the platform and handed it to Gladys.

"It's the right thing to do," Lily said, offering the same answer she had given Jamie earlier.

Gladys put down the heavy bucket and looked into the large hazel eyes of the young woman she had practically helped to raise, "Is it, Miss Lily?"

"You think I'm making the wrong decision?" Lily asked defensively

"Sometimes when we do what we think is the right thing, it may not end up being the right thing at all." Gladys shrugged, "But what do I know? I'm only the *housekeeper*. She lifted the bucket and deliberately walked toward the kitchen.

"Oh for heaven's sake," Lily replied. "I told you I was sorry I said that, but sometimes, Gladys, you do act like you're my mother."

Gladys continued walking and said, as if to herself, "Well maybe you need one right now.

Those words hung in the air and Lily was caught by surprise by the wave of emotion that flooded her. Unbeknown to anyone, Lily incessantly deliberated over and questioned every single choice she made. Throughout Lily's entire life Daisy had made all the major decisions for her and Lily would simply go along with most of them. Since Daisy's death, more nights than she would ever admit, Lily awoke in a sweat, her heart pounding, gasping for air, worrying about the choices she had made and what the future might hold.

Now for the past 24 hours Lily found herself swirling inside an emotional tornado. She didn't feel as if she had the luxury to stop and question her decision to go to Somalia because she felt pressured; time was running out and Robbie's life was at stake. If she loved him, she knew it was expected that she would do anything within her power to save him. When Jamie questioned her, she defended her decision with a bold confidence that she did not at all possess. She truly felt conflicted. If she stayed home, she would avoid being in harm's way, and perhaps as a parent this was the responsible thing to do. But if she didn't go to Somalia, Maniadakis made it clear that he would not proceed with the mission, which could prove fatal for Robbie.

Hours later, after Margaret and Gladys had left for the evening and the baby was fast asleep in her crib, Lily lay sobbing in her king-size bed. For all intents and purposes she appeared to have it all. She had a large group of wonderful, loving friends who would do anything for her. She was so thankful for her perfect, beautiful, healthy miracle of a baby. She had a man so in love with her that he went on bended knee in front of an entire restaurant filled with customers, to ask her to spend the rest of her life with him.

But what the world did not know was that Lily felt empty inside at all times. Besides Daisy Rose, the two people she loved most in the world were forever lost to her. Some days the grief over her mother's death was so heavy that she felt she would collapse under the very weight of it.

On other occasions, when she felt strong, the malaise lay in wait, living barely under the surface, ready to materialize whenever there was a crack in her emotional armor. Would it surprise everyone to know that she cried over the loss of her mother each and every day? Time was not healing her wounds like those who desperately wanted to comfort Lily told her it would. People, even those closest to her, assumed she was well on the road to recovery because she had ceased speaking about her loss. It's just that she couldn't bear the impatience she felt from others when, after two years, she spoke of her mother and how much she missed Daisy.

Lily knew her closest friends would adamantly deny feeling that way. But it evolved to a point where Lily sensed the underlying exasperation of those who desperately wanted her to move on with her life. To get better. To heal. It was time. As if heartache had a gestational period and if you went over the time allotted, it became a burden to those around you.

If not for Daisy Rose, Lily would almost certainly have plunged into a downward spiral of despair over the loss of her mother and by the uncertainty of Robbie's fate. Even now, there were days where she found it most difficult to get out of bed in the morning. But then she would hear her daughter's cry and shift into Mommy mode and Lily would start her day. Sadly, she understood that no matter what she said or did, Lily could never bring her mother back to life. Above all else, Lily often questioned if Daisy would be proud of her and of the decisions she made.

Lily got out of bed and walked down the hallway into the nursery. She had recently strung little white twinkling lights on the ceiling, above the crib. Daisy Rose loved to watch the tiny "stars" sparkle before falling asleep. Lily gently lifted her out of the crib and sat down on the large rocking chair. She held her precious daughter and rocked back and forth until sunrise.

It was there— in the middle of the night, in the stillness of her favorite childhood home—with tears streaming down her cheeks that Lily knew what had to be done.

In the early hours of the morning, she carefully put Daisy Rose back into her crib without waking the toddler. Lily quietly closed the nursery door and walked down the hallway into her office. She sat behind the desk that had once belonged to her mother and wrote a letter that she prayed would never be read:

To my dear daughter, Daisy Rose,

If you are reading this, it means that I am no longer with you and that Auntie D. and your Dad feel that you are old enough to know the reason why. First, I want you to know that I love you from the very bottom of my heart. Last night I held you while you slept. I held you so closely that I felt your little heart beat against my chest. Darling daughter, I want you to know that you have brought such joy into my life. My greatest accomplishment is being your mother.

I have to make a decision that I know may be a dangerous one. If you are reading this it did prove fatal. When I was growing up my Mama, your Grandma Daisy, taught me that if there was ever someone who needed your help or was in danger, it was your moral obligation to help that person. She would say to me 'Lily, you can never turn your back on someone in need, not ever.' So that is what I must do. There is a doctor who went all the way to Africa to help sick children. These children don't have doctors there to take care of them. While he was there, some bad people took him and wouldn't let him go. I promised his mother that I would go to Africa to help rescue him. If you are reading this, I died while I was there and, for that, I am eternally sorry.

I know that you have turned out to be a wonderful girl and your Daddy is proud of you. I am filled with deep sorrow knowing I will never see you grow into a beautiful woman. I will not be there to hear about your first kiss or dry your tears when you are heartbroken. I will not be in the audience when you graduate from school, nor will I watch you walk down the aisle, dressed in white, when you marry the man of your dreams.

Daisy Rose I pray that you are happy. Always know you are worthy of deep love and respect. I will always be your forever guardian angel, watching over you and keeping you safe.

Please forgive me.

xo Mama xo

Lily sealed the letter inside the envelope with hopes that it would never have to be opened.

Now nine days later, with only three more hours to go until they would land at Adden Adde International airport in Mogadishu, Lily closed her eyes and silently prayed to God:

"Heavenly Father, it's me. Lily. I know you must think I'm only in touch when I need something or when I'm scared. That's not true, really. Well maybe it's somewhat true, but I do try to think about you often. But with a toddler and the play just closing and now this whole thing with Robbie, I am crazy busy. Not to say you're not busy too. I can only imagine what you have on your plate with seven billion people to watch over."

Lily sighed because no matter how many times she prayed she always felt like she didn't have a firm grasp on what to say and how to say it. "We both know I'm not really good at this, but dear Lord, I ask you to please watch over me and all these fine men who are putting themselves in danger in order to save Robbie. Please help us return safely to our families. And dear God, please keep Robbie safe and guide these men to find and rescue him. Please soften the hearts of his captors and shepherd them toward good and away from evil. Amen. Oh, and God, can you find my mom and put her on the line?"

With her eyes still closed, Lily imagined that Daisy was seated opposite her, holding her hand and looking into her eyes as she had done all Lily's life. "Mom I'm having a hard time in this world without you. Things don't work the same since you've been gone. Have you been watching Daisy Rose? She has your eyes and curly hair. And Mom, she is as sweet as sugar; you would love her to pieces."

Lily wiped away the tears flowing from her closed eyes. "Mom I haven't felt your presence in the longest time. Please give me a sign that you are still with me. I miss you so much."

With that, Lily wiped her cheeks, put on her sleeping mask, leaned her chair back, and tried to get some much needed rest.

Chapter 15

lindfolded, with hands bound together, Robbie sat in the back of an open jeep, being transported to an unknown destination. Every time the vehicle hit a rock or a hole in the road, he was propelled to one side or the other. He hoped that the AK-47 being held to his back didn't discharge by mistake. What if, after all these months of enduring one brutal beating after another, he was accidently shot due to poor road conditions?

The driver decelerated as the terrain became rougher. Within a few moments the jeep stopped and Robbie was forcefully shoved outside. They walked him inside a building, using the nozzle of the gun to prod him to move faster. Eventually he was brought into a room and pushed into a wooden chair, where they removed his blindfold and untied his hands that had become numb from lack of blood flow. He moved his fingers to bring circulation back.

Robbie looked around the room. It was empty except for a desk and two chairs. His experience with rooms like this was that he would walk in of his own volition but would always have to be carried out, sometimes unconscious and always bleeding. The result of these torture sessions had left him with a lame leg and severe scars. When he felt hopeless, he would touch the scars, his fingers would slowly move up and down each one. He would force himself to remember the events and torment that had led to each wound. His body endured their blows but he refused to allow them to infect his spirit.

Robbie's method of detaching himself from the horrors around him was to think of another time and place where agony did not play a routine role in his everyday life. Many of his go-to memories were of Lily and of the days and nights they spent together. Often when he was thrown into a room such as this one, he would leaf through the pages of his remembrances, like a vast photo album in his mind, to choose the one recollection that would sustain him through the torture du jour.

Robbie decided, as soon as the door opened, that he would visualize sailing with Lily. The Long Island Sound was calm, there was a whisper of wind that barely caught their sails and gently carried them across to Connecticut. She stood at the helm, her face turned up to catch the rays of sun; her long chestnut hair flowed behind her. She beckoned to him to join her, whereupon he walked up to her, moved her hair aside, and kissed her neck. He paused to breathe in the scent of gardenias that always seemed to float a few inches above her skin.

The door opened abruptly and four men entered. As usual, they were dressed in fatigues and were armed. They stood around the perimeter of the room, their black faces stoic, their eyes fixed on him. And they waited.

A few minutes later, the door opened again. There was no doubt, with his easy gait and commanding presence, that the man who walked in was the man in charge. His demeanor was different from the others. He smiled at Robbie, and extended his hand. Robbie tentatively shook it. He sat in a chair behind the large wooden desk.

"So, you've gone through a rough time, isn't that right, Doctor?" Robbie couldn't immediately tell if his accent was Somali or Arabic. Robbie nodded in response.

"First, let me introduce myself. I am Mubaarak Abdikarim. Do you know what that means, Doctor?" Robbie shook his head.

"It means Blessed God's Chosen One. So I am lucky, right? Abdikarim threw back his head and laughed, triggering an immediate reaction among his underlings who also laughed.

He slammed his hand on the desk hard and Robbie jumped. Abdikarim's subordinates stopped in mid-laughter.

He leaned closer to Robbie and smiled. "Luck, my friend, had nothing to do with it."

So now you will think of yourself as Mubaarak: You, too, will be blessed. You are one of the chosen ones and I will explain the reason for this. First, would you care for a drink of water?" Robbie nodded his head.

He barked the order at one of the guards standing in the back of the room and the man left swiftly.

"You live and work in New York City, correct?"

"Yes."

"Ah, Manhattan." Mubaarak sat back in his chair, looked up at the ceiling, and reminisced. "I attended Princeton University and spent many wonderful times in the Big Apple. Even with my meager student stipend I was able to attend many Broadway shows. And several times I attended the Metropolitan Opera. I miss the entertainment—the city that never sleeps—the nightlife is wonderful, is it not?

He looked at the other men. "There is not much night life in Mogadishu in recent years." They all laughed.

The guard hurried back into the room, carrying a large glass of water. He stumbled and spilled half of it near Robbie's feet. Abdikarim glared at the guard as he handed the almost-empty glass to Robbie and walked back to where he had previously stood.

"And the cost of living is high here, but not at all as expensive as in New York City." He clapped his hands together and smiled.

"So would you like to go back to the Big Apple, Dr. Rosen?"

"Yes," Robbie replied warily.

"I would, too. And if we work together, we can both return to New York City. You with your health and life intact and me with some jingle jangle in my pockets to spend at all the fancy restaurants. You and I are going to go into big business together. Doesn't that sound wonderful?"

Robbie was quiet. Abdikarim ignored his silence, folded his hands, and smiled. "So now, you must be wondering to yourself, 'How can *I* possibly be of benefit to a man whose name means Blessed God's Chosen One? He already has so many gifts bestowed upon him.' Well, I will tell you how you can be of service. Dr. Rosen. Did you know that you were hand-selected to be here?"

"I have no idea what you mean."

"Did you think my men came into the hospital compound and randomly seized you?

Robbie shrugged.

Abdikarim smiled, "I assure you, it was not my men. You were taken and tortured by another group. They wanted you for the big ransom that a doctor from the United States would surely bring. The other doctors were collateral damage, unfortunately. And not valuable to anyone." Robbie winced.

Abdikarim stood up, grabbed his chair and dragged it around his desk, placed it next to Robbie, sat down, and crossed his legs.

"When I heard from those uneducated braggarts that they had abducted Dr. Preston Wells's protégé, I was elated. I have wanted to meet you for a long time."

"You could have come in during clinic hours to talk to me," Robbie growled.

Abdikarim laughed and looked at his men. "A gifted surgeon and a sense of humor! He will make good company for the nurses in the operating room. So, getting back to my story, three years ago, you were in Liberia, no?"

Robbie nodded.

"Word got around that you were an exceptional surgeon. So what else could I do when I heard you were taken," Abdikarim paused, "but make them an offer they could not refuse." He threw back his head again and laughed. His men, of course, followed suit.

"Like Marlon Brando, get it?" Abdikarim caught his breath. "I paid for you. You were very expensive, Doctor I assure you. So now you belong to me and we come to the part where you learn why you have been brought here. Before I tell you, I want to assure you that I intend to bring in a doctor—a close friend of ours from Kenya." He smiled at his men, knowingly. "He is a fine doctor and will make sure to treat any damage that my predecessors inflicted upon you. Before long you will be as good as new, because we have built a surgical unit just for you. It is taking longer than I had anticipated, and for that I am so sorry."

A phone rang. It was the phone belonging to the guard who had spilled the water. He took the cell out of his pocket to answer it. Abdikarim glared at him again and the guard quickly put the phone back into his pocket.

"As you can imagine there are many people in the world who need organ transplants to survive. With your help, Doctor, we will be able to get the organs to them and save their lives. You will be a hero and I will become a wealthy man. Sounds like a good partnership, no?"

"I assume these organs will be sold on the black market?"

Abdikarim jumped up, clapped his hands once, and said, "Yes! Hearts, kidneys, livers, even skin. One brave soul at a time will get the opportunity to save many, many lives. Now you understand."

"Who are the donors?"

Again Abdikarim looked at his men, "Well I wouldn't exactly call them donors." Again they all laughed. "Let's call them unfortunate souls who are giving their lives for the good of science. Your job is not only to surgically remove the organs, but also to supervise the packing of them and to act as our liaison."

Robbie jumped to his feet. Within seconds he had three guns pointed at him. Abdikarim waved his hand and the men lowered their weapons.

"I will not do that. I'm a doctor. I cannot kill people."

Abdikarim pushed Robbie back in his chair and stared coldly into his eyes. All pleasantries had vanished. "You will do exactly as you are told to do. Do not underestimate my kindness today as weakness. I always get precisely what I want. And your life is only significant to me if you are augmenting my wallet. If you become worthless to me, well then...." He raised his gun and Robbie stiffened. The guard's phone rang again, and without missing a beat Abdikarim turned and shot the guard right between his eyes. Abdikarim leaned in to the shaken Robbie, winked and whispered, "He was my brother-in-law."

Chapter 16

Lily pulled her scarf down over her forehead, close to her eyes. She slipped the other end over her left shoulder to ensure that it covered her mouth and chin. They would be landing shortly. Remembering Maniadakis's warning that since the culture was Muslim and because they were probably going to be the only white people in Mogadishu, they had to be as inconspicuous as possible. He was worried, with all the security he had hired to surround them, it would be difficult for them to fly under the radar.

Lily had her New York City bank wire $1,000,000.00 into an account in Maniadakis's name in Central Bank, located in the capital city. There was a conference call between the executives of the two banks; an agreement was reached that, due to mitigating circumstances, if and when it became necessary to obtain additional funds, red tape would be circumvented and the money would be made available within hours.

The engine noise diminished as the plane began its descent. Lily turned to David, seated next to her; his eyes were closed and his hands gripped the worn leather arms. The plane landed and the Turkish Airlines flight attendant wished them all a safe journey.

"From her mouth to God's ears," Lily whispered to David. He squeezed her hand. Unbeknown to Lily, David's unflustered demeanor actually concealed that he teetered on the cusp of a full-blown anxiety attack. Earlier, his nerves had gotten the best of him. He'd gone into the bathroom and had breathed repeatedly into a paper bag.

During their layover in Istanbul, while his sister was browsing in one of the many airport boutiques, David picked up a pamphlet at the gate. Its message was foreboding:

Travel Warning: The U.S. warns its citizens against all travel to Somalia. Interclan and interfactional fighting can flare up with little warning, and instances of kidnapping, murder, and other threats to U.S. citizens and foreigners can occur unpredictably in this and surrounding regions.

This was nothing that David didn't already know. He had heard these safety warnings before—from Maniadakis and from others who knew first-hand the life-threatening peril that existed daily in Somalia. However, reading the threat advisory before boarding the plane to fly into the region unnerved him.

Before leaving the bathroom, he splashed cold water on his face. He looked at his reflection in the small mirror above the sink.

What have I gotten Lily into? What kind of man am I?

He was certain that if the roles had been reversed and he had been the captured one, Robbie would have devised a strategy that would never have placed another person in harm's way. David shuddered to think what Daisy would say, knowing that he had positioned her beloved daughter directly in the epicenter of mortal danger. He closed his eyes and made a silent vow. *Daisy I promise I'll do everything in my power to protect your daughter.*

Now that the plane's wheels had touched the ground, he knew that he had to do whatever he could to make sure his brother *and* sister both got home safe and sound.

"You okay, Sis?"

Lily squeezed David's hand. "As long as I have you next to me, I feel safe." David swallowed hard to suppress his urge to throw up.

The cabin doors opened and the passengers got up from their seats. Lily glanced out the window and saw there was only one building in the airport. It was a small, two-story structure with a large sign attached to the front. The words 'Aden Abdulle International Airport' were written in blue and white in English and in Somali; the Arabic translation was in dark-green lettering. Lily looked to Maniadakis, who put his hand up, indicating that she should wait and follow behind him and his men.

When she stepped out of the plane onto the top of the airstairs, Lily was immediately propelled backward by a wall of blistering heat. She had to take shallow breaths because the fiery winds singed her lungs like tiny embers, while the engine fumes scorched her nostrils.

More than fifty men in tan uniforms stood on the tarmac, along with twenty more in full army fatigues and headgear. They shouted instructions to the disembarking passengers, using their high-powered assault weapons to point the direction they wanted the crowd to follow.

Had Lily found herself transported to Mars, it would have been less foreign to her than this airport, swarming with a military presence. Her feet were cemented to the small platform until the crowd pushed into her, forcing her to walk down the remaining ten steps.

Maniadakis and his men stood on the tarmac in front of the plane, speaking with a large group of guards. When she joined them, Lily saw he had provided all their necessary documents. One guard, who appeared to be the leader, examined them, scrutinized their faces as he did so, and then studied their passports. He shook his head, talked with his fellow guards in Somali, pointed to the passports, shook his head again, and finally pointed to three of Maniadakis's men. The other guards nodded in agreement.

When Maniadakis took out folded Somali shillings and transferred the colorful currency into the leader's hand, the guard's demeanor changed completely. He smiled, handed the passports back, and motioned them to move on. Maniadakis would repeat this gesture over and over again as the small group made their way to the building. They walked passed a group of passengers, shouting and fighting over luggage as the pieces were removed from the plane and carelessly thrown onto the tarmac. One young man wheeled his suitcase past an old man who was in the process of lifting his own suitcase up onto his shoulder. The young man grabbed the suitcase away from the older one. They stood for a good minute, tugging and pulling and shouting at one another. Finally the older one acquiesced and suddenly released his grip. The other one fell backward and hit his head hard on the pavement. The older one took the opportunity to pummel him as he lay helpless on the ground. By this time the crowd encircled the two, shouting at them, provoking them. Guards came by, broke up the crowd, and dragged both men through a small door marked PRIVATE on the side of building.

David steered Lily away from the bedlam and through the main entrance of the building. Inside, a man in full uniform approached them. He shook Maniadakis's hand, nodded to David and Lily, and introduced himself as Dalmar Jama, head of their security team. He told them that he and his team would be with them 24/7 while they were in Somalia. The Americans followed him as he walked out of the building to the front parking lot, where three open-bed trucks, engines running, awaited them. Five guards, rifles at the ready, were seated in the bed of each truck. Maniadakis's men split up and got into the other two vehicles.

Lily stepped into the back seat of the first truck's cab, squeezing in between David and Maniadakis. Jama sat in the front seat next to the driver.

"Our first stop will be to get settled and to set up base in Jazeera Palace Hotel," Jama smiled at Lily. "You will find the accommodations very comfortable; it is Mogadishu's version of New York's Plaza Hotel. However, we must be ready to move from there to City Palace Hotel if we feel there is a security breach. Because it is our most luxurious hotel, many high-profile guests and members of the media stay there. It is opposite the U.N. compound. Recently, on the day the new Somali President met with Kenya's foreign minister, it was the site of two suicide bombers. The bombs exploded outside the U.N. gate and unfortunately left eight people dead. Al Shabaab took credit."

"Is it s-s-safe there?" Lily stuttered but fought to regain composure. "I mean, can you guarantee that we will be safe?"

"You must realize that we will do all we can to protect you from the insurgents; but there are no guarantees in Somalia. We have made arrangements with the hotel to do a body search on anyone entering. Trust me, they were not pleased about this, but they have reluctantly agreed to comply."

Lily shivered. She looked out the window as the truck slowly drove through the narrow streets of the city. They passed evacuated, crumbling buildings devastated by explosions. Jama explained that they were the results of the war between Al Shabaab and TFG. These buildings were now reduced to rubble, most with only their foundations and segments of interior walls still intact.

Uniformed soldiers in green berets, four abreast, patrolled the crowded streets. Both sides of the road were congested with slow-moving convoys of Humvees and military tanks. Crowds of people swarmed the streets. A small group suddenly surrounded their truck, pounded on the windshield and shouted angrily at the passengers inside. Lily's stomach twisted in fear.

Their driver honked his horn in rapid short bursts and slowly pushed on the accelerator. The guards in the bed of the truck brandished their weapons, pointing them directly at the rowdy group, who then quickly dispersed.

When they were once again moving, Lily had to take deep breaths to quell her nausea. She stared out the window and to her dismay, saw coral-colored homes that were collapsing—even some that were visibly riddled with large bullet holes. When the truck stopped long enough to allow pedestrians to walk across the road, Lily was able to see into the opened window of one of those homes. An old woman was serving food to her family, who were seated around a large wooden table. The woman slowly walked over to the window, leaned her head out and called to the children playing outside. They answered her and ran into their decomposing home.

The road widened and Jama pointed out the Fakhr al-Din Mosque, built in the 13th century. The entry façade had three doorways that seemed to have been carved from fine marble. For the most part, the ornate religious monument remained intact, rising tall among the rubble.

Bang, bang, bang. Three shots rang out. Lily screamed and David pushed her head down. Jama exchanged knowing looks with Maniadakis. "Nothing to worry about, Miss Lockwood. Soon enough you will get used to that sound and it will not even faze you, I promise."

Lily was certain that would never happen. She sat back up, struggled to regain her composure and took a Kleenex from her purse. She attempted to wipe her eyes, but her hand was shaking so violently she could not hold the tissue. David removed it from her trembling hand and gently wiped her eyes.

It took all the effort she possessed not to scream or plead with the driver to take her back to the airport, to put her on the next plane home. She took a few deep breaths and forced herself to remember why she was there. She closed her eyes and imagined Robbie, tied up in a remote location, his body bruised and bleeding.

When she opened her eyes again, she saw the sign outside the U.N. compound. Even though the entire drive was less than ten miles, Lily breathed a deep sigh of relief when they finally pulled up to the cement wall that guarded Jazeera Palace Hotel. Jama got out of the truck and walked over to the black iron gates positioned at the midpoint of the wall. A guard immediately walked over to him. While the two men spoke, David pointed upward, showing Lily there were two armed guards inside a white tower; its red-tile roof sparkled in the blazing sun.

Once inside the hotel, Lily followed the men as they made their way across the chic lobby, decorated with crystal chandeliers and upfitted with brocade couches and oval rose-inlay mahogany coffee tables.

After checking in, they slowly walked across the lobby to the bank of elevators located on the far-left corner. A group of men in long white linen *dashikis* and *kufi* skull caps stood waiting for the elevator to arrive.

"Do not look at them!" Jama hissed. Lily kept her head down and averted her gaze as the doors to the elevator opened and they entered the small space.

Lily was escorted to the upscale Presidential Suite on the top floor. Jama's men told her to wait outside the room while they went in to perform a security sweep. When they were certain it was safe, they escorted her inside and informed her to remain there until Maniadakis contacted her.

Her hotel suite was exquisitely furnished. The living room had two leather couches and a large flat-screen television. The walk-in closet already had four long dresses with matching *garbasaar* shawls and *shash* scarves hanging.

Once she was alone, Lily put her bags down on the suitcase rack, walked over to the king-size bed, and sat on it. She took one of the over-stuffed feather pillows and hugged it. She had never experienced such fear in her life as she had during the past hour. She rocked her body back and forth in self-soothing rhythm, holding the pillow tightly to her chest. Finally she released the tears she had fought hard to control since leaving the airplane. She sat that way for more than fifteen minutes, sobbing and rocking. Emotionally drained, Lily lay down and within minutes she fell into a deep sleep, unaware of the danger that waited patiently for her when she awakened.

Chapter 17

*C*hloe stepped outside for what they called a 'smoko' back home. It was her first opportunity for a cigarette break since she'd started work at 7:00 a.m. that morning. She squinted against the blazing afternoon sun and examined the long procession of mothers who had waited patiently for their turn to see the doctor.

She was sweating profusely although she was dressed for the heat—a *Médecins Sans Frontières*-issued cotton, short-sleeve t-shirt and khaki shorts. She couldn't imagine how sweltering it must be for those women in their colorful, floor-length *guntinos* and *diracs* made from yards and yards of heavy material, draped over their shoulders and tied at their waists. Most of them also wore an extra layer—a *garbasaar* around their shoulders—and a *shash* wrapped around their heads.

Chloe took off her Aussie cowboy hat—the last purchase she'd made before leaving Melbourne—and rubbed her short blonde hair. She wiped her forehead on the sleeve of her t-shirt, leaving a long, orange sweat mark on the shoulder.

Chloe sighed. Today's waiting line appeared to extend for miles, as mothers stood with their ailing babies cradled in their arms. Others were seated on the ground, their malnourished children draped listlessly across their laps. Chloe knew that many of the mothers had walked for days, carrying their sick children in their arms and on their backs. She knew all too well, that some of the children might die before arriving at the clinic's front door.

When Frosty and Robert were still with them, the two would venture miles into the rural communities, seeking out those inflicted with tuberculosis. If one family member had the fatal disease, then the entire household would eventually be infected. Some days, they would bring whole families back with them and set them up as in-patients in the tuberculosis tent. Since medication—pills and shots—had to be administered daily to these patients, it was imperative they stay at the hospital compound for eight months.

Chloe walked over to the commissary shack and ducked under the lean-to for shade against the cruel midday sun. She sat down on a small wooden chair and stretched out her long legs. They had become cramped because she'd squatted far too long, earlier that morning while examining one small child after another.

She took a drag of her cigarette, inhaling so deeply that it made her lungs ache. She then closed her eyes and exhaled slowly, looking over to the parcel of land that had been designated for the new tuberculosis building. Month after month, Robert had championed the efforts to build a facility; he was like a dog with a new bone. He had overcome every obstacle thrown at him by the powers that be. When the board of directors argued that there was not enough money in the budget to erect this new building, Robert enlisted his family in Texas to raise the funds. They threw a huge charity event and brought in enough money not only to build the facility but also to stock it with enough Ethambutol to last one year. Without Robert's watchful eye, the building efforts had slowed down to a mere crawl.

Chloe missed him; they all did, she imagined. But she and Robert had a close bond, closer than most at the compound. They could talk for hours about everything and nothing. The staff assumed they were sleeping together, since everyone there changed partners as readily as people back home changed underwear.

Their lives, as doctors for MSF, were incredibly stressful. They were always in danger and at any given moment they could be killed. They did not have the luxury of state-of-the-art medical equipment or long consultations with their peers, as they did back in their own countries.

At home, a doctor always shared responsibilities with other doctors. Here, they had to make split-second decisions with imperfect facilities, inadequate diagnostic methods, and limited experience. Whether they would admit it or not, at MSF, every doctor second-guessed themselves whenever their patients died. Did they do everything possible? Would another doctor have made better decisions? Would another doctor have been more talented?

Chloe knew that many days, in the small rooms of the clinic, the acrid smell of her own panic intermingled with the smell of pus and the unwashed bodies of her patients.

It was her first mission when she arrived two years earlier. She was afraid of everything—afraid of possibly catching diseases and afraid of the responsibility. So, given all the daily stressors, when the staff had down time, they partied hard—drank too much booze, smoked too much pot, and never ever missed an opportunity to fuck.

It didn't happen that way with Robert and her. They spent months talking about their lives, sharing their experiences with one another and working side by side every day in clinic.

She knew she had the reputation for being a stone-cold bitch. It was the way she handled fear and stress. She attacked, before being attacked. It was her persona, born from living in the poorest section of Melbourne and nurtured by the many years spent fighting and scratching her way out of the slum.

No one but Robert understood her and knew the story of her past—tossed from one foster family to another. She told him about the beatings and sexual abuse she had endured over the years. With Robert, she could let her guard down—be herself. Finally for the first time in her life, she could allow herself to be vulnerable and discard her past, like a Green Tree Snake shed its skin.

One night, when everyone was drinking and partying, they broke away from the crowd and walked to the other side of the compound with a bottle of vodka and a blanket. After half the bottle was gone, he complained to her about his sore back, which he had pulled while carrying an old man into the hospital earlier that day. She volunteered to give him a massage. He took off his shirt and lay on his stomach. Her hands moved slowly as she took her time to exert the proper amount of pressure across his shoulders and up and down his spine and muscular back.

Once in a while he would let out a moan when she had touched and released a tight knot. Caressing his body and hearing his moans excited her. She had to force herself not to lean down and kiss his back or let her hands move inside his pants. She took a deep breath and looked up at the millions of stars that crowded the black sky. With each gust of wind, the faraway music from the camp floated toward them.

Suddenly, he turned onto his back and put his hands behind his head. He stared at her for a good few moments. Then Robert sat up and put his hands on the bottom of her t-shirt. She lifted her arms and he gently pulled her top up over her head and drew her toward him. Their love-making had an urgency and power she had never known before. When it was finished and she lay next to him, she couldn't help but cry—something she had never done before. The sheer force of her orgasm had left her feeling totally open and vulnerable.

They were closer than friends and knew all about each other's lives and loves. She had told him about her ex-fiancé Philip back home in Australia. She heard all about the woman he was in love with in New York—an *actress*—who she imagined was probably selfish and vain. Chloe had seen Lily Lockwood on the telly and had to admit she was beautiful. She assumed that Lily had been born with a silver spoon in her mouth—one of those privileged women who never had to struggle with poverty or any form of abuse.

Robert spoke often of Lily, sometimes right after making love, and Chloe wondered if Robert had been fantasizing about Lily. She could never ask him, since she knew he would be honest and she feared what his answer would be. More than once Chloe felt the sharp sting of jealousy when he spoke of Lily—how much he missed her and how beautiful, smart, and talented she was. What a mistake he had made by leaving her.

One night, with Robert fast asleep next to her, Chloe lay awake obsessing about him and Lily. She got out of bed quietly and tiptoed over to the bureau drawer where she knew he kept his journal and brought it into the toilet to read in private. As soon as she opened the leather-bound book, she glimpsed a photo of Lily as it fell to the ground. Chloe's heart sank when she looked at it: The actress was truly lovely—a classic beauty with long golden-brown hair and porcelain skin. Her petite features gave her face a pure doll-like quality, while her full lips heaved of sensuality. Ever since her teenage years, Chloe had been told she was attractive, but in an athletic, tomboyish sort of way. What most people did not know was that Chloe had embraced the idea of being a tomboy. She kept her hair cropped short so that no one could see her naturally wavy-blonde hair. And she never wore makeup. Chloe wore runners or Uggs instead of the heels that other girls her age proudly stomped around in. At an early age, she chose to play down her looks and to make herself less desirable to boys, so that hopefully this would ward off the sexual advances made by her foster fathers and brothers. But since meeting Robert, Chloe had, for the first time in her life, felt the urge to make herself prettier and more feminine. She sighed and put the picture of Lily back into the journal and reminded herself that *she*—not Lily—was the one with Robert now. Chloe wanted desperately for Robert to fall in love with her.

Chloe was reminded of the time Robert told her that he thought she was only in Mogadishu because she was hiding—running far away from the responsibility of ever settling down and marrying. This might have been true at one time, since she'd felt suffocated by relationships—until she met Robert. She wanted him and would do anything in her power to help him forget the actress. She never told Robert that she had fallen in love with him. Chloe had hoped that if they spent enough time together, working side by side saving lives during the day and making love each night, Lily Lockwood would eventually become but a distant memory to Robert. And Chloe would finally have the happy ending she thought was only reserved for other girls.

After she carefully replaced the journal, Chloe returned to bed and shimmied close to Robert. That night she made a silent vow: She would do everything in her power to make him fall in love with her.

Fate was not on her side, because later that night Robert was abducted.

They were sound asleep when three armed Somali men burst into the room. It was chaos—the men shouted at Robert and Chloe and held guns to their heads. One man grabbed Robert and the other threw a burlap sack over his head. When she attempted to move toward Robert, the third one shot Chloe in the shoulder. Within seconds, the abductors left, taking Robert with them.

She didn't find out until the next day, while recovering from surgery, that Frosty, Ivan, and Simon had been kidnapped as well. For many months to come, she was unable to sleep through the night. Memories of the brutal abduction gave rise to endless nightmares and she would awaken each morning drenched in sweat.

The kidnapping of the four staff members had sent devastating shockwaves throughout the entire organization. The loss was crippling and they mourned for the "family members" who had been ripped away from them. Chloe was heartbroken and felt as if a part of her had been severed. Ever since that fateful night, she felt only half-awake during the days. At night she would lie in bed and pray that Robert would return safely to her and that she would have the opportunity to be in his arms and finally confess her feelings to him.

She took another drag of her cigarette and unconsciously rubbed the area on her shoulder where the bullet had entered.

"Hey what are you doing: taking the day off?" Chloe looked up and saw Sam Wo, a Chinese doctor and recent graduate from Johns Hopkins, smiling down at her.

Chloe flicked her cigarette butt a few feet away. "Just about to get up." She lifted her right hand. Sam grabbed it and pulled her to her feet. She noticed that his gaze fell upon the neckline of her t-shirt, which inadvertently had been pulled down, revealing her cleavage. Chloe adjusted her shirt and she and Sam walked toward the clinic together.

"Anything exciting happening?" Chloe asked.

"Rondeau sent me over to get you. Seems there's a buzz going around about some dog-and-pony show scheduled to take place later today."

"Meaning?"

"He said there's a group coming here from America and they need to talk to you," Sam smiled.

"Me? What about?"

"Rondeau said it's hush-hush, but he thinks it has to do with guys who were abducted last year. He also said he thinks there's a big-name model or actress who's going to be with them. Kinda cool, huh?"

Chapter 18

The shrill ring of the telephone startled Lily out of a deep sleep. It took her a few seconds to acclimate herself to her surroundings and to remember that she was in her room at the Jazeera Palace Hotel. She picked up the phone and glanced at the clock on the nightstand, surprised to see that she had slept more than three hours.

Clearing her throat, Lily said, "Hello?"

"Hello, Miss Lockwood, I have Mr. Maniadakis on the line. May I put him through?" The hotel operator announced in a thick Somali accent.

"Of course." Lily stood up, stretched, walked over to the windows, and pulled open the velvet drapes. She shielded her eyes against the overpowering light of the midday sun that flooded the dark room.

"Hello, Miss Lockwood. I want you to know that we've taken over the large conference room on the main floor as our headquarters for the duration. If you're up to it, one of my men can escort you down here so that you can be part of the briefing."

"Of course. I can be ready in a few moments." Before she could say anything else, she heard a click and then dial tone. She shook her head and hung up the phone. Maniadakis was certainly not one for small talk. Lily walked out onto the terrace that wrapped around her corner suite and gazed out onto the sweeping city below. The tall white buildings were capped with terracotta roofs and she saw lofty minarets everywhere, poking through dark-green foliage. The war-torn rubble and military presence were not visible from this deceptive vantage point.

Lily walked to the other side of the terrace, and from there she had a view of the Indian Ocean in the distance. The sun's rays, like thousands of tiny diamonds, joyfully skipped across the sapphire spray.

Lily turned her gaze eastward and saw waves of yellow, blue, red, and white orbs—like huge parachutes sewn together—that stretched for miles. Jama had told her those orbs were actually thousands of tarps entwined together to provide minimal shelter for more than 150,000 people displaced by natural disasters or conflict. He went on to tell her that the lack of facilities and clean water created a fertile breeding ground for infection and disease, and that, in the camp, young girls and women were raped daily.

This stark juxtaposition—natural, innocent beauty set against the ruin brought about by malevolent forces—encapsulated Somalia. Lily now understood the passion Robbie had shown for MSF and the life-saving services they provide to populations such as this one. Lily was positive that Robbie had thrown both his heart and his medical expertise into saving as many lives as he could.

She looked around and wondered where in this vast city he might be. Was he even still alive? Tears filled her eyes when she thought of the warning Maniadakis had given her before they left New York: that there was a strong possibility Robbie had already been killed. Or that, if he was still alive, they may never find him.

Lily sat down on one of the terrace chairs and sobbed. After a few moments, she felt a severe pain in her head followed by tightness, as if her skull were being squeezed inside a vice. She closed her eyes and waited for the pain to pass.

Chapter 19

Robbie awoke, his back in full-blown contraction, practically fused into the position in which he had slept. He rocked his body slowly, using abbreviated movements, in an attempt to release the spasm. Hot, searing pain surged along his spine. He yelled as he lifted his body off the pencil-thin mattress that lay on the floor. Once standing, he took a few deep breaths and slowly stretched. His body had withstood one vicious beating after another; this near-crippling pain was but one of the many residual effects caused by the cruel treatment to which he had been subjected.

Since he had been moved to this location, he had not yet been tied up or beaten and was not confined entirely to his room. He had been allowed to walk the compound grounds, under the watchful eyes of several armed guards. The compound, more like a fortress, was encircled by a twelve-foot cement wall—one large building, three smaller structures, and the long, flat hospital facility still under construction—all of which was perched high atop a peninsula, overlooking the Indian Ocean. The ever-vigilant armed guards held AK-47s at their side as they patrolled the grounds.

There was one small window in Robbie's room. From this vantage point, Robbie was able to look out onto the sapphire ocean and watch the surf crash furiously onto the passive shoreline. He yearned to walk on the beach and raise his face upward and bask in the hot sun.

His door opened suddenly and two armed guards barged in. They pointed their guns at him, signaling that he should leave the room. They walked him outside to an area behind the medical building where Robbie had never been. In the distance he saw ten uniformed men standing side by side. They wore black-and-gray *shemagh* scarves wrapped around their heads and faces so that only their eyes were visible.

Startled, Robbie stopped, but one of the guards pushed him forward. As he got closer to the uniformed men, Robbie saw that they were armed with guns and had assumed the firing position. They faced human-shaped targets 150 feet away. On command they fired their weapons. The memory of Simon, Frosty, and Ivan careened through Robbie's consciousness. His knees felt weak and he was certain that he was being escorted to his execution. His mind raced, but he knew that if he bolted, they would surely shoot him. Yet wouldn't that be preferable to being forced to your knees, waiting to be shot in the head at close range? Robbie felt the adrenaline pump through his veins as he took a deep breath and closed his eyes:

The Lord is my Shepherd, I shall not want. He maketh me to lie down in green pastures; He leadeth me beside the still waters. He restoreth my soul; He guideth me in straight path for His name's sake. Yea, that I walk through the shadow of death, I will fear no evil, for Thou art with me; Thy rod and Thy staff, they comfort me.

"Dr. Rosen, so nice to see you again." Robbie opened his eyes and saw Abdikarim standing before him, hand outstretched. Robbie's own hand trembled as he shook the outstretched one. An amused expression crossed Abdikarims's face.

Another round of gun shots rang out. Abdikarim looked at the trainees, put his arm around Robbie's shoulder, and laughed. "My friend did you think you were being brought over to a firing squad?"

Robbie did not answer. He had the innate feeling that the less he spoke, the better it would be. He merely nodded his head. Abdikarim kept his arm around Robbie and led him toward the medical building. He gestured toward the structure.

"*This* is why you are here. As I told you, we are partners. You will do the surgery and remove the organs. They will be shipped all over the world. I get rich enough to buy anything we need to further our cause. And as long as you are doing the surgery, you will remain alive. It's a good partnership, no?"

Abdikarim opened the building's door with a flourish. "I want you to have the grand tour of the medical facility, which is finally ready. Actually, we are waiting for one last piece of equipment scheduled to be brought in later this afternoon and then we get started. Very exciting!"

Despite his weakened state, Robbie walked through the building and saw that the operating suite was state-of-the-art, with equipment that would, without a doubt, rival the finest surgical centers in New York City. The examination and waiting rooms were furnished and well-stocked with all the necessary supplies a doctor would ever need. He thought of the MSF facility and of how their equipment was mostly out of date and sometimes barely usable.

Abdikarim led Robbie into a small office, where there was a large metal desk. He pointed to the desk and smiled, "Have a seat at your new desk, Doctor. Try it out—how do you say it in America, take it for a spin."

Robbie sat behind the desk and Abdikarim sat across from him. Robbie saw that the office was much nicer than the one he had shared with his fellow residents at New York Hospital.

"Explain something to me. If the *donors*, as you call them, won't survive the surgery, then why would you have examination and recovery rooms? It doesn't make sense."

Abdikarim smiled, "Very astute, Dr. Rosen. I have spoken to my superiors and soon many of them will join us, and bring their wives and children. We have decided that you will also be in charge of all their medical care as well. So that is why everything must be the very best."

Robbie saw an opportunity and seized it. "I'll care for your people to the best of my ability, I'll commit to that. But I cannot be involved in the harvesting of organs for the black market. I can't have the death of all those donors on my hands."

Abdikarim leaned in closer to Robbie and whispered, "That is extremely distressing, Doctor. Do you have such little regard for your own life that you would throw it away?"

"No sir, I don't. But I do have the utmost regard for human life. What you are asking me goes against the oath I took when I became a physician. In fact, it's against everything I believe to be right."

"Would it make you feel better to know that most of your patients have agreed to the procedure because their families will be well-compensated? They are all dying, you see, so this is actually an admirable service you will be performing."

"Dying? From what?"

Abdikarim smiled, "From this and that. . .but mostly from AIDS."

"*AIDS?* You can't transplant organs from patients with AIDS. That would be a death sentence for the recipients."

"You are right: It is. But let's just say that I see it as killing two birds with one stone." He laughed in a devilish manner. "Your first day of surgery is tomorrow late morning. I will be in the operating room, eager to witness the talent that I have heard so much about. Now Doctor, I am a busy man, and you must go back to your little world inside your little room." He shouted in Arabic to the guard who was waiting in the hallway. The door opened and Abdikarim nodded to the guard to escort Robbie out. But before Robbie was out of earshot, Abdikarim said, "There is something I want you to think about, Doctor. If you refuse to obey, the treatment you received from the last group will seem like child's play compared to the punishment we have been trained to employ here. Now have a wonderful day."

Hours later, while the sun was setting outside, Robbie lay on his mattress and contemplated his limited options. He knew that he would surely be tortured if he did not obey. But he was convinced that they wouldn't kill him, since the stakes were too high and they desperately needed his services. He thought about all the organ recipients who would be infected with the AIDS virus and who, in turn, might unknowingly infect their own families. It was the perfect storm for terrorists.

Robbie understood what he needed to do; he knew that it would be in his best interest to comply. He sighed and closed his eyes, feeling comfort—a feeling he had not experienced since coming to Somalia—when he thought about his familiar routines as a physician. When he was working at New York Hospital, each time before he performed a major surgery, he would visualize step-by-step every facet of the upcoming procedure.

In approximately fifteen hours, he would meet with his surgical team. Before they entered the operating room, he would make sure they each knew the procedure and what their individual role in it would be. He would ask them to repeat each aspect of the process back to him, so as to ensure that they had grasped the particular rhythm and timing that would need to take place. He would dress and scrub for surgery. He would take his time. He was always fastidious, especially when he scrubbed. Once inside the operating room, he would make sure, one last time that his team was prepared for what he expected of them. He would smile encouragingly at each of them. He would deliberately smile at Abdikarim, slowly lift the scalpel, and feel the familiar weight of the sharp instrument in his hand. Robbie would then calmly proceed to sever his own carotid artery. Within minutes he would be dead.

Chapter 20

Lily and one of Maniadakis's men, the one they called Smitty, walked across the hotel lobby toward the conference room. The young woman, standing behind the front counter, wearing a black-and-gold *shash,* nodded as a signal of recognition; Lily smiled back. She noticed a large clock above the concierge kiosk that was set seven hours behind Somali time, with a sign underneath it—*New York.* She avoided eye contact with four men in white *dashikis* waiting to check in to the hotel. A shiver traveled up her spine as she walked past them.

Smitty turned left into a narrow hallway where two of Jama's men stood guard in front of the conference room. He nodded for the men to open the heavy double doors. Lily walked inside and was astonished to see that that the stark-white conference room had been converted into a high-tech mission-control center that was already a beehive of activity. There were two long rows of computer stations where men and woman, wearing large headphones, sat typing. Live streaming images of streets throughout different sections of Mogadishu played continually on four oversized flat screens mounted on the wall in front of the stations.

Five men—three in tan military uniforms and two in civilian clothes—studied maps drawn on an enormous white board. Photos of individuals and groups of men were pinned to a cork board. Lily looked around the room, but could not find Maniadakis. She spotted David standing with two other men, peering over a woman's shoulder, as she pointed to something on her computer screen. David glanced up and Lily caught his eye. He nodded to his sister, broke away from the group and walked over to her. David gave his sister a peck on the cheek, "Did you get some sleep?"

Lily nodded. "Some." She looked around at the active staff and the high level equipment. "This is overwhelming."

"You don't know the half of it. They have this whole network in place that monitors 'chatter.' If anyone says anything that smacks of a situation that could in any way relate to Robbie, it gets flagged for review." David pointed to the large screens. "And they have satellites that can zoom in on anyone in the streets and listen to their conversations."

"Who are all these people?"

"Most of these people worked for Maniadakis when he was in the C.I.A." David pointed to an older woman, wearing a dark brown suit, her grey hair pulled back into a tight bun and a no-nonsense expression etched on her face. "That woman, Eleanor, was his assistant for twenty years; she says he was a big deal there. Most of these people were in the C.I.A with him."

"Did they share any information with you?"

"Maniadakis said that when you arrived, we should go to his office for a briefing."

David put his hand gently on his sister's back and steered her past the commotion to a private office in the far corner of the room. The door was open and Maniadakis was seated behind a large desk, talking on the telephone. He waved them in and gestured for them to sit down.

"I understand, Frank, you know I do. But if this is what I think it is, then we've got a win-win situation here. You send a team, pick up our guy, and get yourself a few insurgents. Who knows, with just the right coaxing, they may give you the info you need to get you the big kahuna. Then you're a hero with the man in Washington." Maniadakis listened intently while the person at the other end of the conversation spoke.

The transformation in Maniadakis had been remarkable. This mission and the promise of adventure had rejuvenated him. When Ken had contacted him, Maniadakis was at the lowest point of his life. Retirement did not suit him—sitting around for hours talking about his exploits, rather than partaking in new ones, had deflated him. Maniadakis had no wife or children—he had never had time to settle down, since he'd been totally absorbed in the world of espionage. Now, his recollections of more exciting times haunted his days and had begun to seep into his dreams. In recent months, his source of comfort and refuge came from one place: inside a bottle.

One particularly wretched night in Mykonos, after having drunk too much and revealed too many details about past glories to anyone who would listen, he walked along *the limani*. The gentle rocking of the anchored boats in the harbor filled him with an overwhelming sense of loss, loneliness, and guilt. After another few drinks, he stumbled back to his apartment where he promptly passed out on the kitchen floor. At 9:00 a.m. the following morning, the ringing of the telephone woke him up. He was face-down in a mound of his own vomit. It was Ken asking him for his assistance in finding Robbie.

Reacting to something that the person at the other end of the phone had said, Maniadakis suddenly broke into a huge smile and triumphantly slammed his hand on the desk.

"Fantastic! You got it, buddy. As soon as I get that info, I'll be back on the horn. Oh yeah. . . do me a favor and check to see if Preacher and his team are available." There was a short pause. "Thanks. Give Marge my regards and kiss those grandbabies for me." He hung up the telephone, folded his hands on the desk, and smiled at David and Lily.

"Sorry. That was my guy at Langley. So, we're moving right along, doing some digging. Even before we arrived, we had a reconnaissance team on the streets gathering data and we got solid leads that we're tracking." He opened a file on his desk, moved the contents closer to David and Lily, and pointed to a photo of a group of Somali men, all in uniform and carrying high-power guns.

"These guys are part of the Ali Saleeban Clan, known for their piracy and kidnapping activities." Pointing to one of the men, he continued, "This handsome fella is Isse Yuluh, leader of the whole shebang. Our sources tell us that they're the ones who abducted Robbie and the other three doctors. The word is that they've snatched the doctors for the ransom. We don't know what went down, but they executed the other three."

"That means Robbie's still alive?" Lily asked.

David took Lily's hand. "Do you know where they took him?"

"So here's the deal, they don't have your boy anymore."

"He escaped?" David asked.

Maniadakis shifted uncomfortably in his chair. "It seems that one of Jama's men is friends with a guy who has a brother-in-law in the Ali Saleeban Clan. It didn't take too much money for the clan member to spill his guts."

There was a knock on the office door. A balding man in his mid-twenties, wearing thick-lensed oval-shaped glasses, that gave him an owl-like appearance, entered the room. "Sir, we're ready for you."

"Perfect timing. Matt, these good folks are Lily Lockwood and Dr. Rosen's brother, David."

Matt extended his hand to David, then blushed when he shook hands with Lily. "Miss Lockwood... Wow! What an honor! I'm a big fan of yours. My girl and I saw you last month on Broadway and you were awesome. You think I can get a photo with you?"

Lily smiled, "Of course and thanks for all your help here."

"For Chrissakes, Bollinger, stop your damn drooling and get back out there." Matt's face became beet red, he put his head down, and left the room.

"He started working for me at the agency right out of M.I.T. He's a great tech, but the kid's got zero social skills." Maniadakis picked up his files from the desk and started walking toward the door. "Follow me."

They walked out into the commotion that was still going on in the main room. Maniadakis whistled loudly and clapped his hands twice.

"Okay folks, listen up. Someone get the lights." The buzzing ceased and the room became silent. Maniadakis stood up-front, next to the large screen. All eyes were upon him.

So here's what we know: Dr. Rosen and three other staff members of MSF were taken by the Ali Saleeban Clan. Of the four who were abducted, only Rosen survived. There was a proof-of-life photo sent to MSF headquarters in Paris, but that was the only communication. It seemed peculiar, since we know he was taken by a clan notorious for piracy and for kidnapping activities that involve American citizens."

Maniadakis held a projector wire in his hand that had a button on one end. He pressed the button and a photo appeared on the screen of a tall, dark-skinned man in a long *dashiki* with a white *kufi* on his head. "This is Abdulkadir Mohamed Abdulkadir—known as Ikrima. He's currently in Kenya, but is a

Somali and a known senior commander of Al Shaabab. Our intel links him to major Al Qaeda operatives—in particular, to Fazul Abdullah Muhammed and to Saleh Ali Saleh Nabhan, who played major roles in the bombing of U.S. embassies in Kenya and Tanzania.

Now it looks as if one of his top honchos...." When Maniadakis pressed the projector's button, a photo of a bearded Somali in a green uniform appeared on the screen. "This is Mubaarak Abdikarim, a key ethnic Somali, an Al Shabaab planner, and a top guy in what was once a sleeper cell that's recently been awakened. He is known to have been involved in black-market operations—mostly drugs and human trafficking that fund terrorist activities."

Maniadakis clicked the button again and the screen went dark. "We believe that Abdikarim, upon direct orders from Abdulkar, paid the clan big bucks for Dr. Rosen. What we need to figure out is: Why did they want Rosen and where are they keeping him? Once we find out, it's a whole new ballgame. We'll put the drones up and hook into more targeted satellites to babysit them. We'll also have the full support of the Agency, who'll work with us, coordinate efforts with the military, and deploy a squad of SEALs and canines. Their mission will be to capture Abdikarim and Abdulkar, and to rescue Dr. Rosen. From here on in, this mission will be referred to as '*Operation House Call*.' Now all we gotta do to move everything along is to find out where these cowboys lay their heads at night. A piece of cake, right?" A nervous laughter spread through the room. "So why would these two ragheads want our Doctor?"

An attractive blonde woman, seated at one of the computer stations, called out, "Maybe to give medical care to one of the high-ranking Al Qaeda or Al Shabaab leaders?"

Maniadakis scratched his head and thought for a few seconds. "That's what I thought initially, Sharon, but that just don't make sense. They got plenty of doctors. Why pay good money for this one?"

A young man, leaning against a wall in the back of the room asked, "What was Dr. Rosen's specialty?"

"Good question, Gus." Maniadakis turned toward David and asked "Rosen?"

David cleared his throat. "Surgery, actually cardiac surgery. In New York Hospital he worked closely with Dr. Preston Wells."

"Wells is the guru of heart transplants, right?" asked Matt.

David nodded. "Yes. He was grooming my brother to take over his practice when he retires."

"Maybe one of the leaders needs heart surgery," Sharon said.

"We're definitely missing something here." Gus walked to the front of the room. "Boss, you said this guy Abdikarim is into black-market shit, right?" Maniadakis nodded. "Well then why would they need Rosen? Why not hundreds of other doctors within Al Qaeda or Al Shabaab who...." Gus stopped himself in mid-sentence, realizing the answer. "Holy shit."

Lily turned to Dave and whispered, "What?"

David shrugged.

Gus walked up to Maniadakis. "Organs, boss. They're harvesting organs for the black market—that's huge money. We busted that New York doctor, Michael Mastromarino, he was the dude who worked in cahoots with this funeral director, cut out bones, skins, ligaments and tendons, and sold them on the black market. One of the bodies they harvested was, shit, that journalist, what was his name?"

A young Hispanic woman, seated at the computer next to Sharon, said, "Alistair Cooke."

"Bingo." Gus said triumphantly.

Maniadakis folded his arms, smiled, and said to Gus, "If you weren't so ugly, I'd plant a big fat kiss on ya."

Lily stood up, her face red. "Wait, no! Robbie would never do that, ever!" She looked to her brother for support. "Tell them, David."

Maniadakis turned to her and smiled, "With all due respect, Ma'am, when a person's got a gun pointed at his head, he's likely to do things he never imagined he'd do. Remember, we're talking terrorists and I don't need to tell ya, they're mighty persuasive." He looked at two of his men standing by the window.

"Cordova, Mulvaney I need you guys to go over to MSF and see if they still have any of Dr. Rosen's clothes there. If so, grab a few worn items. If we locate him, we'll need these for the dogs to sniff. Okay, people, keep on tracking the intel and see if there's any chatter at all. If there's anything that smells remotely interesting, bring it to me immediately. Otherwise, we reconvene at 17:00 hours."

Without skipping a beat, everyone returned to the activity they'd been engaged in before the meeting began.

Lily walked over to Maniadakis. "Nikos, I would like to join the group going to MSF," she said.

"Out of the question. It's deadly out there. Stay here where you'll be safe. I'll keep you in the loop."

Lily sighed, "I insist."

"You have to listen to him, Lily— he's the expert." David said.

Lily did not explain to them just how vital it was for her to be able to see the compound—the place where Robbie had been abducted. She believed that if she saw the bed Robbie had slept in, where he'd eaten his meals, and saw the clinic where he had cared for his patients, it would bring her closer to him and somehow make his rescue more of a reality.

Lily folded her arms and smiled at Maniadakis. "How far is the MSF compound from here?"

"About ten miles."

Lily could tell he was annoyed. "If, in the middle of the day, your men can't keep me safe for an hour or two, then we're really in trouble, aren't we?"

Maniadakis paused, shook his head, and sighed, "Okay, little lady—point taken. You and Rosen should meet the guys in the lobby in twenty minutes." He looked down at her feet and sneered. "Better change them fancy shoes."

Chapter 21

avid and Lily stepped into the hotel elevator that would take them up to her penthouse suite. When the doors closed, Lily turned to her brother and said, "Is it me or is he the most condescending person you've ever met?"

David smiled. "Well let's just say that Maniadakis can come off as a bit arrogant. But Lily, he's right about your having to be careful. If you leave the hotel, then he has to get a shitload of guys out there on guard detail."

Lily was still brooding, but once inside her room, she kicked off her shoes and put on a pair of sneakers.

"I know what you're saying. It's just the way he talks to me, like I'm this frail piece of china he's afraid may break."

David sat down on the couch in the living-room area and smiled at her, "Don't let him get to you. He's just doing what you're paying him to do."

Lily sat on the opposite couch and tied her sneakers. "Do you think he's right about Robbie?

David shrugged. "We have no clue about what's going on, what Robbie's going through, or what they're doing to him."

Tears sprang to Lily's eyes and this time she didn't stop them from flowing. She grabbed a tissue, dabbed her eyes, and weakly smiled, "Sorry."

"Hey, you don't have to apologize to me."

Lily sighed deeply, "I love him—Robbie, I mean. You know that, right?"

"If I didn't know that before Mom and I visited you, I figured it out pretty quickly. We both did. Your boyfriend Jamie is not too happy about it, I guess."

Lily smiled. "Not so much. But Robbie's *the one*—it's always been Robbie, right from the start. I just never had a chance to tell him.

David smiled, "Well, with any kind of luck, you can tell him yourself, pretty soon."

Later that afternoon, Lily, David, and two of Maniadakis's staff—Miguel Cordova and Sean Mulvaney—along with three of Jama's armed guards were being guided through *Médecins Sans Frontières'* compound by Dr. Alain Rondeau. The hospital compound consisted of numerous buildings and tents where long lines of Somali men, women, and children waited patiently to see one of the eight overworked physicians.

Alain told the group he planned to take them to one of the hospital clinics. As they walked across the facility, they heard snatches of conversations in French, Somali, and English. Alain reveled in his role as tour guide. He had recognized Lily Lockwood as soon as she'd stepped out of the truck and was delighted he'd been chosen to chaperone the actress and her group. In Paris, where he was born and raised, her television shows aired quite often, with French subtitles.

"Our support staff from the area nurses and orderlies act as interpreters between the doctors and the patients who speak only Somali. Without them communication would be frustrating, so you can imagine how vital they are to our day-to-day operation."

He walked toward the clinic, a long white building, where healthy children played and chased one another, laughing and shouting while waiting for their turns to get inoculated.

The group passed a smaller building that Alain said was an emergency triage clinic where sick or wounded children lay lethargically across their mothers' laps. The broiling sun stimulated the stench of blood, pus, and sweat. Flies swarmed the lifeless tiny bodies, targeting their wounded areas. The mothers, with eyes distant and devoid of emotion, systematically swiped the flies away, only to have the insects circle and return a few seconds later.

As they walked past these people, Lily was reminded of the morning she visited Margaret's daughter, Eavan, in New York Presbyterian Lower Manhattan

Hospital. The contrast between the children in that meticulously clean hospital, with its brightly painted wall murals, who were cared for by a full staff of doctors and nurses using the most modern equipment and these poor children who lay dying in front of her, was tragic and heartbreaking.

When they arrived at the crowded clinic, there were three doctors—one man and two women—all wearing matching MSF issued white t-shirts and stethoscopes around their necks. They administered shots and laughed with the children and their mothers. The male—an Asian doctor—was closest to them and Alain walked Lily and the group over to him.

"Sam, these are the people I spoke to you about." He turned to Lily and her group. "This is Dr. Sam Wo, who has a real knack with children. They're the only kids I know who can't wait to get their vaccinations because they get to see the fun doctor."

Sam laughed. "I wish that were true. But it's not me—I have a secret weapon."

Lily was intrigued. "And what, may I ask, is your secret weapon?"

Sam reached into his pocket and produced a few tootsie-roll pops. The children excitedly reached for the lollipops as Sam smiled and put them into the kids' eager hands.

"Ta da, the deep secret to my vast popularity," Sam laughed.

Alain walked over to one of the mothers, nodded to the Somali staff member who signaled that he should act as interpreter. "Sister, please tell these good people why you have come to the hospital."

The staff member spoke to her in her native tongue. He waited for her to respond. "She says that she walks one full day to come here. She does so because she knows that without the special shot, her children will become very ill and may die like many children in her village."

The mother spoke again and the staff member nodded his head, indicating he understood what she was saying.

"She says that soon she will move to the IDP camp for internally displaced people. They have lost everything to a rival tribe who has come in and decimated the area and left them with nothing. No home, no land."

Lily watched the woman speak softly—openly and in a matter-of-fact manner—about a situation that would bring most people to their knees.

She took the woman's hand and asked the staff member to interpret. "I am so grateful that you shared your story with me. I am so sorry for the hardships you and your family are living through." After the staff member told the woman what Lily had said, the woman's face brightened with one of the widest smiles Lily had ever seen.

Lily turned to Alain "May I possibly give her money for food or water?"

"Miss Lockwood, you can make a donation to MSF anytime and this will help all these people. And if you would like, you can purchase food and water for the IDP camp. You can bring it yourself or we can do it for you."

While still holding the woman's hand, Lily looked to David, who nodded and then looked back to Alain. "We'll go to the IDP camp and bring food and water. Is there anything else we can do?

"Yeah, you can take your checkbook from that ridiculously expensive Louis Vuitton purse you're carrying and write a big fat check to open an IDP school for thousands of kids who've never seen the inside of a classroom." The attractive female doctor with the short blonde hair and a thick Australian accent sneered.

"Chloe, that's rude!" The third doctor glared at her fellow Aussie.

Chloe looked at Lily with contempt. "Bugger off Emma, you know what I'm saying is dead on. We don't have time to sugar coat anything here. These people need help and they need it now!"

Alain's face turned a deep shade of crimson. "I am so sorry, Miss Lockwood. Dr. Martin is a wonderful doctor and doesn't mean to offend. She can be a little, how do you say, rough around the edges at times."

"No, it's okay. I asked what I can do to help," Lily said and smiled at the doctors. "She's not wrong." She walked to the side of the room where Chloe was standing and extended her hand, "Lily Lockwood."

"Chloe Martin," Chloe muttered and sighed deeply, attempting to slow down her racing heart. Even though she appeared tough and in control, Chloe was actually nervous standing next to the actress—her nemesis.

The other doctor smiled and also shook hands with Lily. "Emma White and I'm gobsmacked to meet you. I'm a big fan of your work."

Chloe got busy putting away supplies that one of the staff had deposited on the table next to her. Lily thanked Emma and looked back at Chloe. "If you can let me know who to talk to, I would be more than happy to make a donation for the school."

"*Fantastique!*" Alain clapped his hands joyfully. "I will get you that information before you leave. Now I am sure you would like to get to the reason you are here." He nodded to David and looked back at Chloe and Emma, "Ladies, David is Robert's brother and he and Miss Lockwood are here with these other fellows," Alain pointed to Miguel and Sean, "to get any information you think may help them find him. They also need to pick up Dr. Rosen's belongings."

"Come to my room." Chloe instructed and led them out the door.

Once inside her room, Chloe kneeled and pulled out a heavy foot-locker stored under her bed. She opened it up to reveal Robert's personal effects: clothes, jewelry, and his passport. She took out a few folded t-shirts, a pair of khaki shorts, and some blue scrubs.

"These are Robert's clothes; they haven't been washed so the dogs should be able to pick up his scent." As she had done dozens of times before, Chloe unconsciously smelled the folded clothes before handing them to David. "I suppose you will want the rest of his things." She pointed to the remaining items in the foot-locker. David nodded. Chloe took out the pieces of jewelry, holding them each for a few seconds, knowing that she may never see them or their owner again. She quickly handed them to David. "Well, that's that, I suppose," she said, closing the locker in an act of feigned bravado.

"We're going to need his passport, too." Lily said.

"No, he's going to need it when he comes back here." Chloe put her head down so no one should get a glimpse of the tears she was blinking back.

Miguel saw the tears and softly said, "Sorry, ma'am, if and when we rescue Dr. Rosen, it will be helpful for him to have identification."

"You're right, of course." Chloe handed the passport to Miguel. "Do you need anything else?"

Lily turned to Alain. "Can you show us Robbie's room please?" Alain hesitated and before he could speak Chloe responded, "*This* was his room."

"Oh sorry, I thought this was *your* room." Lily looked around and saw women's clothes hanging in the opened closet and strewn on a chair beside the bed. A blow dryer sat on top of the dresser, sharing space with assorted containers of face creams and make-up.

Chloe folded her arms and smiled at the actress, "This is. Robert and I spent so much time sleeping in each other's beds that we decided to give one room up. So this was *our* room."

Chloe walked over to the mirror and picked up one photo among the many that were taped to the glass and handed it to Lily.

Before she looked down at the photo, for a split second, Lily thought that it must be a mistake. The Robert about whom Chloe had been speaking must be a different person than the Robbie she knew and loved. Lily forced herself to look at the candid photo. It was of Chloe and Robbie—his arm was around her waist and he was smiling down at her. Chloe looked so different—so much softer—she was smiling as she looked up into Robbie's eyes. Lily's heart sank and her eyes welled up when she recognized the smile and dimples she had fallen in love with. She couldn't tear herself away from the photograph.

David stood behind Lily and gently took the picture out of his sister's hands. "Come on, we'd better get going." He handed the photo back to Chloe.

Chloe saw Lily's reaction and the tears in her eyes. She smiled at David. "You know he spoke about you and your parents all the time. He missed and loved you all so—"

"—did he ever mention me?" Lily interrupted.

Chloe deliberated for few seconds and shook her head, "No, not that I remember." She looked back at David. "We were planning a trip to Dallas as soon as our mission here was completed—so I could meet his family—before settling down in New York City together." She smiled innocently. Emma shot her a look and Alistair appeared even more uncomfortable than he had been a few minutes earlier.

Miguel looked at his watch. "Well, we have to hit the road; we have a meeting in an hour."

The group piled out of the room, leaving Emma and Chloe alone.

Emma turned to her friend, "You freakin' liar! Why the hell did you say those things?"

Chloe walked over to the mirror and taped the photo back up. "I can say whatever I damn well please."

"What's wrong with you? None of that was true. He never asked you to go to the States with him. And you complained to me that he talked about Lily Lockwood *all the time.* Don't you remember?"

Chloe smirked. "Maybe I do and maybe I don't. Now get the hell out."

After Emma had left the room, Chloe reached into the drawer and pulled out Robert's journal—the place where he poured all the feelings of love and regret that he had for Lily. Chloe now had to accept the inevitable; that whether Robert was rescued or not, he would be forever lost to her. She hugged the journal to her chest, and threw herself upon her bed—the bed she had shared with the man she still loved. Chloe covered her face with her pillow and cried.

David looked at Lily, who was seated quietly next to him in the back seat of the truck, silently staring out the window. She hadn't spoken since leaving the compound. She leaned her head against the glass and closed her eyes. In all the scenarios she had imagined that might unfold, she never thought of the possibility that Robbie would have fallen in love with someone else. She felt stupid. She had felt so connected to him. She thought of the silver cord tied to her heart that she imagined was connected to Robbie's heart. It seemed that he had severed it years before. She thought of the photo of Robbie and Chloe—that photo said it all, in their smiles and in the way they looked at one another. Lily had to face reality, Robbie had totally forgotten her.

David touched her shoulder and Lily turned and looked at her brother. She had gone pale in Chloe's room and David noticed that Lily's color had not yet returned. "Are you okay, Sis?"

Lily shook her head and tried to manage a smile. "You have to do something for me."

"Anything. Whatever you need." He assured her.

"When they rescue Robbie. . ." Lily put her hand to her heart ". . . and I truly have a feeling they will, you cannot tell him that I had anything to do with his rescue. Nothing. Not that I was here and nothing about the money?"

David shook his head. "No, I can't do that Lily. Without you, none of this would be possible. Why would you want that?"

She took her brother's hand in her own. "If he does come back to me sometime, it has to be because he wants me. I don't want it to be because of gratitude or obligation. Can you please promise?"

"How about we wait and see how all this unfolds, huh?

Lily nodded and rested her head on David's shoulder.

Chapter 22

Robbie stood patiently next to the only window in his stark room and waited for the orange and yellow sun, like a massive orb of fire, to gently slide down into the horizon. It would be the last sunset he would ever witness in his life.

When he decided to kill himself, he was instantly blanketed with a sense of peace like he had never before experienced. For years he had thought of suicide as an unfortunate act of weakness—a permanent solution to a temporary problem. But now it had become his shining armor of power. That one deed would remove all control his captors held over him.

After the sun vanished and the streaks of purples and reds left behind were engulfed by total blackness, Robbie turned away from the window. He wondered if life was simply a string of vibrant years consumed by an eternity of darkness. Would his life remain meaningful only in the memory of his loved ones? And when they were also gone, then what?

Robbie knew he was fortunate to have lived a rewarding life. He had been doted on by his family, had a close-knit circle of friends, a career that filled him with pride and accomplishment, had been loved by extraordinary women and finally found, in Lily, the love of his life. He would not sleep that evening, but rather stay awake all night and think of the gifts life had presented him. He would untie the ribbons that had kept those memories tightly hidden away. He would carefully take them out, one by one, and explore them in detail.

Robbie's leg was particularly painful that evening and he massaged the area behind his knee. By this time every evening, after spending the day standing and walking, his leg felt as if it was slowly being severed. Most nights, he would request a pain killer and his guards would comply by bringing him a large syringe filled with Morphine that not only erased his pain— physically and emotionally— but also sent him soaring into a place where time and space had no meaning. Tonight, his final night, he did not want to be anesthetized; it was necessary that he remained sharp and lucid.

Robbie limped over to the small wooden table they had recently brought into his room. The guards proudly carried it in and presented it to him, as if it were an antique Chippendale desk. Taking advantage of their good spirits, Robbie requested paper and pens. When he later returned to his room, he was surprised to find that a notebook and two pens had been left for him.

His plan to spend the evening sifting through his remembrances included writing a letter to his parents, to his brother, and to Lily. He knew they could never be sent and the recipients would never have the opportunity to read them.

He took a drink of water and thought of his fellow doctors at M.S.F and hoped they were all safe. His mind wandered to thoughts of Chloe and a familiar wave of guilt washed over him. He had known, not long after they had gotten together, that her feelings were stronger than his. He made it a point to speak of Lily often as a gentle reminder that he was in love with another woman.

When they first got together, they were simply two good friends who used each another as an oasis against the atrocities and suffering they witnessed daily. He didn't know exactly when it happened, but over the months together, he felt certain that Chloe had fallen in love with him. She became more open with him and her persona, once edgy and sharp, softened. Everyone noticed the change.

He closed his eyes and remembered lying on top of her athletic body—her long legs wrapped tightly around his waist. The guilt he felt now began while they were still together. The last few times they slept together, he closed his eyes and imagined she was Lily. He had never before been *that guy* so after they made love that last evening he decided he could no longer continue their physical relationship. He planned to tell Chloe the next morning that it was unfair to her; he cared far too much for her as a friend and could not hurt her that way. Unfortunately there was never a next morning because he was abducted a few hours later.

The lingering memory was abruptly interrupted by three sharp knocks at his door. Abdikarim walked in smiling and extended his hand.

"How are you this evening, Dr. Rosen?"

"I'm fine."

"Excellent, excellent! I wanted to visit you this evening in order to ensure that you have everything you need for your first surgery tomorrow."

Robbie's legs became wobbly, so he sat down, "Yes, I've gone over everything with the staff and have met the first donor."

Abdikarim smiled, sat on the corner of the table and folded his hands. "Fantastic. Everything must be perfect tomorrow. Because of the momentous occasion, we are honored to have our top officials visiting so they may observe. They will be seated in the room next to the operating room and will watch the surgeries through the glass window. You will not be able to see them, but I assure you—they will be watching you."

"I understand."

Abdikarim leaned in close to Robbie and his eyes narrowed. "Nothing had better go wrong. I will make this promise to you, if anything goes awry, if you pull any stunts to embarrass me, you will be escorted to a 'special' room that we have in the basement." His sneer turned into a smile. "Doctor, have you ever been tied to a chair and had the skin on your arm slowly peeled away?"

Robbie did not respond; he merely stared back into his captor's eyes.

Abdikarim walked toward the door. With his hand on the knob, he turned and again faced the doctor. "I assure you. It is something you would never forget. The first surgery will commence tomorrow morning, 7:00 a.m. sharp. I know you will do the right thing."

"I can promise you I will," Robbie replied.

After Abdikarim left, Robbie limped over to the far side of his room to the mirror that hung over a small sink. He did not look at his gaunt face, but rather focused on the left side of his neck. His right-hand index finger slowly traced the carotid artery from the bottom of his neck up to his ear. He imagined that it would take only a few seconds for him to pick up the scalpel and sever his artery. He glanced at the clock. If all went as planned, he would be dead in exactly twelve hours—at 7:05 a.m.

There were three more knocks at the door and Abdikarim walked in, followed by two of his armed guards.

"I am sorry to interrupt, my friend, but with all our planning and chatting away, I completely forgot one of the main reasons for my visit tonight. Have a seat." Abdikarim sat at one side of the table and gestured for Robbie to sit across from him.

Robbie slowly limped across the room and sat opposite him.

"That leg looks like it is giving you great pain tonight."

"I'm okay."

"You know, I can get one of my men to give you some pain medication, so it will insure that you have a good night's sleep, rested and ready to perform your surgeries tomorrow.

"I said I'm okay."

"Suit yourself." He gestured to one of the guards who immediately took out a large manila envelope and handed it to Abdikarim, who slowly turned the envelope over a few times before he attempted to open the clasp. "These things are the worst to open, aren't they? My fingers are clumsy—not what they used to be." He laughed and handed it to Robbie. "Would you open this for me, please?

Robbie opened the clasp and pushed the envelope back across the table.

Abdikarim opened it and took out what looked like two photographs and laid them face down on the table.

"I want you to understand just how important this enterprise is to my organization. And, since your contribution is vital to its success, we have come up with a way to insure that you remain focused." Robbie's eyes never left the photos on the table.

"So we have called upon our "friends" in the States. And, I assure you, there are many of us across the country. We have a rather large faction in the suburbs of Dallas." He smiled when he saw Robbie's jaw clench.

"We have reached out to them and they have been extremely cooperative." Abdikarim turned over the first photo to reveal a photo of Robbie's mother, Hannah, in the parking lot of a neighborhood supermarket, wheeling a cart full of groceries to her car."

"I am told she is a wonderful woman."

Robbie leapt to his feet, leaned over the table, and grabbed Abdikarim's shirt collar with his left hand while he pulled back his tightly fisted right hand, ready to pound his adversary.

Before Robbie's fist could connect with its intended mark, the guards came forward and pointed their guns at him. Abdikarim stood up, brushed Robbie's hand away, straightened his collar, waved away the guards, and smiled at Robbie. "We all know the love a son has for his mother can be truly heartwarming."

Robbie glared at him "You touch one hair on her head and…"

"…and what, tough man?" Abdikarim laughed. "All you have to do is what is required of you and your dear, sweet mother will be safe and sound." He paused for a second. "Oh, you certainly will want to look at the next photo. Go on."

Robbie turned the other photo over to see his mother, his brother David, and a crowd of people dressed in black standing next to a newly dug grave as a casket is being lowered into the open hole. He looked confused.

"It was a shame what happened to your father. He was a good man and well-respected."

Robbie stared at the photo and shook his head in disbelief. His eyes filled with tears and he shouted, "You son of a bitch."

Abdikarim stood "Yes I have been told that before." Robbie laid his head on the table and sobbed.

Abdikarim stood up, nodded to the guards to open the door. He gestured to a third guard, who had been waiting outside the door, to enter the room. The guard, injection in hand, walked into the room.

Robbie did not fight when the sharp point pierced his vein and darkness filled his room.

Chapter 23

*L*ily was in the middle of a dream when a piercing noise from her computer woke her up. She glanced at the clock on her hotel nightstand and saw that it was already 7:05 p.m. After returning from the MSF compound, Lily had had a raging headache and decided to lie down for what was supposed to be only a few moments—a few hours earlier.

Lily jumped out of bed when she realized there was someone requesting a video chat. She hurriedly situated herself at the computer desk and clicked the green "accept" button.

Donna appeared on screen, which at first was pixelated and fuzzy, but within seconds turned into a crystal-clear picture. Lily was thrilled to see that Daisy Rose was contently seated on Donna's lap.

"Hi, little Munchkin." Lily missed her daughter so much and even though they had only been separated for a couple of days, Lily ached to hold her little girl.

Daisy Rose pointed to the screen and squealed, "Mama, Mama!"

"Yes that's right and Mama's coming home soon to give you a big kiss."

Lily spent the next few minutes playing peek-a-boo with her daughter. Daisy Rose giggled and demanded, "More, Mama, more." Finally when she got bored with the game, the toddler turned her little body around so that she was facing Donna. She put her chubby little hands on either side of Donna's cheeks and ordered "Auntie, down NOW!"

"I guess she's over me already." Lily laughed. "Wait, wait, Daisy Rose, give Mama a big kiss first." Lily said

Daisy Rose put her little face close to the computer and kissed the screen.

After putting the toddler down, Donna repositioned herself and when she looked back up her expression revealed a deep concern. "How are you, honey?"

Maniadakis had made clear, more than a few times, that they were forbidden to discuss any details of the mission. He said that there were eyes and ears everywhere and to ensure Robbie's safety, as well as their own, they had to use extreme caution not to compromise the operation. Lily understood that Donna was trying to ascertain, through any sort of body language or facial expression, how things were progressing. Lily shook her head indicating that they still had not located Robbie.

Donna looked as disappointed as Lily felt. "Well hang in there, Pali, and don't worry about us. We're doing just fine. Your one-year-old daughter is bossing around three grown women and we're loving it. And don't get me started about Ken, Tommy, and Fernando—she has them all wrapped tightly around her itsy bitsy finger." Both women laughed. "Acorn doesn't fall far from the tree, that's for sure."

"Meaning?"

Donna smiled, "Meaning that her Mama also has many men wrapped around her little finger."

"Hardly. As a matter of fact, I found out today there was a hot and heavy love affair going on between surgeries, here in Somalia."

It took Donna a few seconds to understand what Lily was saying. "Darlin' I've learned in my long life you never know what goes on behind closed doors. So wait until he is back where he belongs and then you can sort it out. Agreed?"

Lily nodded.

"Good. Oh before I forget, talk about sorting things out. . ." Donna smiled ". . .Jamie wants to take Daisy Rose to the Central Park Zoo this Saturday. Is that okay with you?"

Lily nodded. "Of course it is. Just remember to pack her up so she has enough snacks and diapers for the afternoon. Oh and don't forget her binky."

Before Donna could answer, Lily's hotel phone rang, interrupting their conversation. "One sec; let me take this."

Lily picked up the phone, "Hello?"

"Maniadakis here."

"Hi Nikos, what's going on?

He cleared his throat, which Lily had long since recognized as his nervous tick. "We have some new developments and I want to bring you and your brother up to speed. I've spoken to David and told him to meet me in your room in fifteen minutes. Are you good with that?

"Sure. I'm here."

Lily hung up and turned her attention back to the computer screen. "Auntie D. I have to get going. Thanks again for taking such good care of the baby. I'll be in touch soon."

"Wait, before you go. Please be careful honey and do everything you can to come back home, safe and sound. I love you."

Twenty minutes later David and Maniadakis knocked at Lily's door. Maniadakis nodded, quickly walked past her, and almost knocked her down in his haste. He then circled the living room, in search of something. He lifted and looked under the books in the bookshelves. He picked up and examined knick-knacks on the tables and desk. He opened all her drawers and started rifling through her clothes.

David shot his sister a 'now what the hell is he doing?' look. Lily shrugged her shoulders. All she knew was that Maniadakis was one strange bird and she had quickly learned not to question anything he did. She noticed he was even more disheveled than the last time she had seen him. He also looked as if he could use a good night's sleep and a change of clean clothes.

After he had finished turning things over in the living room, bedroom, and bathroom, Maniadakis walked over to Lily's iPod that she had left inserted in the portable speakers on the credenza. He lifted it up, scrolled through it, clicked on a playlist, reinserted it into the charger, pressed play, and turned the volume up to the highest, loudest level. Then he motioned them to sit down on the couch. After they were seated opposite him, he leaned over to them and whispered. "You can't be too careful." His face appeared almost animated, which was a complete change from his usual stoic demeanor.

"Oh I thought you were really into Katy Perry." David replied referring to the song that was blasting on the iPod.

Lily laughed but Maniadakis ignored him. "Okay so things have taken a new turn and I wanted to get you both up to speed. The C.I.A. is now on board, so it's a whole new ballgame."

"Does that mean you'll no longer be the point person?" David asked.

"On the contrary, I've been reinstated into the agency and will be spearheading the mission from this end. The reason we have the support of not only the agency but also the White House is because we're confident that Robbie is alive and we've narrowed in on the compound where he's being kept."

"Oh my God that's wonderful." Lily's heart soared and for the first time in days she felt optimistic. She took David's hand and squeezed it. David, on the other hand, looked skeptical. "I don't get it: Why is everyone suddenly on board *now?*

"Well, for one thing, we know he is alive so he is a viable rescue target. And we have extremely reliable intel that at least three of Al Shabaab top bananas are currently in the compound. So now we have even more skin in the game."

David shook his head. "So I guess rescuing my brother is not enough reason for our government to get involved?"

There was an uncomfortable silence that Lily quickly filled. "The most important thing is that they're going to rescue Robbie. Let them get as many terrorists as they want while they do it."

Maniadakis continued. "Now that this is an official mission, I cannot give you all the details. What I can tell you is that a top team will go in there and attempt to rescue your brother and capture the terrorists. If everything goes well, it should go down tomorrow morning. You both need to be packed and ready to go. Once our mission is complete, it won't be safe for any of us. That's another reason we chose this hotel. There's a helicopter landing pad on the roof. We'll get you out of here as quickly as we can."

Lily's heart raced. "When can we see him?"

The plan right now—and remember things can turn on a dime—is if Robbie is alive he'll be immediately transported to the U.S. Medical Center in Landstuhl, Germany. And you'll be taken there, too." Maniadakis cleared his throat. "If he isn't alive and they recover his body, he'll be brought to Virginia. So will you." Maniadakis stood up. "I have to get back downstairs for a briefing."

"Should we come with you, to the briefing I mean?" Lily walked over to her closet and took out one of her scarves.

"No, that's against protocol. Not to worry, I'll keep in touch with you—let you know how things are goin'. Get a good night sleep, tomorrow's going to be a long one." He walked over to the door. "Lily, now that the government's taking over, whatever money is remaining will be returned to your account. Eleanor has already been on the horn with the bank folks and set the wheels in motion. It's being wired as we speak. She'll also fax you an itemized account of expenditures once she's back in Virginia."

"I appreciate it, Nikos, and thanks for everything."

"Just doin' my job, Ma'am" He said nonchalantly.

Lily detected a sense of pride that, in the few weeks she had known him, Maniadakis had not possessed before.

Chapter 24

*S*kipper stood in front of the room and, once again, was filled with an overwhelming sense of pride as he gazed out over the rows of men—*his* men—most of whom he had known for more than five years. He had sat at their dinner tables, celebrated their children's birthdays, and as their Commanding Officer had even received the honor of being called "Godfather" when many of their babies were christened.

He had first met most of these men during their BUD/S Prep—Naval Special Warfare Preparatory School. On their first day, each group of more than 150 already seasoned military men with years of combat experience under their belt are told 'Look to your right, look to your left, look in front of you, look behind you. All of these men except three will drop out before graduation.' And, like clockwork, that's exactly what occurs.

He was part of the prep team and personally witnessed the many months of grueling training, on land and at sea, that each one of these men withstood. Training that would undoubtedly kill the average man.

The Navy SEALs are well known as elite special operations forces. As highly skilled as these men are physically, they are equally proficient intellectually. Their knowledge of technology and engineering would rival that of any Harvard graduate. Whether the mission requires trained killers or the finesse of a surgeon's blade, these are the men who are summoned for the job. The government gives them the highest tech, most classified "toys" invented. Put that all together with unmonitored funding and you got yourself the finest special ops on the planet.

Skipper would be the first to tell you his men are confident, some might even say cocky. He would agree with that. Nothing wrong with having swagger, if you're dedicated, professional, and part of the most exclusive fraternity in the world.

If Navy SEALs are the elite, then the men in front of him—SEAL Team 6—are considered the elite of the elite. And they are the ones being called upon today by the C.I.A.'s Special Activities and Counter Intelligence Divisions.

"Quiet down." The room went silent and the twenty-five men gave their Commanding Officer their undivided attention.

"The mission we discussed yesterday, *Operation House Call,* is now a confirmed go. We have one rescue target and two high-value kill or capture targets."

Skipper turned around to a large screen and pushed the button on the other end of the wire he held in his left hand. On the screen appeared a map of the Gulf of Aden, with Ethiopia and Somalia on one side and Yemen on the other. He clicked the button a second time and it zoomed in on a map of Somalia and the surrounding area. One more click and the area due-south of Somalia appeared on screen. Skipper turned and faced everyone in the room.

"This is Merca. Some of you are already familiar with the area…." Laughter floated through the room. "It's located on the coast, sixty-eight miles south of Mogadishu. You got us hooked into satellite uplink yet, Scooter?"

"One second, sir." A short Hispanic man with long, black hair pulled back into a pony tail sat at a computer, tapped a few more times, then hit the send button with a dramatic flourish. A radiating bull's-eye appeared on screen, and zoomed in on an aerial view of a waterfront bastion.

"And here, folks, is Al Shabaab at its finest—this heavily guarded compound, is located on a peninsula surrounded on three sides by water. Looks to be between twelve to fifteen foot concrete walls, topped with barbed wire. Two security gates, one on the northeast, the other on the southwest—three to four guards on each. The Surveillance shows thirty people living there. No women or children.

The three-story main building is where they're holding our rescue target, Dr. Robert Rosen—code name Tex. These two here are our two kills or captures—we now have been able to make positive identification, through surveillance and intelligence reports that, as of today, they're both inside."

A composite photograph of the two high ranking Al Shaabab leaders filled the screen. "Abdulkadir Mohamed, code name Big Foot and Mubaarak Abdikarim, code name Ranger. Toby emailed you each a one-sheeter on them. If you didn't get it, let her know, she's in the office.

These two are #3 and #15 in the bad-guy food chain and the Oval Office is salivating for them. Number-one priority is captures, but if it can't go down that way and they're kills, then we need proof of identity, photos, DNA… you know the drill. Or, if you can, take them to go."

He clicked again and a picture filled the screen. It showed Dr. Robert Rosen laughing as a Somali boy, who had a stethoscope around his little neck, listened to the doctor's heartbeat. "This is a photo of Tex taken 15 months ago. Scooter, get the copy of the drone feed up from earlier today."

Robbie's picture was immediately replaced by a video: a distant shot of two men walking behind the walls of the compound. A black man, in full military garb, used his high-power rifle to prompt the white one, wearing green scrubs that hung loosely from his emaciated frame, to move faster. The white man had a severe limp and tripped twice trying to keep up the pace. When he fell, the guard kicked him, urging him to stand.

"Zoom in." Skipper commanded.

The faces that were unrecognizable only a second before now appeared crystal clear. "So that's a positive ID for Tex and it looks like you'd better bring a stretcher.

"I have the real-time Uplink, Sir. Want me to put it on screen?" Skipper nodded his head and a live feed of the compound appeared on screen. "Here's the money shot, sir." Scooter tapped on his keyboard again and zoomed in on the last window on the top level. The video showed Robbie standing and looking out of the window.

"Here's Tex." After reviewing all the video we're sure this room is the target's location for pick up." Scooter said.

"Good job. Now we know it's heavily armed, but what we don't know is, if the building is rigged. So I want you to bring a K-9."

The K-9's are highly trained military working dogs that go through the same rigorous exercises as their human counterparts. They have the capability to sniff out bombs, hidden rooms, hidden doors and people who are hiding. They're equipped with mounted cameras, bullet proof vests, night goggles and even have they their own parachutes. They can be sent ahead of the men, armed with communication devices that allow the SEALs to give the K-9's attack and kill commands from far away. When a target sees these dogs running toward them, teeth bared, it's literally a heart-stopping experience. Each K-9 represents one million dollars' worth of training and equipment.

Skipper continued, "You need to get in and out before dawn. We estimate it at thirty minutes, tops. After the mission is complete we need a bird to pick up——" An excited murmur went through the room when the men saw the photo on screen.

"Hey quiet down. From the noise in the room, I guess you all recognized actress Lily Lockwood, code name Twinkle. And this is Tex's brother, David, code name Houston. They're going to need to be lifted from the roof pad of Jazeera Palace Hotel as soon as our targets are in the air.

C.I.A. will aid with chain of custody—final destination for Big Foot and Ranger is Guantanamo and Landstuhl Medical for Tex, Twinkle and Houston. Preacher will take over from here, give out the assignments and answer all questions.

Preacher, the tall, confident Team Leader, walked up to the front of the room and saluted Skipper.

Skipper had been grooming him since Preacher proved his leadership ability after his very first mission in Afghanistan. Skipper knew there were rumblings among the men, especially from Goose, when he appointed Preacher Team Leader. Those two were the best of the best and had a competitive, almost adversarial relationship since BUD/S. Skipper knew it and he was equally certain that the appointment would not only lift Preacher to the next level but would kick Goose's ass into high gear. The team members were closer than most brothers, and sometimes a little sibling rivalry can go a long way.

"Be safe out there men." Skipper said as he walked toward the door.

Preacher scanned the notes on his clip board. "Okay, the core team in the first Black Hawk will fast rope down—myself, Doc, Runner, Goose, D-blast, Stryker, Runt and Popeye.

Skipper left the room with complete confidence that Preacher would lead the team successfully, locate the targets and bring back all of the men— as he had done the last ten missions. Now all Skipper had to do was convince the suits at the C.I.A and the nail biters in the White House Situation Room.

Chapter 25

Lily lay in bed and listened to the thumping of her heart. She took a series of deep breaths in failed attempts to quell her nerves. Lily had been afraid to take a sleeping pill, which would have provided her the much-needed rest that she craved. But because she could be woken at any time and swiftly escorted to an awaiting helicopter, she couldn't chance being groggy.

After Maniadakis had spoken to them, she and David hastily packed their clothes and gave the suitcases to one of his men. Although she had no appetite, David still ordered room service for both of them, simply to keep their minds off the impending mission, scheduled to take place in a few short hours. They spent thirty minutes making small talk and pushing the uneaten food around their plates.

Finally around 10:00 p.m. she and David decided to call it a night and attempt to get some sleep. Maniadakis had suggested that David spend the night on her pullout couch in the living room, so they would be together when it was time for the guards to accompany them to the helicopter. Her penthouse suite, located on the top floor, was merely a short staircase run up to the hotel rooftop.

For the past hour, she lay in bed wondering what was escalating more rapidly, her heart rate or her blood pressure. She thought of the brave men that would soon be risking their lives to rescue Robbie. If all went as planned she would have the opportunity, after two long years, to finally be in the same room as him. Her eyes ached to look at him and her ears ached to hear his voice.

She thought of the day she met Chloe and the request she made of David: not tell Robbie that she had any part in the rescue. Lily didn't want Robbie to feel obligated to be with her. She wanted him to come to her because he felt, as she did, that they were meant to be together. Now that there was a very good possibility that she would see him shortly, everything else seemed insignificant. Even Chloe.

Lily felt her heart almost leap out of her chest so she quickly sat up to try to catch her breath. The last time she felt this way, her mother lay dying in the hospital. No matter how much she willed herself to calm down, it felt as if it everything in her life was traveling at warp speed.

She thought back to when she was a child and suffered from night terrors. She would awaken in the middle of the night screaming at the top of her lungs. Her mother would run in to her room and turn on the small lamp by her bedside.

By then, Lily would be fully awake; her heart racing, her eyes tightly squeezed shut for fear that she would see whatever horrible thing—monsters or boogie man—that had triggered her nightmare.

Her mother would sit on the bed and softly stroke her forehead and say, "Lily honey, everything is all right, it was just a bad dream. You can open your eyes now, my precious girl, Mommy is here. Lily would first open one eye; slowly look around the room to make sure that no evil loomed anywhere. It was not until she was 100% certain the room held no danger that she permitted herself to open the other eye.

Her mother would hand her a cold glass of water, all the while speaking softly, telling Lily over and over again that she was safe. By the time Lily finished drinking, her heart would have stopped pounding and she was able to breathe normally again.

When it was time for her to go back to sleep, the feeling of panic would return. Her mother would say, "Daisy, repeat after me: My Mommy loves me, my Grams loves me, my Gramps loves me, Auntie Donna loves me and God loves me. Nothing can ever harm me." Lily repeated after her mother and when she did, she would inevitably experience a sense of calm enveloping her. Daisy would remain until Lily finally drifted back to dreamland.

Now, so many years later, she took a deep breath and tried to conjure up the feeling of her mother's soft hand on her brow. Tears sprung to her eyes when she realized Grams, Gramps, *and* Mom were all dead. That left Aunt Donna and if she was lucky—God too.

There was a soft knock at the door and David whispered, "Sis you up?"

Lily sat up and turned on the lamp next to her bed. "Yes, come on in."

David came in and flopped down into one the twin club chairs on the far side of the room. "I can't sleep. Too nervous and my mind is racing. I figured I'd see if you were awake. It was either that or I would start plowing through your mini bar." He laughed nervously.

Lily got out of bed and put her arm around her brother. "Two years sobriety is not going to end on my watch, buddy."

"You're the best. I mean it. Did I wake you?"

Lily sat down in the chair next to him and draped her legs over the arms. "Couldn't sleep. You came in right when I was gearing up for a panic attack. I was remembering how my mother—*our* mother— used to come into my room when I had a nightmare and calm me down." She saw David wince.

"Sorry, I shouldn't talk about my childhood—with Daisy, I mean. It must make you feel awful."

"Hey stop that. I'm a big boy. You don't have to edit yourself. I know why she gave me up for adoption and I was lucky to spend some time with her. I just wish we had longer together, that's all." He yawned, stretched then changed the subject. "Do you have any bottles of water?"

Lily jumped up, walked into the living room, and took out two bottles of water from the small refrigerator. When she came back into the room, she threw David the water bottle and sat down.

"You know, ever since Mom passed away, I've wanted to talk to you about something. And since we didn't speak for a while—"

"—I know sorry about that. My bad." David interrupted

"No need to apologize; we've discussed it already. What I wanted to say is since Mom passed away right after finding you, she didn't have a chance to adjust her will. And knowing her as well as I do, I know that she would have changed it.

David looked uncomfortable and waved his hand. "Hey, don't worry about it, truly. Just getting to know her was enough."

"I know it was, but what I'm trying to say is that I spoke with her attorney and asked him to put a portion of her estate in your name. Offhand I don't know exactly how much it is but the attorney's got the list of everything—money, stocks, land. I know Mom would want you to use it to move forward and have a good life."

David chuckled. "You mean stop fucking up, right?"

"No, that's not what I meant. I just mean, you know, she would have wanted you to have it."

David looked over at his younger sister. She had turned red and was desperately trying to do something good for him. He understood that. But unbeknown to her, she had played right into his insecurities. Truth be told, he felt like a complete loser. He had failed the bar exam three times and had no idea what he was going to do. Right now he had no Plan B.

Even though he had been sober for almost two years, no one knew what a daily struggle not drinking was for him. Since his brother's abduction, he had reached for the bottle more times than he would ever care to admit. Thankfully he never went through with it.

Searching for Robbie had given him a purpose in life. It made him feel useful and productive. And Lily's being back was a huge plus. He cherished their newfound closeness and was grateful that she had given him a second chance. He promised himself that he would do everything in his power to keep their relationship intact.

Sleeping was difficult for him tonight because he was worried about his brother's safety as well as their own. He felt guilty that he had put Lily in danger and couldn't wait until he returned her safely to U.S. soil. There was also something else playing havoc with his ability to rest that evening. Even though he prayed that his brother would return safely, he harbored a hidden resentment against Robbie. Given everything Robbie had been through, David was ashamed of his feelings.

In the past, Hannah had never looked to David for anything. She always went to his father when she needed something. If his father was not around, she would then go to Robbie. Before she ever got to David, all her problems and worries were resolved. After his father had passed away and Robbie gone missing, his mother looked to him for support and strength. Then there was Lily— he finally got his sister back into his life. She made it perfectly clear that she needed him. She looked to *him* for strength and support. She asked his advice and truly listened to it. Indeed, she had told him not too long ago: "As long as I have you by my side, I know I'll be safe."

He had no doubt that as soon as Lily and Robbie got back together, as the saying goes, three would be a crowd. It would be natural for Lily to shift her attention to Robbie; he was sure of it. David knew with Robbie back in the picture, neither Hannah nor Lily would have need for him any longer. All that he had now would disappear. He would be invisible, yet again.

Lily interrupted his thoughts "Hey, where'd you go there?"

David shook his head as if to shake away the scenarios that had been playing over and over again. "Nowhere, just thinking about what you said. It's a lot to take in. I thank you for it, I really do. I never expected anything."

"I know you didn't. But I know this is what Mom would have wanted." Lily smiled and as if she had just read his mind said, "I'm so glad we've gotten this close. After this nightmare is over, I want you to remain a big part of our lives—of Daisy Rose's and mine. I love having a brother and Daisy Rose needs an uncle she can boss around."

David chuckled. "Seriously, nothing would make me happier. Now, you better get back to bed and try to catch a few winks. It's going to get rough later on and I'm sure tomorrow will be a very long day. So try to get some sleep.

Lily got into bed, fluffed her pillow, and lay down. "Just think, this time tomorrow, if our prayers are answered, it will be *three of us* talking through the night." Tears flooded her eyes and her voice cracked. "I just know they're going to get him out of there alive. I feel it in my gut. Don't you feel it too?"

David straightened Lily's blanket and kissed her on the cheek. "Yes, I definitely feel it," he lied.

Chapter 26

"Hey Runt, better make sure you got enough in your evasion kit just in case, buddy." Everyone laughed. The SEALs were getting ready to execute *Operation House Call* and they were checking their loadouts and getting into gear.

The loadouts were always at the ready and included camouflage gear and body armor for every terrain and the most sophisticated weapons for any hostile encounter. Each SEAL also had a radio/comm link system in his back pocket, which connected to each other, to the base, and to the dedicated stealth drones.

"Damn when does the statute of limitations run out on that joke?" Runt, who at 6'6" stood head and shoulders above most of the team—actually the shortest male in his family—put on his Kevlar Helmet and checked his camera, night goggles and microphone to make sure they were firmly in place.

"Never, son, that shit's gonna follow you 'til the end of time." D-blast laughed and strapped his pistol to his left leg and slung his assault rifle with special scopes and lasers across his shoulder.

Even though it may not appear to the outsider, those two were closer than most brothers. They hailed from the hills of Kentucky and had bonded since day one. In fact D-blast, who was a good half a foot shorter than his friend, had carried Runt on his back after he had taken two during an ambush.

Runt opened the pocket on the left leg of his pants and checked the evasion kit that contained escape money. Two years before, during a mission not far from Mogadishu, Runt had been in a tight position, separated from the rest, and needed to buy his way back to the Congo.

"He's right, Runt, cause Lord knows, you can't call me in the middle of the night to pick your ass up." Scooter laughed. He checked his blowout kit in his right pocket to make sure his first- aid supplies were intact.

Preacher said, "Listen up. We got four birds—Tier One and Two: Black Hawks, Three and Breach: Chinooks. Three will be positioned nearby the compound and you'll be given the exact coordinate to support the "fight your way out" plan.

The men nodded and walked outside to where the four stealth choppers awaited their arrival. The beauty of the Black Hawks is that they are radar-jamming helicopters—virtually undetectable. The Chinooks are heavy lifting workhorses and designed to tolerate a major ballistic attack.

Once inside and strapped in, Preacher felt the familiar pit in his stomach that he had experienced before every mission. In the fight for freedom, he was charged with getting these men home safely. Nothing was more important to him. SEAL Team 6 was family and spent two hundred days out of every year together. Their lives were intertwined and interdependent.

Preacher looked at his men, some were silently praying— the rest introspective—all of them deliberating on the mission ahead.

Chapter 27

"*T*his is bullshit!" Lily had been tossing and turning in bed for the past hour. Her sheets and blanket were bunched together in a twisted heap. She kicked off the covers and practically jumped out of bed.

When the C.I.A. took over the operation, she and David were kept out of the loop. Granted, Maniadakis had given them the broad-stroke picture, but he had not included them in any of the details, such as: how and exactly when the rescue would take place. She and her brother were told that they would not be allowed back into Control Center; it was against protocol.

Fuck protocol. Lily turned on the light and looked at the clock; it was already 3:00 a.m. She walked over to the closet and took out the only thing she had not as yet packed—the hoodie that matched the sweats she had been sleeping in. Lily took it off the hanger and put it on. She brushed her hair back into a tight ponytail and then pulled the hood over her head.

She left a note for David in case he woke and she was gone. She tiptoed past her brother—snoring loudly on the couch—and walked out of the suite, quietly closing the door behind her. Just as the door clicked shut, she realized that she had left her key card on top of the desk.

During her elevator ride to the lobby, Lily was already planning what she would say to Maniadakis when he refused her entrance into the control room.

The elevator opened to the main floor and she put her head down as she walked past the only person in the lobby—the desk clerk. She turned the corner and saw two secret service types in dark suits, arms folded, standing guard in front of the conference room door.

"I'm here to see Nikos Maniadakis." She said nonchalantly. The younger man's eyes widened in surprise when he recognized who she was.

"Is he expecting you, Ms. Lockwood?"

"Not at this time, no. You can let me in, I'm sure it'll be all right."

"One moment, Ma'am." He touched his ear to activate the tiny wireless headset inside.

"We have Lily Lockwood here, please advise." He listened as the person on the other end answered. He smiled at Lily and said, "Someone will be right out."

The door opened and Eleanor, Maniadakis's uptight assistant, stepped out. "Miss Lockwood, follow me," she commanded through pursed lips.

Lily followed her across the hallway to a small office that the agency had recently taken over. Once inside, Eleanor shook her head. "I am sorry, but it's out of the question and against all protocol for you to be here."

"I've been here from the beginning; I have every right to know what's going on."

Eleanor shook her head. "No Miss Lockwood, it is not your right to know what's going on. Not your right at all. This is now a confidential government matter and civilians have no place in that room."

Lily crossed her arms tightly. "May I remind you that this whole mission would never have taken place if I hadn't been involved?"

"I am sorry, but you cannot enter that room. It is prohibited." Eleanor turned around and opened the door.

"I want to speak to Nikos," Lily said

While her hand was still on the doorknob, the assistant turned around and smiled. "That, I'm afraid, cannot happen. Now please go quietly back up to your room and wait until we call you."

"Eleanor, I will not go anywhere and I assure you I won't be quiet. I insist on seeing Nikos now."

Eleanor glared at Lily. "Very well, remain here." She closed the door hard.

"What a bitch," Lily said under her breath.

After ten long minutes the office door reopened and Maniadakis walked in. He did not look happy. "I hear you've been causing quite a commotion here, Lily. How can I help you?"

"I couldn't sleep. I simply want to know what's going on. I hate being kept in the dark."

"Nothing's happened yet." He replied curtly.

"Okay, then let me join you so I can be there when it does."

"No can do. This is a highly classified mission."

"But there would be no mission if it weren't for me and my money," Lily insisted.

Maniadakis sighed and clenched his jaw. "I'm in charge here, so it's my ass on the line. Do you understand that?"

"I understand that if it wasn't for me the only thing you would be in charge of is a fifth of Scotch." Lily looked at her watch. "And just about this time of night, where you would be? Oh I know— passed out on some street somewhere, dreaming of being back in the C.I.A."

They stared at one another. He blinked. "I'll let you in, but don't say a word about it—now or later. Is that clear?"

"Crystal." She followed him out of the room, across the hallway, past the guards and into the conference room. She couldn't help smiling knowing she had just had a Daisy Lockwood moment.

Once she and Maniadakis walked through the doors that led into the "forbidden room." Lily was startled by how crowded it had become—with twice as many people and twice the amount of high-tech equipment.

"Wow this is what government bucks buy, huh?" Lily whispered.

Maniadakis shot her a warning look. Lily put her hand up to her mouth and simulated putting a key into a lock and turning it.

"I'll believe that when I see it." He gestured for her to move on. "Have a seat in my office."

Lily walked through the room that was a bustling hub of activity. There were quite a few new faces she did not recognize. Most of the newcomers looked startled to see the famous actress pass by.

Maniadakis stood in front of the group, his back to the three oversized screens and clapped his hands. "Okay folks, I need your attention." The room went silent. A phone rang and he nodded to Eleanor, who answered it.

Lily was able to move the chair in the office just far enough to the left, giving her a full view of the room and screens.

"As you know *Operation House Call* has begun execution and four choppers carrying the SEAL team will reach the Merca Compound at approximately 0400—thirty minutes from now. Bollinger, can you run through what we're gonna be looking at." He looked at the MIT graduate.

"You ready?"

Bollinger nodded, adjusted his round glasses and clicked a few keys. Within seconds the satellite uplink of the Merca Compound came on screen.

"This is the real-time uplink. I'll manipulate the view so we can get a 360. He pushed a few more keys and another view filled the second half of the screen.

"The next screen, the screen on your right, will have the camera view from The Core Team's camera. It'll be the night- vision observation. The Core Team will be the ones specifically targeting Big Foot and Ranger." Bollinger wiped the sweat that had begun to form on his forehead and upper lip.

"The second team will specifically target Tex. Their camera view will be on the screen to the far right. It will be a split screen with the other half being the third team who'll be securing the outside perimeters of the compound. That's it for now, boss." Bollinger seemed relieved to be relinquishing the spotlight.

"Great. Thanks." Maniadakis cleared his throat. "As you can see the view of the Merca Compound shows that all is quiet—looks like the guards are snoozing on the job. So the up side—no moon tonight so the teams have the element of surprise as well as the cover of night. Down side—even though they are designed quieter, the rotors may alert the guards before the choppers hover and land." He checked a page on his clip board. "The Breach Teams won't have cameras; they're the ones blowing the hinges off the doors. We might not be able to see 'em but we'll hear them plenty, trust me. We're triangulating audio/video with Langley and POTUS and The National Security team in the White House Situation Room. We also have audio of SEALs base and of course the individuals of the team as well as The Pentagon. When the mission is completed, we'll take over chain of custody if there are captures. Any questions?" No one responded.

"Any of you God fearin'— now's the time to pray." The room became eerily quiet when Maniadakis headed toward his office. Eleanor stopped her boss and whispered something in his ear. Maniadakis looked toward the office and nodded his head.

Lily leaned back in her chair and closed her eyes. Her heart raced when she thought of all the lives that would be forever changed that night. How many would be injured? How many would die? She began to pray, but her prayers were immediately interrupted by footsteps in the room. Lily opened her eyes to see Eleanor in front of her and David a few steps behind.

"Your entourage has arrived." Eleanor announced.

Chapter 28

At exactly 0400, The Black Hawk carrying the Core Team hovered over the Merca Compound. Preacher, Doc, Runner, Goose, D-blast, Stryker, Runt, and Popeye fast roped to the ground.

Three armed guards who were standing watch at the gate opened fire. Runt and Popeye lifted their weapons and fired three double-tap shots that landed with precision—two of the guards got hit between their eyes and the third, in the heart. They were dead before they reached the ground.

One minute later the second chopper landed on the northwest corner. The dog, a Belgian Malinois named Opie, his handler, an interpreter, two intelligence collectors, and four more SEALs emerged. The SEALs secured the grounds while the others headed to the main building to support the Core Team.

The Chinook carrying T Rex and his Breach Team landed outside the main gate of the compound. The SEALs disembarked: Half ran into the building while the rest used plate charges to blast open the gate and a small portion of the cement wall.

Once inside, Opie and his handler led the team down the hall. The dog slowed down by each closed door and sniffed for rigged bombs. As soon as he moved past the doorway, indicating it was all clear, the Breach Team blasted off the hinges so Preacher and his men could rush the room.

"Two on the stairs." Doc yelled as he lifted his weapon and shot and killed the two armed guards before they could press their triggers.

"Closed door left." Popeye shouted. T Rex used a ballistic breach gun to blow the hinges off the door.

Preacher and Popeye burst into the room, leading with their weapons. A man in a long white dashiki and skull cap hid behind a large desk.

"Let me see your hands! Let me see your hands!" Popeye shouted. The interpreter repeated it in Arabic. The man timidly emerged from behind the door with both hands raised.

"Secure him." Preacher commanded. Popeye pulled the man's hands behind his back and proceeded to tightly bind them with a zip tie. Preacher shined a flashlight on the desk, revealing dozens of files and two laptops. He rifled through the files. "Holy crap. Get the collectors in here, this is some good stuff." He walked toward the door and shouted "Movin' on."

Back in the hallway, Runt yelled, "Closed door right." Opie began barking ferociously and abruptly sat in front of the door in an "unassisted sit", which indicated a bomb.

"It's rigged. Closed door right is rigged." Runt shouted and D-blast repeated it for the men bringing up the rear. The team moved forward.

At the end of the hallway they came upon a large corner room with double doors. "Closed door left." Popeye yelled. T-Rex blasted the door and the SEALs rushed in, Preacher in the lead.

Once inside, they encountered a uniformed guard pointing an AK-47. He stood protectively in front of an older man in a dashiki.

Without hesitation, Preacher lifted his gun and put two bullets in the guard's heart. As his body collapsed, it revealed that the older man had been holding a pistol at his side.

D-blast shouted, "Drop your gun, drop your gun!" The man slightly lifted his right hand as D-blast knocked him to the ground with two shots to the head.

Preacher looked at the men sprawled out in front of him, pulled two pieces of paper from his pocket, and compared the photos to the two lying in puddles of blood. He spoke into his microphone: "Wild Falcon, this is Creeper One— Big Foot and Ranger E.K.I.A, repeat Big Foot and Ranger E.K.I.A, over.

The agents at mission-control center sat riveted in their seats as they watched the real-time drama play out on the large screens. The action they witnessed was that of Preachers point of view, which came directly from the night-vision camera mounted on his helmet. Even though the picture was bathed in neon green and shook every time Preacher moved, the agents were able to get a good idea, from the video and audio, what was going down.

When they heard Preacher say, "Big Foot and Ranger E.K.I.A, repeat Big Foot and Ranger E.K.I.A.," a cheer ripped through the room. Confused, Lily turned to one of agents. "What does it mean? Why are they cheering?"

"It means Enemy Killed in Action." He smiled and shook his head in disbelief. "Those sons of bitches got them both—Mubaarak Abdikarim *and* Abdulkadir Mohamed!"

"Let's go up top, get Tex, and bring him home." Preacher said.

Lily grabbed David's hand and squeezed hard. He leaned down and whispered in her ear, "This is it! They're getting Robbie." Lily sobbed with emotion.

Preacher's camera went out of focus when the men ran up two flights of stairs. Once they were on the top floor they went directly to the last door on the right.

"Closed door right." Preacher shouted. T-Rex demolished the door. Once inside, they saw a guard standing behind Robbie, his left arm tightly wrapped around Robbie's chest. He held a pistol to Robbie's head.

"Drop the gun and I won't shoot." Preacher said.

The guard shook his head and shouted, "I will leave now and take him with me, or I will shoot him. Let me go!"

Preacher looked up at the small window then looked back at Robbie and the guard. He said, "Take the shot, now."

As he stood on the roof of the adjoining building, Striker shot twice. The bullets pierced the window and caught the guard in the back of his head. He immediately collapsed to the ground. In mid-fall the guard's gun discharged and the bullet hit Robbie in the chest.

Chapter 29

$\mathscr{L}$ily leaned against the bathroom mirror and cried, releasing the emotions that had gathered within her for so many days. She sighed, leaned back, and stared at her reflection in the mirror. Her eyes were unrecognizable, swollen from hours of crying; there were two bluish-black shadows under them. Her hair was matted with blood and the lump on the back of her head ached. Lily closed her eyes in a futile effort to block out the physical and emotional pain that, in the last two weeks, had become etched into her face.

An extremely pregnant woman waddled into the Ladies Room, looked at Lily and smiled. Lily tried not to make eye contact. She glanced up and saw that the woman standing behind her was staring at Lily through the mirror.

"Excuse me, but has anyone told you that you sorta look a little like that actress Lily Lockwood?"

Lily shook her head and proceeded to splash cold water on her face. She took a paper towel from the holder on the wall and pressed it tightly against her eyes to try to subdue the burning. The woman went into the stall and decided, mid pee, that it was the perfect time to continue the one-sided conversation.

"You know, you look so much like that actress you should do yourself a favor and try out to be her stand in. Or, you know, better yet, you could join one of those companies that hire celebrity look-a-likes. You can make yourself some big bucks."

"I'll keep that in mind." Lily said as she tossed the paper towel into the garbage can. The toilet flushed and Lily quickly exited the bathroom before the woman had time to give out any more career advice.

Lily walked back into the waiting area and saw David asleep on the couch. She sat down in the chair opposite him and thought of the whirlwind of events that had taken place in the past ten hours. Lily sighed and her heart sank when she remembered standing in the conference room, watching the rescue and witnessing Robbie get shot. Lily remembered screaming and then nothing else——-everything went black. David told her that she had fainted and hit her head on the ceramic floor. So much for keeping her promise to Nikos that she would stay out of the way and remain inconspicuous.

When she regained consciousness, she received the glass of water that Eleanor handed to her and she and David were swiftly escorted up to the roof-top to the awaiting military helicopter. The pilot told them that Robbie was still alive, had a medic with him, and was being transported to the U.S. Government Medical Center in Landstuhl Germany.

When David and Lily arrived at the Medical Center the nurse informed them that Robbie had already been wheeled into surgery. She instructed them to have a seat in the surgical waiting room and that she would do her best to update them. So far, she hadn't approached them with any news.

When Lily arrived earlier, she experienced a strong visceral response to the Medical Center and to the smells of the hospital. It was never pleasant to see family members huddled together in their shared worry, their fear like masks on their faces, became impossible to remove.

A young man in a military uniform approached her. "Miss Lockwood?"

"Shh." She put her finger to her closed lips and gestured to the sleeping David. She stood and they walked over to the other side of the waiting room.

"Ma'am, I'm Sergeant Mark Lewis and I was told to come by and help you with hotel arrangements." He had a thick New England accent. "There's a nice one real close by—Pfaelzer Stuben— where most of the families visiting the Medical Center stay. It's quite comfortable, more of a B & B then a traditional hotel. And it has a fine restaurant."

Lily sighed. "Great, if you could give me the name and phone number. . ."

The Sergeant heard her deep sigh and noticed the dark circles under eyes. "You must be tired. I can make the arrangements for you and take your luggage over, if you like."

"Thanks. That would be a great help," Lily smiled, relieved. "My brother and I will need two rooms."

"No problem, Ma'am. I'll check you in and leave the keys with the owners, a real nice couple: Gabby and Gerhardt Mueller. They'll keep the keys at the desk for you. Anything you need while you're here, I'm your point person—just call me." He handed a piece of paper to her.

"I already wrote my number down." He took out a pen and wrote something else on the paper and handed it to her.

"That's the phone number and address for the hotel."

"Thanks so much." She pointed to the area next to the couch where David was snoring loudly. "The luggage is right over there."

"Thanks Ma'am. And it is an honor to meet you, I'm a big fan." He started to walk away, then stopped and turned back.

"Miss Lockwood, I want to tell you: We're all praying for Dr. Rosen. He's been through a rough time, that's for sure."

Lily sighed and smiled.

"Well don't you worry, he's in good hands. Captain Sherman's the best surgeon there is."

"Thanks, that makes me feel better. I appreciate it."

"No problem, you take care." He picked up the suitcases and walked away.

After the Sergeant had left, Lily walked over to the window and looked out over the patio area. She saw patients and their families as well as the military personnel seated at the picnic tables, eating and laughing. One couple sat at a small table, holding hands and gazing into each other's eyes. When the man leaned in and kissed the woman, Lily had to look away.

She turned her attention back to the once-empty waiting room and saw that over the past hour it had gotten crowded. One woman walked in carrying an unhappy infant whose screams were ear-piercing. The mother looked exhausted and embarrassed. Lily smiled encouragingly at her. It wasn't that long ago that Daisy Rose had excelled in selecting the most crowded place to have a temper tantrum.

She missed Daisy Rose so much and couldn't wait to see her again. Lily took solace in knowing that her daughter was in capable hands.

After Lily had arrived at the hospital, she called Donna and brought her up to speed about all that had transpired from the time of their arrival in Mogadishu. Donna was shocked and cried when she heard that Robbie had been shot.

David opened his eyes, sat up, stretched, and yawned. "Anything happening?"

"No, nothing since the nurse came by. Are you going to call your mother?"

David slumped down, put his head in his hands, and sighed. Lily understood how hard it would be for David to make that phone call. Lily got up from her seat, walked over to the couch, and sat next to him. She put her hand on David's shoulder to comfort him.

He opened his eyes. "'I'll wait until Robbie's out of surgery. This way, we'll have a better idea of, you know..."

"Sounds right." Lily agreed.

"How's your head?" David went to touch Lily's scalp and she pulled back.

"Don't. I took a couple of aspirins and it just stopped pounding."

"You need to get it looked at." He stood up. "I'm going to the nurse's station to ask if they could get a doctor to——." David looked at something behind Lily and the color drained from his face.

Lily turned around and saw what had stolen David's attention. Walking toward them was a doctor in blue scrubs, wearing an O.R. hat and shoe covers. He removed a surgical mask from his face. The room seemed to spin and Lily grabbed David's hand to steady herself. He protectively balanced her by putting his arm around her shoulder.

"Mr. Rosen, Ms. Lockwood, I'm Captain Russ Sherman. The surgery was successful and Dr. Rosen is in stable condition. He's a fighter, no doubt about that." He smiled warmly. "And one very lucky man."

Chapter 30

"Yes, Ma, the doctor said they got the bullet out and that Robbie had sustained some minor vascular damage as well as injuries to his lungs." David became silent, listening to his mother's concern on the other end of the phone. "No, they said they repaired it *all*. And that the prognosis is great." He smiled because he never imagined listening to his mother cry would bring him such relief. David understood far too well that this would have been a much different phone call had Robbie not survived the surgery. His mother's tears certainly would not have been joyful.

He switched the phone from his right ear to his left as he listened to his mother speak. He winked at Lily, who was seated across the table from him at the hotel's restaurant.

"Yes, she's right here, Ma. Yes, I'll make sure to tell her. So call or email me with your agenda and I'll pick you up at the airport." He paused again. "Yes, you're right, it is a miracle. Goodbye. I love you too." David clicked off and smiled at Lily as she gulped some German Beer from an oversized, ornate stein.

"I didn't even know you liked beer." Before she could reply, David started to laugh.

"What's so funny?" She asked.

He pointed to her lip. "You have this great big beer mustache." She laughed and wiped it off with her napkin. She looked around the quaint restaurant with its small square tables and pretty red tablecloths stitched with delicate white lace. Along with the grey brick walls and decorative flower pieces, it gave the restaurant a homey feel.

Lily pushed her chair back from the table to give herself more room. "This food is awesome. I'm stuffed, but I feel so good—better than I've felt since, well since you and Hannah first came to see me."

"Oh, my Mom said to tell you thanks from the very bottom of her heart."

"It's my pleasure—really!" She took another swig of beer and wiped her mouth with the back of her hand. "So, since they're going to keep Robbie in recovery for a few more hours and transfer him after midnight to the I.C.U, I'm going to head up to my room and get a good night sleep so I can see him bright and early in the morning."

"Sounds good, I'm going back to the hospital for a couple of hours in case he's awake when they bring him to the I.C.U. They told me that it's less than a fifteen-minute walk, door to door, from the hotel to the Medical Center."

"Okay." Lily didn't know if it was the beer or the circumstance, but she found herself feeling quite giddy. "I'm so happy, I'm going to burst." She giggled.

David smiled. Lily appeared ten years younger than she had only twenty-four hours earlier. And tonight, with the combination of her laughter and the way she had tossed her hair back, made her look like Daisy—so much so that it almost hurt to look at her.

"You go upstairs; I'll sign for the check." David put his hand up to summon the waitress.

"Do you think I can take my beer upstairs?"

He chuckled, "I'm sure of it."

So stein in hand, she kissed her brother good night and all but floated up the stairs to her room.

Lily emerged from the bathroom after a long bubble bath wearing two towels—one wrapped around her body and the other turban-style on her head. She took her ear buds out of her purse, plugged them into her iPod, and turned her favorite playlist on really loud. She danced wildly around the room, moving back and forth, gyrating to the music. At one point she decided there was no better way to express herself than to jump up and down on the bed, trampoline style. After forty-five minutes of dancing, jumping, and twirling, she was completely out of breath and collapsed on the bed.

She removed the ear buds and stared at the ceiling. She was over-the-moon happy and twice as relieved, grateful that Robbie had survived and that in less than nine hours she would finally get to see him She was more than thankful to be away from Mogadishu and the threats that loomed there.

She thought of the conversation she'd had with the woman in MSF who had walked for days so that her young son could receive his vaccinations. She had promised herself there and then, that when she returned home, she would not only donate money but she would also figure out how she could do much more.

She closed her eyes and imagined a time when Robbie was well again. Using her celebrity, they could work side-by-side and truly make a difference, raising awareness and funds for *Médecins Sans Frontières*.

Her thoughts wandered to the day when she had visited the MSF compound. Then it happened: She traveled full speed ahead, straight to what her mother used to call 'The Land of What Ifs.' She had always been a frequent flyer to 'The Land of What Ifs,' especially during her teenage years, when she always gravitated to the worst-case scenarios and lived there. It is a gloomy and shadowy realm—one that has no basis in reality. The longer she remained in that negative space, the gloomier it got and the harder it was to leave.

When Lily was younger, she was often a frequent flyer to the "Land Of What Ifs." Her mother could always recognize the early signs that Lily was sinking into that negative place. Daisy would get in Lily's face and refuse to leave until her daughter latched onto the emotional life preserver she was throwing to her. Lily used to imagine that sunlight and optimism coursed through Daisy's veins and any wisp of negativity that dared to tread anywhere near Daisy would shrivel and die.

Lily never told her mother, but often there were times when she derived great comfort being in 'The Land of What Ifs.' Daisy would never understand that it gave Lily comfort to feel prepared just in case disaster happened. Her friends never understood and when she would have her *obsession du jour*, they would tell her to lighten up or stop being so negative.

After Daisy died and throughout her pregnancy, Lily would often visit 'The Land of What Ifs,' obsessing over terrible things that might possibly occur:

> *What if there were a serious medical problem?*
> *What if the baby was not normal?*
> *What if she or her baby died in childbirth?*
> *What if she was a terrible mother?*
> *What if she didn't love her baby?*
> *What if her baby didn't bond with her?*
> *What if she couldn't breast feed?*

It could go on and on like that for days. And when it did, Auntie D., Tommy, and Fernando would do everything they could to pull her out of the murk.

When Hanna and David told her about Robbie's situation, she was immediately thrown into the whirlwind of activity surrounding his rescue. It was quite interesting that, at that time, Lily did not experience any of her usual anxiety. They were in crisis mode—things were happening at warp speed— and she was surrounded by frightening events. She'd had no time to imagine or obsess over things that could possibly happen. But tonight, on the eve of what conceivably could be one of the happiest days of her life, she lay in bed and virtually booked her passage and voyaged to the worst-case scenario.

Tonight's journey to 'The Land of What Ifs':

> *What if Robbie never loved her?*
> *What if he'd felt relieved when he left her?*
> *What if Chloe, not Lily, was the love of Robbie's life?*
> *What if Robbie was disappointed that it was she and not Chloe visiting?*
> *What if as soon as he was well he went back to Chloe?*
> *What if he never got well?*

Two hours later, she drifted off to sleep.

The alarm clock rang at exactly 7:15 a.m. Lily pushed the "off" button and continued to apply her mascara. She had awakened an hour before the alarm was scheduled to go off and had already showered and gotten dressed. The thought of seeing Robbie launched a flutter of butterflies in her stomach—a welcome relief from the shackles of fear and anxiety that had held her captive fewer than ten hours earlier. She shook off the memory of the past evening and concentrated on Robbie. He had survived an ordeal that could certainly have killed him—that's all she planned to focus on.

She'd received a text from David at 5:00 a.m. telling her that he had spent the night at Robbie's bedside in the I.C. U. and that Robbie was doing so well that they planned to move him to the surgical floor in the morning. David had just gotten back to the hotel and wanted to get some sleep, but would meet her later at the hospital.

Lily took one last look in the mirror and was relieved to see that the dark circles from the day before had now disappeared. She took a deep breath and held it before exhaling. After two long years, she would finally get to see the love of her life.

The nurse at the desk pointed to the last room on the right—435. As Lily walked down the hallway, she recalled the first time she had met Robbie. It was coincidentally also in a hospital. After Daisy's accident, she had left her mother's hospital room to visit David, who had also been admitted to the hospital. At that time, Lily had no clue who David was and what his relationship was with Daisy. She certainly did not know that he was the son Daisy had given up for adoption. She was visiting him because he had been in the car with her mother when they'd had the accident that killed Daisy. Lily did not yet know if he was Daisy's friend or even a younger man with whom Daisy had been having a secret relationship. Lily wanted to find out the events that led up to the crash.

When she walked into David's room, she saw someone seated next to the bed, his back to the door. Both of them were laughing.

She smiled at David. "Hi, I'm Lily. I promised I would stop by, but if you have company…"

The visitor stood up and turned around. Lily felt as if the air had been knocked out of her. It was more than just the stranger's wavy dark hair, blue eyes, and dimples. He had a special aura about him. She felt an electric shock go through her as she looked into his crystal-blue eyes. When he introduced himself and shook her hand, she felt a palpable electricity. A few weeks later, as they lay in bed during an afternoon of lovemaking, Robbie confessed it had felt exactly the same to him.

Dear God please make him be happy to see me. Please let him love me.

She took a deep breath and walked in. There were four beds in the room, with privacy curtains drawn around each one, so she could not see which bed was Robbie's. The room was unusually still, with only the beep, beep, beeping of the heart monitors fracturing the silence. She walked outside and quickly scanned the list of names on the side of the door. There it was: R. Rosen, Window Right.

She reentered and walked to the far-right corner of the room, to the bed next to the window. She cautiously moved the curtain a few inches—just enough to see inside.

Tears filled her eyes. Robbie's face was extremely pale and skeletal—his skin appeared to be stretched to the breaking point over his protruding cheekbones. He did not move. He did not blink. He stared at the ceiling.

Lily opened the curtain wider and the rustling of the fabric captured Robbie's attention. He looked up and stared at her, but his expression remained stoic. *Oh my God, he doesn't know who I am.*

Robbie blinked his eyes a few times and then they widened. His chin began to quiver and his eyes filled with tears. The two stared at each other and Lily was unable to move. Slowly, Robbie lifted his right hand to her— his eyes never left hers.

She moved closer to him, took his hand in hers, and sat beside his bed. Tears streamed down both their faces. She lifted his hand and kissed it.

Robbie was so weak that when he spoke it was barely a whisper. Lily had to lean in to hear him say, "Lil, I have dreamed about you and imagined you so many times, that when I saw you standing there, I didn't think you were real."

Lily put his hand on her heart and at that moment she was certain that, while New York City was 4,000 miles away, she had finally come home.

Chapter 31

The next couple of days and nights, Lily and David took turns seated by Robbie's bedside while he drifted in and out of sleep. The parade of nurses and doctors seemed unending. Robbie would awaken for short intervals, say a few incoherent words, and float back into a drug-induced slumber.

One afternoon, after Robbie had fallen asleep, Lily was seated on the chair by his bedside, thumbing through fashion magazines. Robbie began to moan and slowly rock side to side. He started breathing rapidly and put his hands up, palms toward his forehead, in a defensive gesture, then started screaming while tears streamed down his face.

Lily rushed over to him. "Robbie, you're safe. It's Lily, wake up." When he opened his eyes, he was covered in sweat and seemed wrought with fear. Lily wiped his face with a damp cloth until his breathing returned to normal.

He stared at Lily and the terror in his eyes rapidly devolved into shame and embarrassment. Robbie swiped the towel out of Lily's hand and rolled on his side. "Go away."

"It's going to be okay, Robbie, I promise." Lily said soothingly

He grabbed the rail on the side of his bed and pulled himself up. He put his other hand on his chest and winced in pain. "I said get out."

Tears stung her eyes and Lily hastily left the room. She walked over to the nurse's station to find Esther so that she could inform her of what had happened.

The nurses at the hospital were adept at their jobs and, from what Lily had gathered in the few days she had been there, calm in the face of emergency. The one nurse Lily connected with almost immediately was Esther Cohen. She was an attractive woman with salt-and-pepper, shoulder-length wavy hair and smiling eyes that looked perpetually amused, as if she was always on the verge of sharing a funny anecdote. Lily found her down to earth, compassionate, and quick-witted. There was something about her that reminded Lily of Daisy—not in looks but in the way she lived her life. Esther seemed to take things in stride and had Daisy's flair for immediately sizing up a situation and giving the perfect advice.

Esther listened to Lily's account of what had just taken place and her heart went out to the young woman. She did not know much about Robbie's story or of his involvement with the actress, but had gathered bits and pieces from information that had been flying around the base since the first day Robbie was brought in. Months earlier, they had all heard of an Al Shabaab abduction involving an American doctor working with Doctors Without Borders in Mogadishu.

Of course the appearance of the famous actress, Lily Lockwood, sent her colleagues into a marathon chinwag. One afternoon, while Esther was in the nurses' lounge, the gab fest reached a new crescendo and she told them firmly to keep quiet—and to focus on giving the patient the best care possible and to cut out the gossip. Since Esther was their boss, the chatter stopped—or at least they refrained from talking about Robbie or Lily whenever Esther was within earshot.

Esther looked at the beautiful but distraught young woman standing in front of her. Her heart went out to Lily, all the more so as Lily seemed to be about the same age as Esther's niece Laurie. She could not imagine Laurie being alone, so far from home, having to deal with a situation as serious and as emotionally charged as this one. From the stories she *had* heard, not only was Lily a talented actress but also a certifiable hero.

Esther smiled at the young woman. "I'll look in on him. As a heads up to you, Dr. Rosen is on a lot of morphine, so don't worry about what he says or doesn't say. And the nightmares, well those are to be expected. He went through a traumatic experience that is bound to play out in his dreams. Add the morphine to that and...well, you saw what happened."

"Yes of course, you're right. It just shook me up a bit, that's all."

Esther's heart gave a tug when relief sweep over Lily. "For now, why don't you go outside, take a walk, and clear your head a bit. Captain Sherman will be back from his meeting by early evening. I know he wants to sit down with you and Robbie's brother when he reaches the hospital."

Esther smiled. "Meanwhile my shift's over in about twenty minutes. Why don't you come with me for a bite to eat? The change of scenery will do you good."

An hour later Lily and Esther were seated in a small restaurant outside the Burg Nanstein—Landstuhl's famous castle, 6 kilometers away from the medical center. Even though portions of the castle, built in 1162, were in ruins, the grandness of the fortress's sweeping, grey stone walls, wood-covered terraces, and stone turrets remained intact. The view from the outdoor restaurant was breathtaking. Lily and Esther could look out over the quaint village below and see charming white homes with clay- colored roofs nestled among the lush dark green forest and small knolls.

"That church is beautiful." Lily pointed to a statuesque white steeple that stood tall among the smaller buildings. "Oh my God, is that a Mickey D's?" Lily pointed to a tall sign that had the familiar "M"—recognizable all over the world as the symbol for the fast food restaurant. It towered over the Autobahn exit.

Esther laughed. She took off her thick black glasses and wiped the lenses with a cloth napkin. "Sure is. There are so many Americans here, because of Landstuhl Regional Medical Center and Ramstein Air Base, that the franchise decided what better place to bring burgers and fries than to the Village Melkerei?"

Lily laughed and looked below. She leaned back in her seat, took a deep breath, and relaxed for the first time in days.

The waitress, a tall blonde, walked over to them and handed them menus.

"Lily Lockwood, I am such a big fan of yours. It's an honor to serve you today. May I please have your autograph?" She handed Lily a piece of paper and pen.

Lily smiled and graciously, "What is your name?"

"Katja, K-a-t-j-a."

Lily signed her name and handed the paper back to Katja who quickly seized it as if she feared Lily might have second thoughts about allowing the waitress to keep it. By that time, a buzz floated through the café and the patrons at the other tables turned in their seats to look at Lily.

When Katja walked away, proudly holding the autograph, Esther shook her head. "I imagine this happens all the time, huh?"

Lily chuckled. "Yes, it's all part of the business."

Esther looked over the menu at Lily, who seemed transformed from the distressed young woman that she had been a mere sixty minutes before.

"Don't think you are the only celebrity in this area. I will have you know that this small area of only nine thousand people was the birthplace of Rob Thomas, lead singer of Matchbox 20, and of LeVar Burton, as well as of a few well-known athletes whose names I've forgotten.

Katja returned to take their orders.

"I'll have the mushroom Schnitzel plate and salad." Lily said

"I'll have the Leberknoedel with extra kraut please. And a beer." Esther pointed to Lily. "Make that two beers."

After Katja walked away, Lily looked at Esther and smiled. "I want to thank you for inviting me for a bite. It's a welcome change of pace."

Esther smiled and made a toast with the beer stein in front of her. "To Robbie's complete recovery."

Lily raised hers and said, "I'll drink to that. So Esther, tell me, how did you end up in West Germany?"

"Well, I lived on Staten Island and was a nurse for many years at Staten Island University Hospital. You may already know that many of the firefighters who lost their lives on 9/11 lived on Staten Island. Several friends and relatives of ours were among those killed.

"My husband Phil was a firefighter with Ladder Company 3 and on 9/11 was one of the first responders. He and his company were responsible for saving hundreds of lives. Many of the people Phil guided to safety contacted me to make sure I knew what a hero my husband had been. Phil was last seen in the North Tower on the 40th floor." Esther took off her glasses and touched her eyes with her napkin. "He had always been a hero to me. On 9/11, he became our country's hero."

"I'm so sorry."

Esther smiled and shook her head. "When I kissed him goodbye that morning, I could never have known that it would be our last kiss." She took another sip of beer and feigned a smile, "So, I ended up enlisting. I felt like I had to do something to continue the legacy that my Phil and the rest of the firefighters had started. I've been here ever since."

"Do you have any children?"

Esther shook her head. "No, we had just started trying to get pregnant the summer before. Guess it was not in the cards for us."

Katja brought the food over and placed the steaming dishes down in front of the two women.

"Dig in," Esther said with a bravado she did not at all feel. Even so many years later, every time she spoke of Phil and of his tragic death, her stomach would be in knots for hours.

Lily took a bite of her Schnitzel and her eyes widened. "Oh my God, this is amazing."

"Delicious, right? I'm addicted to the Leberknoedel. I have to have my fix once or twice a week.

"What is it?"

"Liver dumplings in broth. Want a bite?" Esther lifted her spoon.

"Uh. . . no thanks." They both laughed.

"How long were you and Phil married?" Lily asked

"Only five years, but we'd known each other since Mrs. Spadafore's fourth-grade class. You could say we were soul mates or, as our mothers used to say, our relationship was *bashert*—we were intended for each other."

Lily was amazed to hear that word, *bashert*, from Esther, because she'd just been thinking of the story Robbie had told her about his grandparents and about the silver cord that tied their hearts together.

Lily told Esther the story of Chaya Ruchel and David and the silver cord that kept them connected and how, after so many years in the concentration camp, they had been reunited. Esther's eyes misted up a number of times during the story. She shook her head when Lily told her about Chaya Ruchel's years in Auschwitz.

Esther said, "You know, Lily, it's ironic that here Robbie is recovering in Germany, after being held captive in Somalia. Many of the German staff in the hospital may have been descendants of the Nazi's that held his grandmother captive in the concentration camp.

Lily shook her head. "Wow, I hadn't thought of that."

Esther replied, "It's amazing. What's also remarkable is that David knew, even as a young boy, that Chaya Ruchel was his *bashert*."

Lily paused, lifted her beer, and finished it off. "You know, I feel the same way with Robbie. I've always felt there was a bond—" Lily chuckled nervously "—very much like the silver cord. I had no idea Robbie had been abducted, but I felt an undeniable force pulling me toward him." Lily paused, embarrassed. "Do you think I'm crazy?"

Esther leaned in closer to her new friend. "It worked, didn't it? You followed the silver cord 8,000 miles, all the way to Somalia. I wouldn't call that crazy, I would call that *bashert*.

Chapter 32

ater that afternoon, Lily and David were seated in Captain Sherman's office, waiting for the doctor to arrive. She told David about the event that had taken place earlier in the day—when Robbie had kicked her out of the room.

"He's not himself. You understand that, right? He's going to be okay, Sis, I know it. Robbie is tough, he'll get through this." Lily nodded in agreement but couldn't stop thinking about the terror she had seen on Robbie's face.

Captain Sherman walked in, shook their hands, and sat down behind his desk.

"When Dr. Rosen first arrived, we performed a thoracotomy. We needed to contain the hemorrhaging, remove the bullet, and repair the damage to his chest cavity and lungs. Even though the recovery from that surgery is usually difficult and painful, it was a necessary resuscitative procedure. Infection is always a major concern and right now his white blood cells are slightly elevated, so we are monitoring him closely.

"How long will it take for him to be well enough to go home?" David asked

"If he lived nearby, I would say ten days to two weeks. Since he has to travel to the States, we're going to keep him here longer so he is healthy enough to withstand the long trip."

He folded his hands on his desk. "That brings me to our other concern. When Dr. Rosen is weaned off the pain medication, our psychiatrist Captain Tremont will see him and conduct a psychological evaluation. With patients who have been in hostage situations, especially with terrorists involved, the physical damage can be bad but often the psychological wounds can be far worse. These patients often suffer from PTSD— post-traumatic stress disorder. If they are not treated properly with psychotherapy, they can suffer devastating consequences.

You have to understand that talking about the events that occurred may be extremely difficult for victims of hostage situations. Without the proper care and therapy, coping from a significant event of this enormity, is almost impossible. Without help they may isolate themselves from friends and family because they feel that no one they know has ever had the same experience—and they are usually correct in this assumption. They may act fearful and mistrusting and angry to family, friends, and strangers. Or they may turn inward and suffer from self-loathing or lack of self-esteem. So it's important to know this in order to understand the stages that Dr. Rosen may go through and to encourage him to continue therapy after he leaves the hospital."

Thirty minutes later, David and Lily left the doctor's office and walked in silence to the hospital restaurant. Their heads were spinning and they gave each other the space to process the information.

Seated at the table, David broke the silence, "Like I said, he's tough; I know he'll be all right." It sounded to Lily as if David were trying hard to convince himself. "We'll make sure he gets the right help so he can move forward with his life." David sounded confident but inside he was riddled with doubt. He knew from his own therapy that psychological demons could last a lifetime.

"Of course he will. We'll make sure he feels our love and support." Lily smiled at David and wondered if he had any indication just how scared she was.

Even though Lily was hesitant about going back into Robbie's room after his earlier outburst, she wanted to check in on him before she went back to the hotel for the evening.

When she walked into the room, Robbie was asleep. Lily sat next to his bed and took his right hand in hers. It looked swollen. She looked at his left hand and it too looked as if it had become puffy since her earlier visit that day.

Lily walked into the hallway to see if any of the nurses were available. When she couldn't find one, Lily walked to the nurse's station and saw a clerk talking on the telephone. As Lily approached her, the clerk held up her index finger to let Lily know that she would be right with her. She hung up the phone and smiled at Lily.

"Can I help you, Miss Lockwood?"

"I don't know if I'm imagining it or not, but Dr. Rosen's hands look like they've swelled up since earlier in the day."

"Okay I'll ring for his nurse, Patricia, to have her check on him. Meanwhile I must inform you that visiting hours are over, you really must leave."

"Yes I understand, I'll go as soon as I speak to Patricia." Lily turned around and headed back to Robbie's room before the clerk could respond.

Within a few minutes, Patricia walked into the room, nodded to Lily, and went over to Robbie's bed. She picked up Robbie's hand and pressed the top of his hands with her thumb. She then examined his fingers, separating each one from the other. She removed his blanket so she could see his feet. She pressed his ankles.

"You're right, his hands and feet look swollen. It looks like he may be retaining water. I'll let Captain Sherman know after I take his vitals."

Patricia wrapped the blood pressure cuff around Robbie's left arm and pumped. After she had marked down the results she took out the ear thermometer and pulled his left lobe down. Her demeanor changed and she appeared concerned.

"What's wrong?"

"Well, he's running a temp of 102 and his blood pressure is lower than usual. I'll be right back." Patricia walked out of the room.

Lily moved her chair closer to Robbie and put her hand on his forehead; he was burning up. When Patricia returned, she was carrying a bag of fluids that she hung on the pole. She removed the bag that was previously dripping medicine into the intravenous line and connected the new one.

"Captain Sherman is starting him on antibiotics. We're going to take blood and urine to determine where the infection is coming from." She put her hand on Lily's shoulder as she walked by. "Listen, visiting hours are long over, so why don't you go back to the hotel and get a good night's sleep? I'll be here until the morning, so I'll take care of your man, here. He's in good hands."

Chapter 33

At 6:00 a. m. the phone rang in her hotel room, piercing the veil of slumber. Without opening her eyes Lily reached for it, and, in the process, knocked over the pitcher of water that the housekeeper had left for her on the nightstand. The water spilled on to the bed, soaking the sheets, blanket and Lily.

"Shit, piss, and corruption!" Lily said angrily. It was Daisy's favorite "go to" curse whenever she was frustrated. Lily had happily adopted it after her mother's death. She clicked on her phone, put a few pillows against the headboard to support her back, and sat up.

"Hello?" She scooted over to the left side of the bed, pulling all the pillows with her, to avoid the puddle that was rapidly invading the right side.

"Hey Sis, it's me," David said.

"David! What's up? What time is it?" She squinted so she could see the clock.

"It's about Robbie—"

"Uh oh, what's going on?"

"Look, don't get excited— promise me you won't panic." David had been with Lily before and witnessed, first hand, what she was like when she was on the verge of an anxiety attack. His sister was a conundrum. When things got rough or complicated, she could go two ways: fly off the handle and become paralyzed with fear or charge in like a bull and take control of the situation. Hopefully today the latter would prevail, because the last thing he needed was to expend his energy talking her down.

Lily's heart began to race. "I promise, now tell me."

"Well, the nurse called me at the hotel a couple of hours ago. I didn't want to disturb you because I know you must have gotten in late. She let me know that there was a problem. Robbie's white blood cells were elevated, his blood pressure had dropped really low, and he was running a high fever. He had been put on antibiotics earlier and now they were increasing his meds. I rushed over to the hospital and when I got to his room, I saw that Robbie was breathing really fast and was shaking. They said they're bringing him to I.C.U. in a few minutes."

Lily remained silent for fear of breaking down. Her heart raced and she felt tingles of perspiration on her forehead and under her arms.

"Hello? Are you still there, Sis?"

Lily struggled to compose herself. She wiped her face and took a deep breath, "Yes I'm here. Just trying to process everything. So what happens next?"

"I think they just keep on doing what they're doing until he comes around." David said.

"I'm going to get dressed and will be right there." David breathed a sigh of relief.

It was past noon and Robbie had already been back in the I.C.U for more than six hours. The swarm of nurses and doctors going back and forth in the past hour increased and David and Lily learned that Robbie's condition had taken a turn for the worse. When Robbie opened his eyes he was so delirious that he did not recognize anyone. One of the nurses instructed David and Lily to leave the room and stay in the waiting room where Captain Sherman would be with them shortly.

Soon thereafter, Sherman joined them. "Robbie developed an infection that we've been treating for the past couple of days." He reached into his brief case and extracted a thick manila folder, glanced at the pages, then looked back up at David and Lily.

"Unfortunately he has not yet responded to any of the antibiotics or steroids we've given him. They're working overtime in the lab trying to figure out from his blood and cultures where the infection is originating and what kind it is. Unfortunately it rapidly progressed into sepsis which is extremely serious. Basically the infection travels through the blood to all the body's organs. The danger is that one by one it affects each organ and shuts it down.

The doctor thumbed through Robbie's hospital file. "If you remember, this morning, you signed a consent allowing us to put a central venous line in his jugular vein. Which we did. I just want to make sure that you understand its function. It's a catheter that will allow us to get the medicine delivered into his heart faster and more efficiently.

"I don't understand why you can't figure out where the infection is or even what type it is. They have to—he's been through so much already!" Lily stared into the doctor's eyes as if her sheer will would somehow motivate him to uncover the one thing that would insure Robbie's recovery."

Captain Sherman pulled his chair closer to Lily. "I understand, Ms. Lockwood, but we are doing everything in our power for him."

He turned the pages of the file until he had found the data he had been searching for. "Robbie's creatinine level is high; he has low urine output and edema—all indicators that his kidneys have stopped functioning properly. The plan is to start him on dialysis as soon as they stabilize his blood pressure. I want you to know sepsis can be fatal if we cannot isolate the source of the infection and treat it. Unfortunately, because all the organs are involved, things can deteriorate rapidly. I want you both to fully understand the gravity of the situation.

Lily did not respond. She appeared shocked and sat silently wringing her hands. David realized that his brother was in deep trouble.

"We understand. We'll be back in the I.C.U. with Robbie, if you need us for any reason." David shook hands with the doctor.

When they stood, Lily stumbled and David grabbed her arm. While Captain Sherman was speaking Lily's color had grown pale. Now she appeared frail, as if she had aged twenty years in the past ten minutes.

When the doctor began talking, Lily felt that familiar feeling—the room spun and she became lightheaded. When she stood, it was like being on that Tilt-a-Whirl ride at amusement parks.

Lily sat back down and looked at David, who was more than a little concerned. She didn't know how much more either one of them could take. Just when they thought Robbie was out of the woods. . .

"I just need to sit down for a few minutes. Can you bring me some water, please?" Lily asked. David seemed relieved to be given a task.

When Robbie was brought back into the I.C.U, everything started feeling all-too-familiar for Lily. Memories of Daisy's last days flooded back to her. How her mother's condition seemed to get worse as each hour passed. Lily remembered all the meetings she had had with Daisy's doctors. How each time she met with them the test results and condition were less encouraging than the time before. Until finally there was nothing more to discuss, no more tests to administer and no doctors to speak with. The final act was the admission of her mother into hospice care. The flurry of activity that had surrounded her mother the weeks after the accident ceased abruptly. Lily found the hush to be much more unsettling than the commotion had ever been. Once her mother was settled on the hospice floor, it was either one of the nurses or social workers, she couldn't recall, who gave her a palliative care handbook. She remembered how surprised she had been when she read all about "active dying" describing, in detail, the last stages of life. She learned a person actually goes through different physical phases during the dying process. Their breathing changes, as does their color. . .

Lily began to panic. Robbie's symptoms mirrored those of her mother during the last days of her life. Was Robbie *dying*? How could that be? Would Robbie, who had survived the abduction and unimaginable torture in the hands of the terrorists, die because of an infection? It didn't make sense.

David returned with the water and Lily took the cup from him with trembling hands. She pressed Kleenex against her eyes and said, "David I need to go to a chapel to pray."

Lily closed her eyes and folded her hands:

> *Dear Heavenly Father, I cannot believe that this happening—that you and I are here again. Please help me to understand why this is so. Is this some grand plan of yours? I cannot imagine it would be, because it seems so senseless and wrong. You know that Robbie is a good man who heals the people that most of the world has forgotten. How could you allow him to be kidnapped, tortured, and then, with your intervention, be rescued—only to die in a hospital bed?*
>
> *Please, dear Lord, heal Robbie. I understand that everything is your divine will. I get that; I really do. But please, oh Lord, use all your power and love to make him well. Take pity. He is such a good man. All he wants from life is to heal people and make the world a better place. There is so much more that he has to give and so many people he could help.*
>
> *You must know that Hannah just buried her husband. How could she survive the death of her son, too? This will kill her, but then you know that.*
>
> *Please don't leave me alone in a world that has no Daisy and no Robbie. When my mother died, my life went from oil colors to pastel. If you take Robbie those colors will be gone and I will be left with nothing but black and white.*

While his sister was praying, David closed his eyes. But he did not pray. He needed to determine what he would say when he called his mother to tell her that Robbie's condition had taken a turn for the worse. How could he prepare his mother for the possibility that her youngest son may very well die.

David needed a drink—bad. He had been sober and working the program faithfully. At home, he attended at least four meetings a week—more when he was going through a difficult time. It had been weeks since he'd attended a meeting and he knew he needed to call his sponsor. Maybe that should be his first phone call before he telephoned home. He opened his eyes and looked at his watch. Dallas was eight hours behind, which gave him plenty of time to make both phone calls.

His sponsor would help him put together a plan. But who would help him cope with the guilt weighing heavily on his soul? He looked over at his sister who was praying so fervently, hands clasped, eyebrows furrowed. How could he have put her through all this grief?

How in the world would he ever come to terms with the shame that weighed so heavily on his conscience? There was a time when he almost wished that Robbie would not be rescued so that his mother and Lily would continue to look to him for support and advice. David thought that once Robbie was back in the picture, he would be forgotten and cast aside. But now, Robbie may not survive. And how could David ever live with the guilt?

I could really use a Scotch—just one shot to calm my nerves and to be able to talk to Mom. One shot, I can handle it. It doesn't mean I'd have to take a second. No way—one shot, done. Then when I get back home, I'll get right with the program. I don't need to tell Lily. No need for her to worry. One drink is shit, I could handle that, easily. And who knows, this could be a test. If I could handle it, maybe I could be like everyone else—a normal drinker. Keep it under control. Get home from work, have dinner, a drink or two and go about the rest of the night. I could be cured, and unless I test it, how would I ever know? As soon as I leave here, I'll go out for one drink.

Once he'd made the decision to have a drink, the thought of it became encompassing. Everything else faded into the background.

When she was finished with her prayers, Lily reached for David's arm to help her rise from her kneeling position. She faced David and knew that he felt the responsibility to be strong for the both of them. She looked at his face—tired beyond his years—with eyes that mirrored the anguish and worry he couldn't dare reveal.

Lily held her arms up and David walked into her embrace. Even though David stood a good foot taller than his sister, she reached for his head and pulled it down to rest on her small shoulder.

"Robbie and I are lucky— you are a wonderful brother."

David licked his lips. He could taste the Scotch.

Chapter 34

After leaving the chapel, Lily and David returned to the I.C.U. to check in on Robbie. His condition had improved slightly and the lab technicians planned to bring in a portable dialysis machine. David left suddenly, saying there were a few loose ends that he had to take care of. He told Lily that when she was ready to leave, she should text him and he would pick her up in the car he had rented the day before.

Lily had a suspicion about why David had left so abruptly. She felt the thought of dialysis probably brought back terrible memories for David. After the car crash in which he and Daisy had been involved, David's both kidneys were damaged. For the few weeks before he was the recipient of a kidney transplant, he had been practically tethered to the dialysis machine to keep him alive.

Lily moved closer to Robbie and gently brushed his hair from his forehead and whispered, "The silver cord is tied from my heart to yours that can never be severed. Robbie Rosen, you are the love of my life."

The nurse asked her to leave before they hooked Robbie up to the machine. As Lily walked out the hospital's entrance, she texted David to let him know that she was ready for him to pick her up. Lily waited outside the hospital for almost thirty minutes. When she tried calling him, it went directly to voice mail.

"Hey David, it's me again. Where are you? I'm waiting for you, in front. Okay, guess I'll see you soon."

Lily stood by the entrance and watched visitors enter and exit from the hospital. Some people did a double take when they recognized her. Lily smiled to herself because she actually saw a few of them shake their heads as if to dismiss the crazy notion that the famous actress was actually standing in front of them.

After waiting an hour, Lily felt aggravated. It was unlike David to keep her waiting. A blue Saab pulled up in front of her and the driver rolled the window down. Lily was pleased to see that it was Esther.

"Hey there. Need a ride?"

Lily felt relieved that she didn't have to walk or call a cab to take her back to Pfaelzer Stuben. "Actually yes, I just need a ride back to my hotel."

Esther unlocked the passenger door. "Climb in."

While Lily was buckling her seat, Esther smiled. "Do you want to come with me? I was just going to get some sushi at this fantastic little place in town. When we're done, I'll run you back."

"Perfect."

While driving the few minutes into Kaiserstrasse, the main street in town, Lily told Esther that they had just started Robbie on dialysis as she was leaving. Since Robbie had been moved into Intensive Care, Esther did not know how he was progressing.

"Putting him on dialysis could be a slippery slope. His renal function has been affected, meaning his kidneys are not functioning properly. So the dialysis, while it will remove waste, will also remove the antibiotics and steroids from his system that are meant to help fight his infections. They're going to have to bump up his dosage after dialysis. I'll take a peek in on him tomorrow."

Lily was grateful she had an ally to whom she could turn, someone who could interpret all the medical jargon that was being thrown at them. Esther made a right turn onto an exceedingly narrow side street. Even though it was a two-way street, it did not seem wide enough to accommodate two cars going in opposite directions. When a car passed them, Lily held her breath.

"Shit that was close."

Esther laughed, "You get used to it, believe me."

They turned on to the main road, lined with quaint restaurants and shops. Esther pulled up in front of the sushi restaurant and stopped behind a car that was pulling out of the space. With a few deft turns, Esther parallel parked. When Lily stepped out of the car, she noticed a man stumble out from the Irish Pub across the street. He got into his car and accelerated so fast that his tires screeched. Lily shook her head, because, in his haste, the driver almost hit a pedestrian. When the car passed by, she looked at the driver. Lily was shocked to see it was David.

"David, it's Lily and it's 6:00 a.m. Where the hell are you? I'm really worried. Please, whenever you get this message call me." Lily hung up. It was the fourth message she had left him since the night before. After she saw David drive away from the pub, she was troubled. David was in A.A.—so unless he had relapsed, why was he coming out of a bar? When she saw him stumble and witnessed the hazardous way he drove, Lily was certain that David had fallen off the wagon. She was so upset that she could hardly eat her sushi or carry on a conversation. She finally told Esther why she was distracted.

"You know, Lily, we can't control other people—only ourselves. If he's been drinking, then it's up to him to pull himself together, yet again. Just take care of yourself and of Robbie. David will have to figure out his own way."

Once back at her hotel, Lily knocked on David's door. There was no answer. Lily was frightened that David could be drunk somewhere or, worse, lying in the street hurt. What if he'd gotten into an accident?

She slept fitfully, tossing and turning, until 5:30 a.m., when she gave up and took a shower. Visiting hours weren't for another few hours, so she decided to call the hospital to check on Robbie.

"Good morning, Landstuhl Regional Medical Center, how may I help you?"

"Hello. May I please be connected to The I.C.U? Lily asked.

"One moment, please." Lily heard a series of clicks before the connection went through. Lily unknowingly clenched her fist when the phone rang and rang. After the fifteenth ring someone eventually picked up.

"I.C.U. West, Pembroke speaking, how can I help you?

I'm calling to find out how Dr. Robert Rosen is doing. He was brought into the I.C.U yesterday.

"Sorry, I can only give that information out to immediate family, Ma'am."

"This is his uh. . . *fiancée*," she lied.

"Oh excuse me, if you can give me the code, I'll be able to let you know how he is doing,"

"What code?"

"When a patient is brought into the Intensive Care Unit they choose a code and give it out to the family members who have permission to receive the information." Pembroke replied by rote.

"He was not conscious when they brought him in, so he couldn't choose a code." Lily explained

"Sorry Ma'am, then I can't give you any information."

"Can you at least tell me if he has improved since yesterday?" Lily was losing patience and had to work hard at not sounding annoyed.

"I *can* tell you his brother is here with him." Pembroke said.

"David? David is there?" Of all the places Lily could imagine David would be, it never occurred to her that he might have gone back to the hospital.

"Yes Ma'am."

"Great, can you please put him on the phone?"

"Sorry Ma'am, visitors are not permitted to use the phone."

To release her frustration, Lily stomped her foot. "Then can you please ask him to call Lily?"

"I certainly can, but you should be warned that the use of cell phones is forbidden in this unit. So he may not call until he is out of the hospital building."

"I understand. Please ask him to call."

After she hung up, Lily couldn't decide if she was relieved that David was safe, or angry that he could not be bothered to return her calls. Surely he must have listened to her many messages and could tell that she was beyond distraught. Esther was right: The only actions she could control were her own. Now that she knew her brother was safe, she lay down on the bed to rest her eyes. Within minutes, Lily drifted off to sleep. But a knock at her door startled Lily awake. She glanced at the bedside clock and was amazed that she had slept for more than two hours. When she opened the door, she saw David standing there. Lily just looked at him.

"Aren't you going to let me in?" he asked sheepishly

Lily did not let him into her room, nor did she say a word to him. She simply folded her arms and stared at her brother.

David chuckled, "Okay, I get that you're mad, but at least let me explain myself."

Lily shook her head in dismay and granted David entrance into the room.

Once inside, he tried to give his sister a hug and she fervently shrugged off his attempt.

"You have got to be kidding me. Why didn't you return all my calls? Do you know what you put me through—how worried I was?"

David smiled, "I'm sorry Sis, my phone died and I spent the night in the I.C.U with Robbie." He sat down.

"Don't make yourself comfortable, you're not staying long."

David looked confused, "Why are you so angry? I apologized for not answering your calls."

"How about for keeping me standing outside the hospital waiting for almost an hour and—"

David interrupted "— you're right, I'm sorry. I just got caught up in stuff."

Lily stared in amazement, surprised at how easily David could lie to her. "Don't give me that crap. I saw you. I was in town and I saw you leave the pub—you were drunk!"

David smiled. "Ah, now I get it. You think I went on a binge."

"I saw you stumble outside the bar and then drive like a maniac."

"Sis, sit down and let me explain, it's really not what you think. When we were in the chapel, I got all sorts of jammed up. Everything hit me at once and I needed a drink. You're right I went to the pub."

Lily crossed her arms and sat back. It seemed that finally David planned to tell her the truth.

"I got there and ordered a shot. The bartender poured it and put it in front of me. I sat looking at it for more than thirty minutes. I didn't drink it, Sis, I left. And I tripped over something as I rushed out." He chuckled. "And the driving—I'm not used to a clutch so I popped it, then pressed on the accelerator so it wouldn't stall."

"Then why didn't you call me back, right after you left? It was only 6:30 p.m." Lily asked, still not convinced.

"Well, little sister, I found out they run an A.A. meeting on the grounds of the hospital—building 3703—Wednesday's at 7:00 p.m., so I rushed over. I made the meeting and after it was over, I sat and talked for a couple of hours with a few of the guys. I went to call you, but my cell was completely dead. Since I was near the hospital, I figured I'd duck in to the I.C.U. I ended up staying all night."

Lily felt as if a weight had lifted from her heart. "Why didn't you tell me you wanted a drink? Why didn't you let me know so I could've helped you?"

David shook his head. "As much as I love you, you can't help me Lily. I have to figure it out myself. It's a process—*my* process. So yesterday, I figured it out. While I'm here, I'll work the program—go to meetings."

Lily was visibly relieved and hugged her brother. "I'm sorry if I acted like a bitch, I was really worried about you." She pulled back from their embrace. "Just know that whenever you need to talk or anything, I love you, I'm there for you."

David smiled and pulled her ponytail. "I love you, too."

"Now that we got that straightened out, tell me about Robbie." Lily's face went from relief to concern. "How's he doing?"

"Why don't you get dressed, I'll take you over, so you can see for yourself."

When they got to the Intensive Care Unit, David stepped back and let Lily walk in first. When she opened the door, to her surprise Robbie was sitting up in bed eating. Tears started streaming down Lily's face. She was so astonished, she couldn't move.

Robbie looked up and smiled when he saw Lily standing there. His eyes never left hers. He said, almost to himself, "God, I forgot how gorgeous you are." Startled, Lily could not move or speak. Robbie looked at his brother and they exchanged smiles. "Lil, I've been waiting a long time to kiss you." Lily practically glided across the room, into Robbie's arms.

Chapter 35

*L*ily slapped the card down on the table. "Gin!" She stood up, raised her arms, and did her best impression of Rocky Balboa after he'd knocked out Ivan Drago. "And the crowd roared". Lily made the sound of a roaring crowd and, with her arms still raised, danced around in a circle.

The brothers looked at one another and, as if on cue, rolled their eyes and shook their heads.

She looked at them, feigning innocence. "Hey, what's with the eye-rolling, I don't understand?

David chuckled. "Oh I don't know, *Wyatt Earp*, maybe because this is the fortieth time you've beaten us in last fourteen days."

Lily threw back her head and laughed. The sun caught her face at the perfect angle and caused Robbie's heart to skip a beat. It was as if, at that moment in time, the sun was an enormous spotlight whose only function was to transmit Lily's happiness to the world.

She was overjoyed, which had nothing whatsoever to do with the game of Gin. She looked at Robbie and said a silent prayer of thanks for the way he had transformed physically and emotionally since they first arrived. Sixteen days had passed and she, David, and Robbie were seated at the same picnic table, in the courtyard of the hospital, as the couple whom she had seen kissing the first day she was there. Lily recalled how she had had to walk away from the window because watching them had almost brought her to tears. Now, looking at Robbie and knowing he was on the mend, intensified Lily's joy. He was still in a weakened state, but he was becoming stronger every day and his doctors were optimistic that he would make a complete recovery.

David glanced at his watch and smiled. "Well kiddies, as much as I would like a chance to win back some of my hard earned cash from Doc Holliday, I'd better get to the airport to pick up Mom." He kissed Lily and gave his brother a hug.

Lily looked across the table at Robbie and smiled. "Want to go for a romantic stroll?

"You know, the leg is giving me some problems today." He pointed to a bench on the edge of a pond, underneath a large shade tree. "If you don't mind giving me a hand, let's go and sit over there."

She stood, walked around the table, and picked up the cane that was hooked on to the arm of the empty seat next to Robbie. He pushed his chair back, took a deep breath, and stood up. The pain in his chest from the surgery was only secondary to the pain in his knee—the one that had been crushed by the sledge hammer. The doctors were convinced that he would benefit greatly from a knee replacement.

He put his arm around Lily's shoulder and using his cane for additional support, he walked slowly with her toward the bench.

"You know you're luckier than most girls."

"Oh yeah, and why is that?"

"You get to see what it's going to be like in fifty years, when you have to help me get around this way, all the time." He teased.

Even though he was poking fun at himself, her heart leapt when he spoke of the future. Because, finally after all they'd been through, they had a chance to have one—together.

"Well just remember I'll be old and wrinkled then and constantly complaining that the kids and grandkids never visit." Lily teased.

Caught by surprise and visualizing the scenario, Robbie laughed. Lily looked up at him and smiled. Robbie's laughter was music to her ears.

They arrived at the bench and sat down under the tree. A delicate breeze whispered softly through the leaves. Lily looked up at the sky, then faced Robbie. "It doesn't get much better than this."

Robbie put his hands on either side of her face and gazed into her eyes. A surge of love for the beautiful woman next to him sent electric shockwaves through his body. He gently kissed her forehead, then slowly kissed both cheeks.

Their lips met and finally their tongues found one another. The years of yearning and heartache collided together.

She wrapped her arms around Robbie, holding him closer than she had ever held anyone. Finally, she leaned back and tilted her head as she looked into his eyes.

Tears filled Robbie's eyes. "That's it!" He pointed his finger. "That look—do you know how often I thought of that look when I was…away?" He wiped his eyes.

She leaned in and kissed him again. "You are the bravest person I know."

An odd look crossed Robbie's face as he turned his attention away, feigning interest in a bird perched on a limb in a nearby tree. The bird squawked three times before flying into the pond. Robbie sighed deeply, turned his attention back to Lily, and took her hand in his.

"You know a lot has happened in the past two years." He closed his eyes and shook his head. When he reopened them, he leaned in to Lily and softly said, "Some things were really terrible. But I've spoken to the doctors here, and I'm going to get through it, I know. I have to.

Other things, I'm not proud of. . ." He thought of the decision he had made to commit suicide.

"We don't have to talk about it, now. Lily interrupted. "I want you to know I'm here for you whenever you're ready to talk. And there will be no judgment, ever."

"Thank you." He realized, when his brother told him about the events that had led up to his capture, what an amazing woman Lily had become. She was stronger than most. He couldn't imagine anyone risking their life to save his, as Lily had done. If it wasn't for her, he would still have been a hostage—or worse. The thought that Lily Lockwood—whom fans knew her only as a great actress and trendsetting fashionista—almost singlehandedly, through her resources and sheer will, commandeered his rescue. It was mindboggling to think that the whole undertaking had escalated into a C.I.A. Mission and Navy SEAL rescue.

When David filled Robbie in on their visit to the MSF compound and the conversation they had while they were there, Robbie understood it was important for him to talk with Lily about Chloe. This way, Lily would never have to question Robbie's feelings.

"David told me about your visit to MSF," Robbie said and Lily moved around uncomfortably.

"I know what Chloe said to you. Look. I'm not proud of the fact that the type of relationship she and I had was totally physical. I never told her I loved her and I was clear with her about my feelings for you." His eyes narrowed and his face became flushed. "And it was an absolute lie that I was planning to bring her home to meet my folks. And I certainly never planned for her to live with me in New York."

Robbie took Lily's hand in his, "I was wrong because I knew she had feelings for me, that I didn't have for her. Yet I continued sleeping with her."

Lily put her hand on his cheek. "It doesn't matter now, Robbie, I promise you. We have a chance at a new beginning—a new life—and nothing will come between us. I refuse to let that happen."

She looked so sincere and so sure of herself that Robbie couldn't help but smile.

"And, you didn't get upset that I hadn't been forthcoming about my pregnancy." Lily said.

He kissed her on the cheek, glad of the conversation shift. "If Daisy Rose is anything like her Mama then I am truly a blessed man. I can't wait to meet her. Did Donna send you anymore photos?"

Lily pulled out her phone and clicked on a recent video Donna had sent her that morning. It was of Daisy Rose singing *Itsy bitsy spider*.

"Wow, she's a cutie." Robbie said. Lily looked at him and her heart sang when she saw the expression on his face. She had no doubt that Daisy Rose would love Robbie and visa-versa.

"You know, I was thinking. . ." Lily smiled

"Uh oh, that could be dangerous." He began to laugh. His laughter devolved into a series of coughs.

Lily continued, "Well you told me that Captain Sherman said you definitely need knee surgery, right?" Robbie nodded. "Why don't you fly back to New

York, have it done by one of your colleagues at New York Hospital, and this way you could stay with me and I can take care of you."

Robbie paused for a few seconds. "I know what your angle is, Lil."

Lily was taken aback. "Angle, I don't have an angle—what do you mean?"

"I'm going to be in your bed recuperating—on my back—and each and every time you walk into the room, you're going to jump my bones. You're using me for my body!"

"Lily threw her head back and laughed. "You got that right and if we weren't in a public place that's what I'd be doing at this very moment, Dr. Rosen." She looked around to make sure there was no one nearby and took his hand, placed it under her tee shirt, and let him cop a feel.

"No bra? Baby, you're killing me."

Lily took his hand out from beneath her shirt. "Okay, that's enough. I just want you to know there's more where that came from. Much more."

"Okay then, I'll take you up on it. I'll stay with you."

"Awesome. Since your mom will be here to take good care of you, I'm going to get a flight tomorrow. I really need to get back home to Daisy Rose. This way, I can get the house ready for you."

"I understand, but I'll miss you like crazy." He gently touched her face. Do you know how beautiful you are?"

Lily batted her lashes and laughed. "Yes, but you can tell me anyway."

"You are the most beautiful woman I have ever met. Inside and out. And brave. Seriously, you were beyond brave to go to Somalia. I owe you my life. I will never forget that."

"I would do it again. I mean it—

"There's something else I've been meaning to say: I was stupid and am I am beyond sorry that I left you like that—at your mother's memorial. I regretted it almost immediately."

Lily took his hand. "It's water under the bridge, no need to talk about it."

"I really needed to say it" Robbie looked uncomfortable. "There's something else on my mind that I've been trying to say correctly. And since we are being open and forthcoming. . ."

Lily felt a wave of dread wash over her. "Just say it."

"Look I know that everything is happening fast, but one thing that I've learned from the horror show I just came from is that life can change without a moment's notice. I don't want to be apart from you ever again."

Lily smiled and hugged him.

"Excellent, so it's a deal Ms. Lockwood." In a mock gesture, he extended his hand for her to shake.

She looked around, shook his hand, and promptly put it under her t-shirt again.

Chapter 36

$\mathcal{L}$ily looked at her watch. In fifteen minutes David was scheduled to pick her up from the hospital and take her to the airport. Lily's stomach sank when she realized soon she would be in a car speeding away from Robbie.

Saying goodbye to him was bittersweet. She hated to leave, yet she knew that if all went as expected, he could very well be on a plane heading for New York in less than a week.

Robbie held Lily's hand and they slowly walked around the grounds of the hospital. Lily was so grateful that Robbie was getting stronger every day. She thought of all the work that had piled up while she was gone—scripts that needed to be read and decisions to be made. Arthur Thomas's film had been delayed so it wasn't slated for preproduction for five more months. Franny had spoken to the producers of *St. Joes* to see if Lily could rejoin the cast, not as a series regular but as a recurring character. This way she would be free to accept film roles. Franny had said, because the ratings had fallen after she left the show, they would take her back any way they could—and give her a fat paycheck to boot.

But now that Robbie was going to be with her and recovering from knee surgery, going out to L.A. immediately was out of the question. Her two priorities were Daisy Rose and Robbie, and she planned to spend all her time with them.

Eventually, when Robbie was fully recovered, they talked about moving out to California together. Robbie told her that after he healed and was ready to go back to work, he would speak to a friend of his at U.C.L.A Medical Center about the possibility of joining their Cardiology team. This way they could be together on the West Coast, where Lily would be spending most of her time.

"A penny for your thoughts."

"So not worth it." She laughed. "Just work stuff."

They stopped to sit down at "their bench" and Robbie lifted a flat, black stone, threw it across the pond, and it skipped four times before it disappeared.

"So when you get back are you going to see Actor Boy?" He asked nonchalantly.

"You mean Jamie? I'll see him only when he visits Daisy Rose or picks her up for the day." She put her hand on his, reassuringly. "There is absolutely nothing between us. The last thing we talked about was my feelings for you." Lily kissed him. "I don't want you to worry at all, promise?"

"I won't." He smiled, relieved.

Lily snickered, "And also, please stop calling him Actor Boy."

"Yeah—now that I can't promise." He laughed and Lily swatted his arm.

She stood up and grabbed his hand to pull him up. "Time for us to go up front. David will be here in five minutes."

They walked together toward the front entrance of the hospital.

Robbie broke the silence, "What am I going to do here, without you?"

Lily slipped her arm through his. "Well, you are going to do everything you can to heal fast, so that you will be on a plane this time next week.

"It's a plan." Robbie said.

They were midway up a small hill when Robbie became breathless and began to cough. He coughed non-stop for several minutes. Lily was concerned; she didn't like the sound of the cough. It was the kind her mother used to call "productive." When he finally stopped coughing, he took her hand and continued to walk.

"Did you tell the doctor about the cough? Because, to me it doesn't sound good—it sounds sort of phlegmy," Lily said.

"So now that we have the symptoms, what may I ask is your diagnosis, *Dr.* Lockwood?" Robbie teased.

"Seriously, Robbie, I'm worried. Please tell me that you'll notify the doctor today. Promise me. Otherwise I'm going to be worried the whole plane ride home."

"Even though I know there's nothing to be concerned about, I'll have my nurse contact the doctor. Does that make you feel better?"

"Much." She said.

"I promise I'll do everything I can to get home to you."

They continued to walk in silence. When they turned the corner, they saw David leaning against the car parked by the front entrance of the hospital.

"My brother's here," they both said in unison. They looked at each other and laughed.

"Now how do you suppose we're ever going to explain to people that I am deeply in love with my brother's brother?" Lily joked.

"Just tell them we come from an *extremely* close family and that's just how we roll."

They were both laughing as they approached David. He opened the passenger door with a dramatic flourish, "Your car awaits you, Madam."

Tears filled her eyes when she looked up at Robbie. He wiped away her tears and kissed her. Then, he leaned down and whispered in her ear, "The silver cord is tied from my heart to yours that can never be severed. Lily Lockwood, you are the love of my life."

The Lily Lockwood Series: Book Three: The Family Bond will be published 2016.

If you enjoyed the The Silver Cord, please leave a review on amazon.com.
Keep up-to-date with book signings and releases:
www.alisoncaiola.com
blog: alisoncaiolawriter.blogspot.com
facebook: alisoncaiolaauthor
twitter: @AlisonMCaiola
Instagram: AlisonWrites
The Lily Lockwood Series: *The Seeds of a Daisy, The Silver Cord, The Family Bond.*

Made in the USA
Middletown, DE
03 September 2020